St. Martin's Paperbacks Titles
by Charles Wilson

DIRECT DESCENDANT
FERTILE GROUND
EXTINCT

EXTINCT

CHARLES WILSON

St. Martin's Paperbacks

EXTINCT

Copyright © 1997 by Charles Wilson.

ISBN: 0-312-96212-6

Printed in the United States of America

St. Martin's Paperbacks edition/May 1997

10 9 8 7 6 5 4 3 2 1

To Linda, as always

ACKNOWLEDGMENTS

My special thanks to those many people whose knowledge, research, and advice made this novel possible.

In particular: Dean A. Dunn, PhD in oceanography and paleontology, former shipboard scientist for Glomar Challenger expeditions in both the Pacific and western North Atlantic, and current Professor of Geology at the University of Southern Mississippi (Dr. Dunn is also the webmaster for GeoClio, World Wide Web site for the history of Geosciences—Oceanography, Geology, Meteorology, Geophysics, at http://geoclio.st.usm.edu). Dr. David M. Patrick and Dr. William Odom, the University of Southern Mississippi. Major Gen. Dave Robinson, U.S. Army, Ret., of Ridgeland, Mississippi. E. B. Vandiver of Fairfax, Virginia. Wesley and Craig Harris of American Aquaculture, Inc., of Jackson, Mississippi. Rayanne Weiss, Jimmy McIntyre, and Mike Filippi, of Gulfport and WLOX-TV. Julian and Rowella Brunt and Ralph Hyer (former charter boat captain) of Biloxi, Mississippi. Alice Jackson Baughn of Ocean Springs, Mississippi. ATF Special Agent Ron Baughn of the Gulfport, Mississippi, office. Rankin-Madison County District Attorney John Kitchens, Ridgeland, Mississippi. Lisha Edwards of Florence, Mississippi. Derrick Groves, charter boat captain at the Broadwater Marina in Biloxi.

Dr. Steve Hayne, M.D. FCAP DCMEI, pathologist at Rankin Medical Center, and medical director for Renal Care Group Laboratory and the Rankin County Morgue. Al Jernigan, Assistant U.S. Attorney, Jackson, Mississippi. Bos'n Mate Third Class Todd Anderson, Bos'n Mate Third Class Beck Shane, and Fireman Michael A. Schmitt of the Gulfport, Mississippi, U.S. Coast Guard Station, who helped me with Coast Guard boats, regulations, and equipment. My oldest son, Charles P. Wilson, Jr., J.D., who helped me with the legal aspects, and my son-in-law, Cas E. Heath, III, M.D., who helped me with the medical facts, both of Brandon, Mississippi.

Finally, my thanks to two special friends of mine from Brandon who made criticism contributions to this novel from the time it began to take shape to its finale: first, to Tommy Furby, whose help on all my previous manuscripts has been above and beyond, but who helped more with this work than any before—especially with his intricate knowledge of the Mississippi coast and its "creatures"; and, to Alison Orr, who refused to let my opinion overpower hers—though I tried hard.

After all the highly knowledgeable help given me on this work, it goes without saying that any factual errors there might be contained in the text are solely attributable to me.

CHAPTER 1

Dustin pointed his finger in the six-year-old's face. "This is as far as you go, Paul—I mean it."

Paul stared at the finger, and then past Dustin to the river spreading out across a wide channel behind the teenager's back. Nearer the water a second teenager smiled at the confrontation as he unbuttoned his shirt. Dustin looked at him. "You going to help me, Skip?"

"You're the one who let him come with us," Skip said. "Tie him to a tree."

Paul narrowed his eyes. Dustin tried again. "I know you can swim fine, bud, but I told your mother you wouldn't go near the water."

"What about you?" Paul asked.

"I told her *you* wouldn't go in the water, not us," Dustin said.

Paul stared past him again. Across the river a heron suddenly flapped up into the bright sunlight. Curving its long neck back into an S above its body, the bird turned across the vast expanse of marshland extending out from the far side of the channel toward the long Interstate 10 bridge in the distance—and Paul's gaze followed the bird's flight.

"I've got some gum," Dustin said.

Paul's eyes went to the pockets of the teenager's jeans.

Dustin pulled out a flattened pack of Wrigley's Spearmint. "I'll give you this now and buy you a sucker the next time I'm at the store."

Paul weighed the offer with one eye nearly closed. He held out his hand.

Dustin said, "You promise?"

Paul nodded.

"He's lying," Skip said. He had his shirt off now and was stepping out of his jeans.

Paul reached for the pack.

Dustin pulled it back.

"Promise," Paul said in a low voice.

"I heard a big bull alligator got after some people here yesterday," Dustin said.

Paul smiled mischievously.

"He knows you're lying now," Skip said. In his undershorts now, he stepped to a frayed rope hanging down from a limb of a tall oak leaning out toward the river. Catching a grip high up the rope, he took a step backward, then jumped off the ground and sailed slowly past the bank, dropping into the warm brown water with a splash, sending ripples fanning out in wide circles toward the center of the channel and back against the bank.

Paul took the gum. "I'm warning you," Dustin said. He pulled his T-shirt off over his head. Paul, pulling a stick of gum from the pack, theatrically stuck his foot out closer to the bank.

"*Paul.*"

The boy smiled.

Dustin slipped off his jeans. "You stay here and I'll let you take a drag off a cigarette when we finish."

Paul pulled his foot back and began to unwrap the gum. Dustin caught the rope and, stepping back a couple of feet, jumped and grabbed it higher and swung out past the bank. Reaching the peak of his swing, he kicked his feet over his head and somersaulted backward into the water.

A large black Labrador trotted out of the trees behind Paul and stopped by the boy. It wagged its thick tail as Paul patted its head.

Skip splashed water in Dustin's face.

The Labrador edged closer to the bank and barked loudly.

But the dog wasn't looking toward the boys. Instead, its muzzle was pointed downstream in the direction the river dumped into the Sound and, beyond that, the Gulf of Mexico. A hundred feet in that direction, the water sloshed gently against the bank.

The Labrador barked again.

Dustin got his hands on Skip's head and pushed down. Laughing, barely able to get a breath before he was dunked, Skip disappeared under the surface. Dustin splashed away from the spot so Skip couldn't grab his legs. Near the bank, he turned and waited for his friend to reappear. The Labrador barked again. Now it was looking directly at Dustin.

Skip did not reappear.

A few seconds more.

Dustin's brow wrinkled. Slowly, he began to breaststroke toward the spot. He began to stroke faster. The Labrador barked repeatedly.

Close to the spot Skip disappeared, Dustin took a quick breath and dove under the surface.

Paul walked past the Labrador to the place where the bank started sloping steeply down to the water.

The dog came up beside him.

Paul looked at the foil wrapper from the stick of gum. He used his finger to shape it into a trough and sent it sailing toward the water. It curved in the air and landed at the bottom of the bank, where it sparkled in the sunlight.

Paul stared at the shiny scrap for a moment, then turned

and, moving his leg backward down the slope, caught a grip on the edge of the bank and began sliding toward the water.

Carolyn Haines leaned back from the ledger sheets she worked on at the desk in her study. She slipped her glasses off and fluffed her hair off her neck. She looked toward the thermostat next to the glass doors leading out onto the sun deck, then stood and walked to the control.

She adjusted the temperature and started to turn back toward her desk but hesitated and looked toward the doors. She listened for a moment, then walked to the doors and slid the glass back.

Duchess's loud barking reverberated through the trees between the rear corner of the house and the river.

Carolyn stepped out onto the sun deck and looked through the thick growth.

"Paul," she called.

She waited a moment. The Labrador's barking grew more agitated.

"Paul! Dustin!"

Duchess barked at a feverish pitch now.

Duchess, her forepaws in the mud at the edge of the bottom of the bank, her head and neck stretched out over the water, barked rapidly, one sharp sound after another. Paul stood next to her. "Stop it, Duchess," he said.

She didn't.

He pulled at her collar. "*Duchess.*"

She suddenly moved sideways, bumping into him. He barely kept his balance. "*Duchess*," he said, frowning down at her. She barked toward her left now. Paul looked toward the center of the river. Then he looked down the channel to his left. His eyes narrowing, he pulled a wad of gum from his mouth and looked up the bank to his right. Twenty feet out in the water in front of him, a gentle swirl twisted the surface and a faint ripple moved in a line toward the bank.

"Paul!" Carolyn yelled as she came out of the trees. "You'll fall in!"

He looked up at her as she slid awkwardly down the bank and grabbed his arm. Tugging him back up the slope, she saw his questioning expression. Somehow she knew it wasn't because of her pulling. At the top of the bank, he looked back at the river again.

Her gaze followed his.

"Dustin?" he said in a low voice.

Carolyn looked at the clothes scattered under the oak. Her eyes went back to the water. She looked down the river with the current and upriver to her left.

"Dustin?" Paul said again.

He kept staring toward the center of the channel.

Carolyn brought her hand up to cover her mouth.

CHAPTER 2

BILOXI, MISSISSIPPI—AN HOUR LATER

Alan Freeman came up the side of the street at a fast jog, running effortlessly, his thick, dark hair whipping gently in the breeze, his loose T-shirt damp with perspiration clinging to his wide shoulders. Slowing for a Lincoln Town Car entering Boom Town Casino rising back to his left above the shoreline of Back Bay, he shortened his stride, then came around the automobile's rear, resuming his pace. A couple of hundred feet farther he passed dozens of shrimping trawlers berthed close together off to his left, their long booms pointed up at an angle out to their sides.

Running past a rambling, broken line of aging boat repair shops, old ice houses and the shuttered front of an abandoned fish-processing plant, he kept his pace. Moments later, he began to slow and came to a walk. He raised the tail of the T-shirt to his face and wiped the perspiration away.

A hundred yards farther, he turned off the pavement onto the graveled area at the front of a wide, one-story concrete-block building. A van sat next to his Jeep parked close to the big, block letters AMERICAN AQUACULTURE, INC., painted in red across the building's front.

To the side of the entrance a wooden sign proclaimed in bright orange letters:

Dr. Ho Hsiao
Dr. Alan Freeman
Proprietors

As Alan passed the sign he knocked on the wood. He felt stickiness and looked at his knuckles, now brightly illuminated with round spots of orange.

Mrs. Hsiao, a small woman of fifty with coal-black hair hanging down the back of her print dress to her waist, sat behind her desk in the reception area.

"Ho touched up the sign again," he said, reaching to the desk to pull a tissue from a box of Kleenex.

She smiled as she looked at his knuckles. "He thinks he was an artist in his former life. Your aunt called. She wanted you to call her as soon as you came back."

He wiped as much of the paint from his skin as he could, dropped the Kleenex in the wastebasket at the side of the desk, and reached for the telephone. "Whose van is that outside?"

"A Mr. Herald. He called Ho yesterday and asked if he could bring some boys from a local boxing team over to view an aquaculture operation. Ho is back there practicing the speech on them he's giving to the Chamber tonight."

His aunt's line was busy. He replaced the receiver. "I'm going to take a quick shower."

As he walked across the hall toward the rest room and showers, he looked down the hallway past the open, double doors at its far end. Ho stood just inside the wide rear area of the building with his back to the doorway. His thin body clad in a white, knee-length lab coat, his long hair hanging against his shoulders, he leaned forward on the side of the fingerling tank, a container closely resembling a child's wading pool with sides three feet high. Beyond the far side of the tank a dozen boys of widely varying heights seemed to be paying close attention to his words. Alan walked toward the door.

"Water cover seventy percent of world," Ho was saying. "People in past always think it inexhaustible supply of food." He raised his long finger. "But, as I tell you while ago, most sought-after food species in oceans decline two, three percent a year. Population grow more than that each year. Soon not only most sought-after species but all food species begin to decline. If this so, then nature's balance in seas as we know it not stay the same. To not let that happen, big aquaculture must be world's future. Grow fish in controlled environment for eating, leave fish in oceans to people for fun catching—if not catch too many."

As Ho stopped his words he smiled broadly. "So that it. How you like speech?"

The boys, most of them wearing dark windbreakers with BILOXI BOXING CLUB arched in white block letters across their backs and appearing to range in age from around ten or eleven to their early teens, remained silent.

"Questions?"

The deep voice came from Mr. Herald. A large man, he stood off to the boys' side. His gray hair unruly, and dressed only casually in a short-sleeved pullover hanging out over a pair of faded khakis, he nevertheless presented an impressive appearance with his erect posture and taut arms that belied his age.

Two of the younger white boys on the team wiggled to the front of the mostly black youths to get a better look inside the tank's light-green waters, bubbling with oxygen and swarming with the inch-long baby fish.

"What about you, San-hi?" Mr. Herald asked, looking at one of the oldest boys in the group, a thin Vietnamese with shoulder-length coal-black hair.

"He explained it fine," the boy answered.

"Armon?" Mr. Herald said.

A stocky black youth about the same age as San-hi said, "Got it all here in my mind."

"Any you others?" Mr. Herald asked.

A boy at the rear of the group looked behind him at the half-dozen larger tanks spread out across the concrete floor, each of them six feet high and twice as big around as the fingerling tank. Conveyor belts rumbled as they angled over the rims of the tanks, lifting a shiny-looking coating from the water and carrying it to a garbage-dumpster-sized container against a far wall. "What's that stuff?" the boy asked.

"Algae and fish droppings," Ho said. "We recycle for fertilizer—nothing go to waste. When we build new facility, we send droppings and old water to pond where plants grow. Plants make food and same time filter droppings from water where water come back clean to tanks. Called hydroponics—and save money for not having to buy more water." Ho smiled broadly again.

"Anybody else?" Mr. Herald asked.

When none of the boys responded, he turned and reached toward a tall stack of slim, white Styrofoam cartons on a metal folding chair behind him. Lifting the cartons and balancing them against his wide chest, he nodded across his shoulder toward the open, double doorway at the rear of the building.

The boys stepped toward him and started stripping him of his load. "Easy, men," he said. "Out in back to eat. Don't let any of the trash end up in the bay."

In a moment the boys, each with a carton, were hurrying toward the doors. Mr. Herald looked at Ho. "Thank you for your presentation, doctor. They don't often say much, but they're listening." Then he followed the team from the building. Ho walked toward Alan.

"I do good horse and dog show, Alan?"

Alan smiled at his friend's misquoting of the saying. "It's dog and pony show, Ho."

"What different?"

The wall telephone at the side of the door leading toward the front offices rang. A few seconds later, it buzzed. Alan stepped to it and lifted the receiver to his ear. "Uh-huh?"

"It's your aunt," Mrs. Hsiao said. "Line one."

He pushed the button. "You're feeling guilty because you haven't invited me to dinner this week," he said, and smiled.

His aunt didn't come back with her usual fast words.

"Alan, I just saw on TV—Julie's boy drowned."

CHAPTER 3

Alan looped his tie around his neck and tied it, using his elbows to guide his Jeep along the narrow blacktop passing in front of a mixture of old and new houses backed up against the Pascagoula River. Julie and Barry's home, an older one-story brick, was near the end of the street, next to a newer two-story stucco contemporary. Two Jackson County Sheriff's Department cruisers and a yellow Toyota with an empty boat trailer behind it sat off the side of the road. Alan parked behind the trailer, lifted his sports coat from the seat beside him, and walked toward the house.

An older woman answered the front door.

"I'm Alan Freeman, a friend of Barry and Julie."

"They're down at the riverbank, Mr. Freeman. They haven't found the bodies yet."

The place where the boys had gone into the water was along a wooded stretch of river where no houses backed up to the bank. Out in the center of the channel the Sheriff's Department's Flotilla Search and Rescue Team pulled grappling hooks behind an eighteen-foot aluminum boat. The Biloxi Fire Department's Marine Unit had come from Harrison County to join in the search with their seventeen-foot Mako. A young couple Alan guessed to be the parents of the boy who had been with Dustin stood near the water, their arms around each other as they stared toward the boats. Farther up the bank, a dozen people who lived along the river silently watched the search. He spotted Julie's long blond hair. She and Barry stood close together back in the trees. Julie was shaking her head and crying softly while Barry, his face ashen, tried to comfort her. Standing next to them was a tanned brunette wearing a short-sleeved pullover and loose-fitting shorts; her bare legs were tight and very feminine. Alan thought there was something familiar about her. As he drew closer, she looked at him, holding her stare for a moment, then looked back at Julie and Barry.

Then Barry's eyes met his. Dressed in the blue trousers and gray shirt of the Mississippi Highway Patrol, where he had served for fifteen years, Barry was a lean, strong man with chiseled features and swept-back blond hair, a man normally commanding respect by his very appearance, but who now looked suddenly frail. As Alan stopped next to him, Julie, tears running down her cheeks, shook her head slowly back and forth. "We've lost Dustin, Alan," she said. Her hands came up clasped and trembling in front of her chest.

Feeling a great sadness for her, Alan took her gently into his arms. She laid the side of her face against his chest. "What are we going to do now?" she asked.

"I'm sorry," he said, knowing how hollow the words sounded, but not knowing what else to say. He could feel her hands moving against his shirt. The brunette looked at him. Then at a murmur rising from the onlookers, she turned her face toward the river.

The rope trailing the Mako had tightened. The fireman at the rear of the boat started pulling it in as the other man in the craft leaned over him to help. Julie turned toward Barry's arms. The deputies in the aluminum boat stared toward the Mako.

In seconds, the boat had been pulled backward where the

rope ran straight down into the water. The fireman continued to pull it in.

A greenish black shape . . .

And a slime-coated Christmas tree broke the surface.

Julie started sobbing loudly.

By that night, still nothing, though a pair of divers had been
down and two more rescue craft had joined the search.
Spaced a few feet apart, the four boats moved in slow for-
mation along the center of the channel pulling ropes disappearing into the water behind their sterns. Occasionally,
a man at the bow of one of the boats would flash a light
through the tall marsh grass along the far side of the river.
A small aluminum boat coming up the river slowed and
moved to the far side of the channel to give the boats pulling the grappling hooks plenty of room.

Eddie Fuller, his squat body hunched at the bow of the
small boat, tugged at the neck of his coveralls and shook
his head.

"Somebody's not coming home no more," he said.

The thinner man holding the outboard motor's steering
arm said, "Makes you want to sit closer to the middle of
the boat, don't it?"

They moved slowly past the other craft.

As the small boat cleared the dragging area and resumed
its speed, Alan, sipping from a cup of coffee as he looked
out a window at the rear of Barry and Julie's living room,
turned his eyes back toward the deputies and firemen. He
sensed the brunette stop beside him.

She had changed into a skirt and blouse. "Barry asked
me to thank you for helping get Julie back here," she said.
She glanced past a group of highway patrolmen talking at
the center of the room to the hall leading to the bedrooms.
"She's doing better now, but she doesn't want him to leave
her alone."

Her face came back to his. "I'm sorry, I'm Carolyn Haines."

"Alan Freeman."

She nodded. "I've seen you on WLOX talking about aquaculture. My father's the one who coaches the younger members of the boxing team. The ones who came by today."

He now realized that what had looked familiar to him was her father's face in hers: her high cheekbones, the shape of her chin widening back smoothly toward her hair, even her dark eyes.

"Julie told me you two used to date," she said.

He nodded. "I've known her since high school." He raised the cup of coffee toward his mouth, but stopped it before it reached his lips. Using the cup as a pointer, he gestured toward the kitchen. "They just brewed a fresh pot, if you would like me to get you a cup."

She shook her head. "No, thank you. I'm going to have to leave. I need to check on Paul. My son," she added.

Alan had already heard the boy's name from the older woman in the kitchen. Paul had been with the boys when they went into the river. Carolyn, living four houses up the street, had heard Paul's dog barking and came down to the water. She had called 911 and then came here. The older woman had seen her as she stood at the front door, hesitating, her hands at the sides of her face as she tried to gain the courage to ring the doorbell. She had sent Paul to his grandmother's house so he wouldn't be present when the bodies were carried from the river.

Now Carolyn glanced at the patrolmen again.

"They have you blocked in?" Alan asked.

"They're about ready to leave, I think." She looked toward the window. Seeming to speak to herself as much as to him she said, "With them still lying there under the water . . . I'd be in worse shape than Julie."

When she looked back at him, she forced a polite smile.

"I'm glad to have met you. I know Daddy really appreciated your letting the boys come by." Then, without waiting for him to respond, she turned toward the patrolmen. As she neared them, Barry stepped into the entrance to the hallway and called her name, and she changed directions, angling across the carpet toward him.

Alan watched them until they disappeared down the hallway, then turned back to the window.

A thick cloud had moved across the moon, casting the river in dim shadow. The boats were out of sight, but an occasional flash of light reflected off the water and came through the trees to his right.

Back to his left, the river ran into complete darkness.

TWO MILES FARTHER UP THE PASCAGOULA RIVER—10:00 P.M.

The outboard motor cut off and the small aluminum boat glided though the dark toward the wide gap in the beaver dam. Eddie Fuller shook his head in dismay. "Some son of a bitch blew it," he said. It made him mad as hell. The fish that had been trapped in the slough behind the dam had first eaten up all the little bugs and decaying matter, then had eaten up each other until there was nothing left in the slough but some of the biggest fish he had ever caught. "And now some son of a bitch do that," he repeated. "Who was the dam bothering anyway but the fish this far back on the river?"

At Eddie's words, Luke scratched at the gray stubble on his protruding chin and pushed his bill cap back on his head. "Sure enough. Jes' my luck. 'Course if it weren't for bad luck, I wouldn't have none a'tall."

Eddie leaned his wide body forward, caught a grip on the dam, and pulled them closer to the gap. In a moment he had wrapped the boat's bow rope around a protruding branch and they came up onto the structure of small logs and limbs cemented together with mud. Luke tucked his rod and reel under his arm and pulled a half-eaten Snickers bar from the pocket of his overalls. Taking a step as he unwrapped the bar, he slipped and fell to his knee, nearly dumping his minnow bucket.

Eddie smiled out of a corner of his mouth. "You're gettin' clumsy in your old age," he said. Eddie raised his arms out to his sides and, a cane fishing pole held in one hand and his minnow bucket in the other, mimicked moving along the top of the dam like a man on a tight wire.

"Did you fart?" Luke asked.

"Not in the last little bit."

"What's that smell then?"

"Somethin' dead, I'd say." His wide hips swaying, his arms still raised out to his sides as if for balance, Eddie continued on the tiptoes of his boots toward the thick trees growing in the darkness at the end of the dam.

Luke looked back at the water between the ends of the break. "I think I'll just park myself here and try to catch me a big'un when they come through from the river."

"Better chance they're already feeding at the mouth of the creek," Eddie said across his shoulder.

"Then I'll catch me one when you scare 'em this way," Luke said.

"Wanna bet who comes out with the most tonight, Mr. Silence?"

"A dollar."

"Don't be such a big spender, Luke."

Luke didn't hesitate. "Two dollars."

"You're on," Eddie said as he stepped down to the soft ground at the end of the dam. He continued on with his arms raised, this time doing his balancing act alongside the slough, angled in a gentle arc toward the mouth of the small creek, a couple of hundred feet in the distance.

When a warm gust of air came through the trees, bringing with it a stronger smell of the terrible stench, he dropped his arms to his side, glanced once into the darkness between the tree trunks, and continued on toward the creek, leaving the prints of his wide boots behind him in the soil.

Carolyn's mother, a diminutive woman with graying brown hair, quietly opened the door. Her husband's large frame came around her into the room. Paul lay on his back, his breathing quiet and slow. The flattened pack of Wrigley's Spearmint had fallen out of his hand and lay on the sheet.

Mr. Herald picked it up, placed it on the night table, and retraced his quiet steps to the door. Mrs. Herald closed it behind him.

In the living room she looked at her husband.

"It's a normal reaction," he said, "not wanting to let go of something Dustin gave him just before he went into the water."

The telephone rang and he reached to the coffee table to answer it.

"Fred Herald," he said, and then, "Hi, baby." He mouthed silently to his wife, *It's Carolyn.* "He's asleep," he said into the phone. He listened a moment and said, "It seemed like it took forever to get my bunch back home. If Dr. Hsiao hadn't delivered half of them for me, I don't believe I could have stood the time it took. I kept thinking how Paul was needing a man to talk to."

Mrs. Herald shook her head at her husband's words. "She's wanting to hear he's okay," she said.

Her husband nodded. "He's going to be fine," he said into the receiver.

Alan sipped his coffee and glanced through the window once again. Then he looked toward Carolyn, speaking on the telephone at the bookcase across the living room.

"What, Daddy?" she said. With her question, her voice rose a little from the soft tone she had been using. "What did he say about it?" she asked.

She listened a moment. "I know, Daddy, but what did Paul say?"

As she listened this time, Alan saw her eyes turn toward his. She held her gaze on his for a moment, then turned back to the phone as she said, "In the morning, Mother and I'll take him somewhere he likes—try to get his mind on something else for a little while anyway." She smiled a little. "The bumper cars—he can drive them better than I can."

A moment later she said, "'Bye. Love you."

As she replaced the receiver, she caught her lip in her teeth. She looked across the living room as the doctor Barry had called stepped inside the house. He spoke to one of the highway patrolmen and followed him toward the hallway. As they disappeared toward the bedrooms, she kept staring in their direction. Then she caught her lip in her teeth again and looked toward the front door. Alan walked toward her.

"If you need to go on," he said, "you should."

"Julie said she wanted me to stay here for awhile."

"She wants all of us to stay here," he said. "She doesn't want anything to change. But it already has."

Carolyn looked directly into his eyes now. He thought she was going to ask him something, but she didn't. "Paul's already asleep," she said. "I'll see him in the morning."

Then, almost as if the words flowed out of her without her meaning them to, she said, "Dr. Freeman, I feel guilty worrying about my own son. I should be thanking God he's okay. But I keep wondering how this might affect a six-year-old's mind. He thought of both of them almost like brothers. Dustin was at the house nearly every day and now he's not going to be there any . . ." She took an audible breath. "I'm sorry. A mother worrying about—"

"That's normal," he said.

She looked strangely at him. "That's what Daddy said." She stared at him a moment longer and then said, "Dustin gave Paul a pack of gum just before he went into the water. Daddy saw it when Paul took it out of his jeans before he climbed in bed—he went to sleep holding it.''

She waited now. Waiting for him to respond to her worry, as if she had nobody else to talk to. He looked at her wedding ring. He wondered where her husband was.

She still stared.

''He'll be okay,'' he said.

Eddie Fuller stared at his cork floating in the water, turning dark as a cloud passed across the face of the moon. He turned his face toward the beaver dam a couple of hundred feet around the curving arc of the slough. A tendril of steam curled off the water nearest the dam. The light grew dimmer. He had watched the late movies on TV the night before. Bertha had warned him what that did to his mind. He remembered the character in *Friday the 13th* slinking through the trees. He didn't want to, but nobody was around to see him, so he glanced back across his shoulder into the dark trees behind him. Then he looked toward the dam again. His tongue washed his upper lip.

''Hey, Luke, caught any big'uns yet?''

He waited a few seconds, then raised his voice higher. ''Hey, Luke, buddy, caught anything yet?''

Seconds passing and still no answer.

''Luke, you deaf or something?''

Still no answer.

''Luke, damn it. Quit fooling around.''

He brought his hand up to scratch the side of his face.

A moment later he stuck the butt of his pole in the soft soil and started around the curve of the slough toward the dam.

Nearing the rough structure, he caught the stench again. He had been upwind from it while he fished. He looked into the trees, then back to the dam. Luke must be sitting down. The moon was bright enough to see him standing.

"Hey, Luke, ole buddy?"

Eddie climbed up on the dam. A puzzled look crossed his face, then he frowned. "Hey, Luke, I'm not in the mood for no games."

He walked a little way along the structure. The break in the thick tangle of branches and logs was easy to see now. The only place Luke could be and not be seen was sitting down over the edge of the break by the water. *Or taking a dump,* Eddie thought.

He glanced toward the trees on the far side of the slough. But Luke would've had to go through the water to get there. *If he had come back this way, I'd have already passed him.*

"Luke, now damn it, you know I scare easy." He was close to the break now, steeling himself for Luke suddenly springing up and growling at him.

He noticed something at the edge of the break.

Luke's rod and reel.

He walked to it—and spotted Luke's cap floating in the still water at the bottom of the break. His stomach tightened. Luke's chest had been bothering him lately.

His brow now deeply creased, Eddie worked his way around the protruding branches and limbs to the bottom of the break and reached for Luke's cap.

He didn't know why, and he never had time to think it out, but, suddenly, he felt a cold sensation run down his back to thud at the bottom of his stomach.

Its great jaws agape, its cavernous maw red, the creature's wide head thrust up through the surface in an explosion of water and seized him, lifting him off the edge of the break much as an alligator might snatch a rabbit off a floating log.

Eddie's arm stuck out of the great, partly closed mouth. His hand opened, then closed, as the giant fish sank beneath the surface. The water boiled. Bubbles rose to the surface.

In a moment, the water was quiet again.

The small aluminum boat, its bow rope pulled loose from

the dam by the buffeting of the water, drifted slowly out toward the middle of the channel, the rope trailing along the surface behind the craft.

Alan drove slowly along Interstate 10 on his way back into Biloxi. Across the median the eastbound lanes were crowded with traffic, vacationers on their way to Florida.

That's where his parents had been going, he thought. He remembered his aunt shaking him awake with the news they had been killed in a car accident. He had been nine.

He remembered the terrible grief and instant loneliness, the men patting him on the head, some of the women hugging him, everybody saying how sorry they were. But he also remembered nobody thinking to ask a nine-year-old if he had any questions. Mixed in with his grief had been his wondering who but his parents loved him enough to take care of him with them gone, even such simple things as who was going to take him to school each morning—was he even going to be allowed to keep attending school? Thoughts that wouldn't occur to an adult, but questions very important to him at that time. But he couldn't ask anybody what he wondered—how could he be so selfish as to be worrying about himself when his parents had been the ones to suffer, he remembered thinking at the time.

Carolyn had said she was worried what might be going on in her son's mind. Why didn't she simply ask him?

And Alan wondered why he hadn't told her that.

The bow rope trailed the small aluminum boat, drifting backward down the channel.

A long ripple behind the craft.

The massive head thrust up through the water. Water streaming in rivulets back around its black eyes, the head continued to rise until several feet of the great fish's body hung suspended above the surface. With a twisting action, the head and wide upper body moved forward over the boat and came down hard, driving the craft under the surface with a great splash.

Two-foot waves crashed against the banks and rebounded toward the center of the channel.

The water slowly calmed.

Nothing could be seen but the wide channel stretching out endlessly into the dark.

Suddenly the boat shot halfway out of the water, splashed back against the surface, and drifted half-submerged and partly on its side down the river.

A moment later it began to gain speed, and moved rapidly along the center of the channel.

CHAPTER 4

BILOXI—THE NEXT MORNING

Mrs. Hsiao raised her face from her computer as Alan came inside the building.

"Have they found the boys?" she asked.

He shook his head no.

Her husband, his hair hanging against the shoulders of his plaid shirt, was speaking on her telephone. "Governor Childress," he mouthed. He pointed toward the telephone on the empty desk to the far side of the area.

Alan reached for the receiver without going around behind the desk.

Ho said, "Governor, Alan's on line now."

"Dr. Freeman, how are you doing?"

"Fine, Governor. How's the weather down there?"

"Hotter than hell. But as I was telling Dr. Hsiao, not as hot as it's going to be if I don't get some federal aid to help locate those damn Z-nets. They're killing us. Especially between Miami and the Keys. We get rid of the foreign fishing vessels and then we learn how many of those damn nets they lost, down there God only knows where, their mouths gaped open, rolling around on the bottom, thousands of fish swimming into them every day. Just great damn killing machines. I've got our charter boats, all the sports fishermen, everybody and their kid brother bitching about the fishing declining.''

As Childress paused, Alan heard him take a deep breath, and then he spoke in a more settled voice. ''Well, you don't need to hear about my problems, doctor. I'm certain you have enough of your own. It's only that I have a meeting with an environmental group in an hour. Wanted to be positive we still have ourselves a deal. Want to be able to announce some good news anyway.''

''You'll have half a million fingerlings a month for release in your waters starting your way in thirty days.''

''Guaranteed?''

''Guaranteed.''

''I hope so. I'm going to hear in an hour that the state's had dealings with other companies who weren't able to live up to the terms of their contracts.''

''The others didn't have Ho,'' Alan said.

Ho smiled broadly at that.

''Okay,'' the governor said. ''Fine. Good. Only don't let me down.''

As Alan replaced the telephone receiver, Ho smiled again. ''Good to have more demand than product,'' he said.

A moment later a serious expression replaced his smile. ''Still find no more mature red snapper females available at any hatchery. How we produce so many babies we need with only one mother? Maybe she get tired.'' His mouth moved toward the side of his thin face as he thought. ''Maybe Chang in Los Angeles—he import live fish.'' He reached for the telephone on his wife's desk.

''Ho, you keep using the phone here, how am I going to answer it?'' she said, looking up at him.

Frowning, Ho walked toward his office.

Roland Carroll, a forty-year-old copilot for Southern Air Shuttle, a small, privately held company based in the Keys, stared from the cockpit at the starboard engine of the twenty-seat craft. "It's not sounding right," he said. "I keep telling Jack if he doesn't maintain these planes better he's going to get a bunch of passengers killed one day—not to mention me." He glanced down toward the blue-green water below the plane.

"Look," he said.

The pilot looked down.

Barely visible under thirty feet of water, a long, narrow speedboat lay upturned on the bottom. Roland ran his eyes across the water in every direction. There was no sign of a life raft or people floating in preservers. He reached for the radio mike.

The pilot shook his head. "Probably been down there for years," he said.

"I didn't see it any other time," Roland said.

"You probably didn't look down at this exact same spot, Roland. You thought of that?"

Roland moved the mike to his mouth and started transmitting anyway.

Alan leaned forward at his desk and looked through the folder Ho had handed him on the fingerlings' latest survival ratio. When companies trying to meet the demand for more seafood started growing saltwater varieties in a controlled environment they encountered a grim surprise. They had already known the seas were the most dangerous places on earth. While mortality rates of seventy percent in such places as African game parks were said to demonstrate how deadly such places were to the animals living there, that rate paled in comparison to the mortality rates routinely found in the ocean. It was not unusual for as few as two to three percent of fingerlings ever to reach thirty days of age.

The low survival rate, coupled with the pressure of fishing and pollutants, the overheating or overcooling of particular spots in the oceans, the creating of deadly algae, was the reason entire species of fish often disappeared temporarily from large sections of water stretching over thousands of square miles. And that was one of the reasons most seafood restaurants featured "Fish-of-the-Day" on their menus. It was not because the restaurants were offering their customers a service by providing a varying menu, but because they had no choice—they often didn't know until the fish were delivered to them each morning what kind they would be serving that night.

So several companies had seen the opportunity for profit in establishing a dependable supply of seafood.

The surprise had been that after the companies started trying to grow the fish, they were able to increase the survival rate of most species only a meager five to six percent above what it had been in the wild.

This had to do with the mechanics associated with raising the fish, and the fish themselves. Many of the saltwater species turned out to be cannibalistic when contained close together in the comparatively small grow-out tanks, and that accounted for up to sixty to seventy percent of the mortality rate. The remainder of the deaths were due to the ocean algae. The fingerlings couldn't live without them, for the algae were not only the vital first nutrient in the baby fishes' food chain, but among the algae strands were contained rotifers and copepods, minute crustaceans that were to become the second and third steps in the chain.

The problem had been that immediately after the fingerlings were hatched they were even smaller than the crustaceans, and were eaten by them until the fish became large enough to turn the tables on these creatures. By then, combined with their own cannibalistic behavior, less than ten percent of the fingerlings survived.

There had been some improvement over the years. In using the coarsest algae from among the ninety thousand species found in the oceans, the companies had discovered that the fingerlings were provided a place to dwell safely once they reached the inner strands where they fed. Though the rotifers and copepods still were present, their slightly larger size prevented them from getting deep into the algae in pursuit of the tiny fish until the fingerlings were large enough to swim back out and attack their erstwhile nemeses.

Ho gave their company an edge here. His research had developed an even coarser algae than was used by—

"Alan," Ho said, and Alan raised his head.

"Chang not have any red snapper either. He said maybe next week. So what we do? Wait?"

Alan closed the folder. "We get them ourselves."

"How we get them when none available?" Ho asked.

"Catch them, Ho. Like everybody else does—go fishing."

"We have to have them not harmed."

"We can net them instead of using a gaff. Rig up some kind of live tank to get them back here."

Ho had a strange look on his face. "Why we not do that before?"

"The curse of convenience, Ho. Everybody always orders from the labs."

"More case of bureaucracy, Alan. We must watch that in future." A pleased expression swept Ho's face now. "And I know perfect boat to ask to rig live tank. Mr. Herald say he do us favor when he can for me showing boys around. He retired and help out some on boat at Broadwater Marina."

Paul ran his bumper car into one driven by a boy several years older. The boy frowned across his shoulder at being jolted and spun his steering wheel. In a moment he drove his car hard into Paul's and kept following him, bumping him no matter which way he turned. Carolyn frowned.

"I'm getting ready to go to jail," she said to her mother. "For teenager abuse."

Martha smiled a little. She looked at Paul and back at Carolyn. "Your grandfather died when you were six, Carolyn. You cried yourself to sleep that night, and more than once after that. But the worst eventually passed. It will pass for Paul, too."

Carolyn knew that. It was logical. And who else was more logical than she? Her father said she had decided on math for her major in college because it was the only thing she could find where two and two always added up to four—no matter what. Completely logical-thinking. Except when it came to Paul. Not that she wasn't at first—right at the very first.

The delivery had taken an especially long time. She had already decided it best her child come naturally and had resisted the doctors who wanted to deliver Paul by cesarean rather than let her labor continue any longer.

He had been born with one leg slightly shorter than the other and slightly smaller in circumference. His shoes only needed a slight thickening of one sole; no one could tell without measuring. But she knew. Despite the doctors saying the length of time she was in labor had nothing to do with the slight impairment, she had never been able to completely accept that.

And now, instead of being logical in raising her child, she had to be careful to keep from being too protective—and hurt him again in that way.

It had already happened in the hours since Skip and Dustin's deaths the day before. She knew she needed to do what she could to keep Paul from having the tragedy on his mind, and she knew what he liked most, to anchor the boat and swim and play in the clear water off the barrier islands. They had done it a hundred times. Yet, now, every time the thought passed through her mind, she felt a surge of nervousness. That certainly wasn't logical. She would be with him every second he was in the water. Yet the thought still bothered her.

"And he's to worry about?" her mother said. "He's going to be fine."

The older boy and Paul had left the small vehicles and were now talking friendly about something as they walked toward the miniature golf course at the front of the complex.

Carolyn watched them for a moment, then turned her face across the four lanes of Highway 90 bordering the small amusement complex. Past the pavement, the white sand beach ran down to the Mississippi Sound, its wide, murky waters spreading out toward the barrier islands, seen in the far distance only by the tops of the trees growing high above their low shapes.

Beyond them were the gentle breezes and crystal-clear waters and quiet anchorages stretching to the Chandeleur Islands.

She made up her mind.

"I don't have a charter booked tomorrow. I'm going to hold the boat open and take Paul out to the islands."

Her mother nodded. "He'll like that."

Carolyn nodded. "Me, too. I need to have something else on my mind." She started to say how she had awakened with a start during the night after dreaming that Paul *had* gone in the water with Dustin and Skip. That all three of them . . .

She was pulled out of her thoughts by Paul walking toward her. He had his thumbs hooked in the pockets of his shorts, and his head hung down.

"I'm tired," he said.

That's what he always said when he didn't want to do something.

"You're not having fun?"

"I'm tired," he repeated.

CHAPTER 5

A Coast Guard boat, its bow marked by a diagonal orange stripe, floated at anchor under a bright sun shining down on the water off the Everglades. Known in Coast Guard jargon simply by its length in feet, the "forty-one" had responded to the report of a sunken speedboat lying upside down on the bottom in thirty feet of water.

A pair of divers were down.

One of them, Petty Officer Matt Rhiner, lowered his head and, shining his watertight light ahead of him, peered under the speedboat. No bodies lay with the hull on top of them. He hadn't expected there to be. But neither had he expected what he had seen when he first dove down to the boat— long, narrow slashes up and down its hull. The damage *had* to have been caused by the craft having slammed hard into the jagged protrusions of a reef. Yet there wasn't a shallow-water reef projecting near the surface anywhere close to the area. And the damage actually didn't look to Rhiner much like what would come from a reef's protrusions. Rather, each of the slashes started with a round puncture at one end, narrowing almost to a point at the opposite end of the cut, similar to the marks that would be left if a construction crane had let down a big steel bucket and its metal teeth had dug into the craft's hull before then pulling through the fiberglass, and slipping loose.

But the most unusual circumstance was where the craft lay—over seventy miles from where it had been reported missing some three months before off the west side of the Keys and, supposedly, on its way down the chain toward Key West.

That not being a heavily traveled route, Command had first thought about the possibility of drug smuggling. Yet smugglers didn't take drugs south toward the end of the Keys, but north toward the mainland. And the possibility of smugglers had gone completely by the wayside when it was learned that the two men on the boat had been prominent, older doctors off on an annual two-week fishing party without their wives.

So with the craft being found, instead of answers being given, new questions were raised. Rhiner pushed himself away from the hull and looked across his shoulder through a school of small brightly colored fish to the second member of his diving team, gliding slowly a few feet above the bottom, searching for any sign that might have to do with the boat. Rhiner used his flippers to push off against the craft's hull and swam out over the sand.

The sun was almost directly overhead, its strong beams passing easily through the light-green water and reflecting off the sand almost as if it was a polished surface. Everything could be seen. It was a good time to search.

But for what? He looked back across his shoulder at the boat. Was there something obvious he was missing? He moved his gaze toward the sand beneath him, the current flowing there expressed in the slight leaning of the sea grasses below him. He quit swimming, holding his hands and flippers motionless, and watched the grasses.

Slowly he felt his body pushed gently forward, the

grasses starting to move backward underneath his form. As he neared the low remnants of a reef that had once flourished with color but was now a gray, dead chunk of rock, he noticed his drift was forced slightly to the side by the current moving around the structure. But the current's movement—at least at this point in time—was directed generally south, in the opposite direction of the way the speedboat would have had to drift to come to where it lay. Besides, despite this lesser-traveled area off the Everglades, the route wasn't completely devoid of traffic. Somebody would have spotted an empty, floating boat in the time it would have taken to drift here, wouldn't they? But the fact was they hadn't.

Then deciding to leave such technical speculation to the investigators and oceanographers who would be familiar with the reefs, the currents, and what they could do, how far they ran, and from where, he started kicking his flippers again. In any case, he now had a creepy story to tell his children, he thought—about a boat so far from where it should have been, and empty of its occupants—his own personal version of the *Flying Dutchman*. A smaller, two-man speedboat version, he thought, but *his* version. When he was older and the story grew exaggerated in his mind, it would become a *really* creepy story to relate to his grand-children. He smiled to himself.

Then he caught sight of a sparkling reflection below him.

He waited until the sun reflected off the object again, then tilted his head down and let the work of his flippers carry him toward the spot without using his hands.

He saw it more clearly. It was an off-white or a light beige, but shiny at the same time. Drawing near it, he saw the object was triangular in shape, with its blunt base notched with a curving indentation at its center. He kicked his flippers a last time and reached his hand out.

Even before he touched it, he knew what it had to be— the shape, its tapering sides serrated—a shark's tooth. But as he lifted it into his hand, he couldn't believe its size—three to four inches wide across its base and at least six or seven inches in height.

Letting his feet settle toward the bottom and his shoulders rise, he kept staring. The tooth's age was evident, the normally ivory surface having turned darker with time. But once, however long ago, a huge . . .

His gaze went back over his shoulder toward the speedboat. Though knowing how ridiculous his thought had to be, he kicked his flippers, propelling his body back toward the sunken craft.

Reaching its side, he lifted the tooth on top of the hull and pressed the pointed end down into a puncture at the beginning of a slash. The puncture was so wide that had he not continued to hold the tooth it would have fallen through to the sand beneath the hull. His thought *had* been ridiculous. Now the other diver swam up beside him. Rhiner held the tooth out flat in his hand. He saw the man's eyes narrow behind his faceplate.

The shadow began to creep over them.

They jerked their faces toward the surface as one.

Above them, the rounded hull of the forty-one continued to swing around on its anchor line, extending its wide shadow farther out across the bottom.

Alan slowed his Jeep as he neared the stoplight at the west entrance to the Broadwater Beach Hotel and Marina. In past decades a sleepy luxury stop for yachts traveling the Gulf between New Orleans and Mobile, the complex now operated at a more frenetic pace as the Broadwater Beach Hotel and Marina—and President Casino. Alan turned into the marina.

Shaped in a wide, deep square, with enough area of water at its center to allow even the largest yachts to make a complete turn, the complex's sides and near end featured the much-photographed concrete-roofed slips that gave the vessels nestled under their shadows protection from the weather. He turned his Jeep toward the charter fishing boats lined side by side at the marina's northwest corner, drove into a parking space in front of the slips, and stopped.

The first person he saw was Carolyn's father. He stood in the fishing cockpit of a thirty-four-foot Silverton, one of the older boats there with the sailboat-like curving lines of craft built in the sixties and seventies. He held a wrench in one hand and a five-gallon can in the other. His large frame was clothed in a yellow jumpsuit with smears of grease down its shoulder. He was looking toward his feet, turning around and around slowly, as if he had dropped something small and was trying to find it. At that moment, he looked toward the Jeep and waved the wrench in greeting. Alan stepped to the concrete, lifted his sports coat from the Jeep, and walked behind the boats toward him.

"Dr. Freeman."

Slipping the sports coat on over his shoulders, Alan nodded his greeting. "Mr. Herald."

"Thinking about going fishing?"

"Sort of."

"Well, you've come to the right place. Best charter boat captain on the coast. She always finds fish."

She?

"Woman's intuition," Mr. Herald added, nodding at the craft's name, *Intuitive,* stenciled across its rear. "Works every time." He grinned. "Of course maybe with a little help from all the expensive locator equipment she's put onboard. Carolyn said she met you last night. Oh, yeah, I really do appreciate Dr. Hsiao letting me bring the boys by." His expression turned serious. "Terrible about those children at the river. Have they found them yet?"

Alan shook his head.

"Terrible," Mr. Herald repeated. "Here yesterday morning and then gone just like that." He shook his head sadly, then walked toward the side of the cockpit to come up out of the boat onto the narrow concrete walkway running back toward the parking area.

As he did, Alan looked at the wide beam of the boat, setting backed into its berth with little room to spare to its sides. A woman's touch would be more than adequate in the deft maneuvering it took to dock such a craft during crosswinds and the changing current created by rising and falling tides—a woman surgeon's delicate hands could be more exact than a male surgeon's. But there were also the bulky rods and reels to be handled, and a gaff not only used to snag a fish as it was reeled close to the boat, but then to lift that catch from the water over into the cockpit when some of the larger species could routinely weigh forty to fifty pounds or more. He could visualize a *big* woman being up to the task, but Carolyn couldn't weigh much more than a hundred fifteen to a hundred twenty pounds. On the other hand, a captain could remain always at the controls and leave the heavy work to a mate. He looked at the large frame of Carolyn's father, who had stopped before him. He imagined he was looking at the mate.

Mr. Herald pulled a soiled rag from his hip pocket and scrubbed his hand vigorously. But it remained dark with grease. He shrugged and smiled instead of reaching to shake hands. "You said *sorta* thinking about going fishing?"

"I need to catch a few red snapper—females."

Mr. Herald grinned. "You care about the sex?"

"I need females to spawn. And they can't be injured. So we'd have to use a net instead of a gaff to bring them on board."

"Bringing them back alive," Mr. Herald mused. He looked into the cockpit. "There's the cooler, maybe." It was a fiberglass container built into the front of the cockpit against the cabin. It was a little over five feet long and two feet wide. "Possible we could get a couple in there. We would have to cushion the box. Maybe use foam rubber.

They'd still be fighting it, trying to get out, and probably at each other. I wouldn't guarantee they'd live after we got them back here. But if you want to pay for the charter, that's the business Carolyn's in.''

Alan nodded. ''I'll tranquilize them—but I don't know if a couple will be enough.''

Before Mr. Herald could respond, a figure stepped out of the rear door of the boat's cabin. It was one of the boys from the boxing team, the thin Vietnamese named San-hi. He was barefooted, had his khaki pants rolled halfway up his skinny calves, and a long shirt hanging down past his waist. He held a rag and bucket in his hands. ''Mr. Herald,'' he said, and nodded back across his shoulder. ''It's clean as I can get it. You want to inspect it?''

''Clean as you can get it?'' Mr. Herald asked.

''Yes sir.''

''Then I don't need to inspect it, do I—if you can't get it any cleaner.''

''Same here,'' a voice said from the far side of the cabin. Armon's stocky, dark shape came around the rail. Dressed in jeans and a T-shirt stretching to contain his muscular shoulders, he also held a bucket and rag. He pointed at the rail. ''How's that?'' he asked.

The rail glistened as if it had been shined with polish. In fact, the whole boat did.

''Looks fine, Armon. I guess I owe you two a meal now.''

''Not to mention the fifteen bucks apiece,'' Armon said.

Mr. Herald smiled. ''So long as you let Carolyn think I did this all myself.''

''No skin off my bal . . . teeth,'' Armon said.

Mr. Herald stared at him.

''Teeth,'' Armon repeated.

''You all wash up so you don't look like a couple of bums when I take you in.''

Armon's eyes went to the grease across the shoulder of

Mr. Herald's jumpsuit. San-hi smiled. "Come on, Armon."

They stepped inside the cabin.

As they did, Mr. Herald said, "Here's the boss now."

Alan looked across his shoulder as Carolyn drove a Ford Ranger into the parking space next to his Jeep.

She stepped outside in an orange sundress exposing her tanned shoulders.

Her son was with her.

Alan couldn't help but stare at the boy.

CHAPTER 6

It was as if Alan was watching himself as a small child walk toward him. Paul's hair was thick and dark like his own, his coloring not quite as dark as Carolyn's, more like mine, Alan thought. He visualized the scrapbook photograph his aunt had of him the day he entered the first grade. Carolyn leaned to say something to the boy as they came toward the boat.

The boy nodded—and looked directly into Alan's face.

Alan moved his gaze back up to Carolyn as she stopped in front of her father.

"The boss," Mr. Herald repeated, and nodded down at Paul.

Carolyn said, "Paul, this is Dr. Freeman."

The boy reached out his hand, and Alan shook it.

"Dr. Freeman wants to charter your boat," Mr. Herald said.

Carolyn smiled politely. "What date do you have in mind?"

Alan took his eyes away from the boy's. "Tomorrow would be fine, if that's all right with you."

"I'm sorry, but I'm booked for the weekend."

Her father said, "I thought you still had tomorrow open."

"Filled it a few minutes ago," Carolyn said and looked down at Paul. "So Monday would be the earliest possible time, Dr. Freeman. I'm sorry. You might try the other captains, but I don't think you'll find a boat not already booked—the weekends are our busiest times."

"Is it clean enough?" her father asked.

Carolyn looked at the boat. "You did a perfect job."

San-hi and Armon smiled at each other. Paul stepped around his mother and walked toward the two boys.

Mr. Herald waited until Paul was out of hearing, then spoke in a low voice. "How has he been doing?"

Carolyn shook her head. "He was having fun at the bumper cars, and then suddenly wanted to leave."

"It'll come and go for awhile."

She nodded.

"Well, I have to get San-hi and Armon home," he said. "I'm going to pick them up a sandwich. You want me to bring you one back?"

"No. I shared a po'boy with Paul."

Alan looked toward the boy. He was smiling at something one of the older boys said. At that moment, Paul's face turned toward his, and Alan smiled pleasantly back in his direction.

"Do you want to check with the other captains?" Carolyn asked.

"I can wait until Monday," Alan said, bringing his eyes back to hers.

"He's going to stick hypodermics in red snappers," Mr. Herald said and grinned. "Has to be females. Let him tell you about it." He looked toward San-hi and Armon. "You two ready?"

Armon smiled and rubbed his thumb and forefinger together in Mr. Herald's direction.

Mr. Herald frowned.

They started toward his pickup.

"Thank you for cleaning the boat, Daddy," Carolyn

said, and then her eyes came back to Alan's. "Hypodermics?"

He explained why he needed the fish as her father and the boys drove off in the pickup. When he told her about needing to rig up some way to bring them back unharmed, she looked into the cockpit.

He said, "Maybe I could bring one of the smaller fingerling tanks down here and we could figure out a way to mount it on the forward deck."

Carolyn nodded. "We would need to put something under it to cushion it. To protect my deck as well as make the ride smoother for the fish. Whole-day rate starts about as early as you want. Give me a time and I'll meet you down here Monday morning with what you bring and we'll see if we can fashion something that'll work."

He nodded, then looked at Paul, his back to them as he stared down into the water between the *Intuitive* and the boat beside it. Alan thought for a moment. He glanced at his watch. "It is about lunchtime. You sure you wouldn't care for something?"

Carolyn shook her head.

"I'm hungry," Paul said, turning in their direction.

"You just had a po'boy," Carolyn said.

"I'm hungry anyway."

Alan looked toward the marina restaurant and lounge at the far end of the line of boats. Music from its outdoor speakers floated back through the air to them and people crowded the tables arranged around the outside of the main structure. "We could catch something down there or back in the Broadwater."

"I want to eat in the hotel," Paul said. Alan noticed the boy was looking at him instead of his mother.

"Paul, Dr. Freeman isn't—"

"I don't mind at all," Alan said.

"Mother?" Paul asked.

"Okay," she said in a low voice.

* * *

She said nothing more as they walked toward the hotel. Alan glanced down at Paul as the boy came around to his side and walked at the same pace as he did. Alan noticed Carolyn glance down at Paul once—and the barely perceptible tightening of her jaw.

They took a table by a window overlooking the tiered swimming pool across a patio from the restaurant. Carolyn sat directly opposite Alan, and Paul sat in the chair to their side. "You want the buffet?" she asked.

Paul shook his head. "A chicken sandwich."

"Only tea for me, please," she said to the waitress.

"I want a Coke," Paul said.

"Tea and a chicken sandwich will be fine," Alan said.

"Separate checks," Carolyn said.

"I'll catch it," Alan said.

"Separate checks," Carolyn repeated. Alan looked at her. She didn't look back at him.

As the waitress walked away Paul asked, "Can I buy some gum?"

"After you eat."

"I won't chew it until then." He held his palm out across the edge of the table toward his mother.

Alan started to reach into his pocket, but didn't.

Carolyn handed Paul a dollar from her purse.

He slipped from his chair and hurried toward the front of the restaurant and the hotel lobby. Alan watched him for a moment, then looked back at Carolyn. She turned her gaze out the window toward the pool. He stared at her for a moment.

"I don't know any way to be but blunt," he said. "Have I done something to put you off?"

Carolyn's face came back around to his. "Paul wanted to eat with you because you look a lot like his father."

Before he could respond in any way, she said, "I'm not married."

He looked at her wedding ring.

"I wear it so men chartering my boat don't keep trying to corner me against a bulkhead. Chartering is how I make my living, I can't afford to be telling my customers off. And some of them wouldn't leave me any other choice. It usually works except with the worst of them."

She didn't specifically say he was one of them, but her glance at her ring and back at him said it for her.

Irritated, and at the same time amused, he lifted the side of his mouth in a sarcastic smile.

She stared at him now.

"Listen," he said, "you're as nice looking as you evidently think you are, but your ring did work on me."

She started to say something back to him, but it was his time to talk now. "I asked you if you wanted to eat lunch partly because . . . partly because you were worried about Paul last night and all I said when you told me you were was that he'd be okay. I thought maybe you might still want to ask something. And partly because of Paul. I don't know. I thought . . . Hell, maybe it was because I thought he might want to ask me something. It's none of my business though, is it?"

Her stare slowly softened.

"I believe you're serious," she said.

"Really? Well I guess I should be thankful that—"

"No, I do. . . . I'm sorry."

He stared back at her.

"I'm sorry," she repeated.

The waitress leaned over the table to set their tea before them. Carolyn nodded her thanks, then looked back at him as the woman walked away from the table.

"We'll fix your tank where it'll work," she said.

She smiled softly now. "I might order a salad after all,"

she added, "if you have time to wait. I'm sure they already have your order about ready."

Her eyes stayed on his. He nodded.

"Fine," she said.

He looked at her ring.

She opened her fingers and looked at the band. "To make a long story short—I guess I owe you—he left me right after Paul was born. But don't start crying. He left the papers to the house signed over to me, lying on the kitchen table. I guess he felt like he owed me something after three years of dating and a year of marriage. He definitely didn't want a child. He made that plain the first few months I was pregnant. I guess he stuck around a month after the birth to make sure I was going to be able to handle Paul by myself—he said I was too stupid. Or maybe it took him that long to figure out where he was going to go where he wouldn't be bothered by me trying to get some child support."

She paused a second. "I'm not a man hater. I wasn't even really irritated with you. It's only that you look so much like the pictures of his father Paul found in the attic. And then you're standing at the boat and Paul's eyes widen. I was afraid he was going to hop out of the Ranger before he realized you weren't his father—and it made me angry. Not at him. At his father. And Paul wasn't hungry—he hardly touched the po'boy—and then he wants to eat with you. Is that some kind of transference? He's already facing Dustin and Skip drowning, and now seeing you brings his father back into his mind—that he was deserted. I . . ."

She spread her hands. "No excuse. I shouldn't have taken it out on you."

He was silent a moment. "He's a nice kid."

"Not always," she said, and smiled. A soft smile. It hadn't escaped him how attractive she was when he had seen her at the river, but with Julie and Barry on his mind he hadn't dwelled on her looks. Now, looking directly into her face, she was as attractive as he first thought, maybe even more so.

She looked at her ring again. "I don't wear it all that much really." She grinned. "Even when I'm on a charter. Just when I'm in a bad mood basically and don't want to be bothered by anybody. I forgot I had it on. Maybe I've used it so much when I'm in a bad mood, it casts a spell now."

She smiled once more, then looked across her shoulder in the direction Paul had gone—giving Alan her profile: her dark hair and high cheekbones, her full red lips, and the olive hue of her skin. *Damn*, he thought at what he was about to say.

"At the risk of getting us back to where we were a few minutes ago," he started.

She faced back toward him.

He nodded toward her ring. "Now that I know that doesn't mean anything, I wouldn't mind maybe taking you out to dinner."

He quickly held his hands up in front of him. "A simple no will suffice."

"I'd love to, really," she said easily. "But I'm going to stay close to Paul for awhile. . . . Maybe another time."

"We can take him along."

"You have to be kidding."

"About what?" Paul said as he stepped to his mother's side. He had two packs of gum in his hand. Neither of them were opened, but he was chewing something.

"I said I'd like to take you and your mother out to dinner tonight—if you'd like to go."

Paul smiled broadly.

Carolyn frowned, but only half-heartedly.

"Mother?" Paul asked.

She closed her eyes and nodded.

Paul smiled again.

"Eight o'clock?" Alan asked.

"Seven," she said. "Paul has to be in bed by ten."

Paul frowned.

Alan's cellular phone rang.

He grinned as he pulled it from inside his coat. "Ho wondering if I've found a boat yet." He unfolded the phone and lifted it to his ear.

"Hello."

"Alan, I have to have my baby back to bury. Please help me find him." Then Julie started sobbing uncontrollably.

"Alan." It was a different voice—Barry's. "Alan, I apologize. They've stopped . . . they've stopped dragging with all but one boat." His voice was about to break, too. "Julie can't bear to think that we might not find . . . I . . . I apologize, Alan. I'm sorry." Alan heard the receiver placed back onto its cradle. He hadn't said a word.

Carolyn's eyes were on his expression. "It was Julie," he said. "They've stopped. . . ." He looked at Paul, listening.

Then the waitress set Paul's chicken sandwich in front of him. "Be careful," she said, "the french fries are hot." Alan looked at the plate. The waitress repeated her warning as she set his order on the table. Outside the window the sunlight shone brightly down on the pool, glistening off the water. *Warming its water.* He didn't like what he was thinking. He came to his feet.

"I'll call you later," he said to Carolyn. He patted Paul on the head and said, "You be ready by seven now—I'll see you then."

He looked back at Carolyn again.

"I'll call you," he repeated, and walked toward the front of the restaurant.

CHAPTER 7

Alan stopped at the riverbank. Only the *Mako* remained on the water, as Barry had said. The two firemen in the craft were slouched, obviously tired, one of them leaning on his hand and looking off through the marsh as he smoked a cigarette. They were only going through the motions of dragging now. What they were really doing was waiting. It had already been a little over twenty-four hours since the boys had disappeared. It couldn't be much longer until the warm water would do the job everybody knew it would finally do and the bodies would come floating to the top. Unless they were snagged on something.

And if that was the case, it would quickly reach the point that there wouldn't be any bodies worth recovering—at least that their parents would be able to face.

That was the thought that had passed through his mind as the waitress had warned about the french fries and the sunlight had glistened off the pool outside the restaurant window. He thought of Julie's sad voice again, how Barry sounded. He kept staring at the water. It was so damn murky. Only two divers from the search-and-rescue units had gone down. They could have easily been within a few feet of the bodies and had no chance at all of glimpsing them.

But the fish would have no such problems in finding them. And the turtles. Especially one turtle . . .

He had been diving in Norfork Lake in north Arkansas a few miles from the Missouri border. A storm had passed through the area only a couple of days before and the visibility wasn't much over five feet. Swimming near the bottom, he had almost blundered into an alligator snapping turtle as big as a pickup-truck tire, the creature's feet lightly touching the bottom, its long neck thrust forward and its jaws gaping, big enough to ingest a softball, its eyes staring up at him.

Small turtles and fish would go after the eyes and ears and lips first, the soft parts of the bodies. Yet as horrible as that thought was, a mortician could mold the lips and ears back and close the eyes. But a snapping turtle like he had seen at Norfork. . . . And the Pascagoula River and marsh swarmed with the big turtles, with their ridged backs and wide, hooked beaks giving them the appearance of prehistoric monsters. One of them, given only a little time to work on a body, would leave behind a carnage that nobody could fix—that no mother or father could stand to see.

He punched a number into his cellular phone and lifted it to his ear.

When a voice answered he said, "Bert, this is Alan. I'm going to need some help—some volunteers who can dive."

The Coast Guard forty-one's bow threw spray out to both sides, the craft both plowing through the swells and riding up and down with their motion at the same time. Petty Officer Matt Rhiner stood at the flying bridge atop the main structure at the center of the boat. He held a radio mike in one hand and the giant tooth in the other. Only twenty minutes earlier he had reported the damage done to the sunken speedboat, and twice had been asked to repeat the dimensions and condition of the tooth. Now he had been contacted again and asked to stand by. As he waited, he watched the swells building in front of the forty-one. Some of the waves were starting to lose their tops to whitecaps. He looked at the clouds rushing toward the craft. The forty-one suddenly yawed to the left and he had to grab for the front of the bridge to keep his balance. He looked at the young woman at the wheel. She only glanced at him from the corner of her eyes. "Sorry," she mumbled. She held both hands on the wheel now.

"*Stand by*," came over the VHF radio, "*for Admiral Kendrick.*"

Admiral? Rhiner was taken aback.

"*Petty Officer Rhiner.*"

"Yes, sir."

"*This is Admiral Kendrick. I understand you have something unusual on board. I wanted to hear it for myself. Close to seven inches in slant-height?*"

"Yes, sir; roughly six and three quarters by the ruler."

"*An indentation in the center of the base; the tooth overall nearly heart-shaped, you reported?*"

"Yes, sir. I've seen a White Shark tooth; a lot like that except for the indentation and its being so much larger, sir."

"*Still smooth to the touch? Dark in color?*"

"Off-white, sir, maybe a light beige."

"*Well make certain you hang onto it son; I have an old friend that's going to be quite interested in it.*"

"Yes, sir."

"*Out.*"

Seaman Rowella Brunt grimaced as another hard swell bore into the forty-one's bow at a quarter angle, but she held the boat straight.

"Good job, Seaman," Rhiner said.

"Thank you."

He nodded his reply. His gaze went to the tooth again. This time he also thought of the dark shadow that had passed over him, and a chill swept across his shoulders.

* * *

It took less than an hour for the volunteers to assemble after Alan made his calls. Two friends who had gone to college with him and owned their own businesses in the area, two off-duty deputies from the Jackson County Sheriff's Department, three off-duty highway patrolmen, Carolyn's father, and two neighbors living along the river and a man one of them had brought with him had responded. A dozen of them in all—enough to form a tight line sixty to seventy feet wide across the bottom. In repeatedly moving back and forth from one side of the channel to the other, they could cover better than the length of two football fields in ten or so passes—more than enough area in which to find the boys, even if their bodies had drifted a distance before settling to the bottom.

Actually, there was one more man prepared to dive. But Alan knew there was no way he was going to let him go down.

He looked at Dustin's father. In a pair of swimming trunks and standing with the three similarly clad highway patrol volunteers, his hand rested limply on an air tank propped upright on the ground beside him as he stared at the water. Carolyn stood a few feet behind him, watching him with a deep sadness apparent in her face. Alan walked toward him.

Barry's face came around to his. "Barry, this isn't something you need to be doing."

"Julie's going crazy."

"I know. But we have enough help to cover the bottom. We'll . . ."—looking at the pain in Barry's face, Alan had to take a breath—"we'll find them."

"I have to help," Barry said. "I told her I would."

"Then you mark the side of our passes each time we come back to the bank—make certain we don't leave a gap."

"Alan, I want to dive with—"

"Barry, with you in the water, everybody is going to be thinking about you finding them—how you're going to react. They wouldn't be concentrating on what they're doing."

"Maybe he's right," one of the patrolmen said in a soft voice.

Barry looked at the man and then, without another word and leaving his tank propped where it sat, turned and walked into the trees toward Julie. There wasn't any reason for him to wait by the bank. Barry knew nobody was needed to mark the passes.

Alan slipped his tank up around his shoulder to his back. The others did the same. Carolyn's father, his wide chest matted with a thick layer of graying hair, finished buckling his tank's backpack around his waist and lifted a coil of nylon rope from the ground.

Alan spoke in a voice low enough it wouldn't reach up through the trees. "With them down there twenty-four hours now, I don't know how they're going to look. Whoever does find them, knock on your tank with your knife. We'll come to the sound. If they look too bad, a couple of us need to come back and try to prepare their parents before we bring them up."

"Not me," a voice said in an equally low tone. Alan looked to his right at the youngest of the men, a lean, tanned blond in his mid-twenties. Alan didn't know him personally, but knew his first name was Donald. He was the one who had come with a neighbor of Julie's and Barry's. "I couldn't handle that," Donald added.

Carolyn's father said, "I'll do it if it comes down to it, son." He handed the young man an end of the rope and the other men moved to form a line. He walked in front of them, each of them catching onto the rope at four- to five-foot intervals. Alan stepped to the middle of the line, caught the rope as one of the deputies moved down the line to make way for him, and they started forward.

At the very edge of the water the flippers were slipped on.

"Ready?" Alan asked.

Everybody nodded. Alan pulled his mask down over his face and fitted his mouthpiece into place. The firemen in the *Mako* looked toward the bank as the line of men stepped ankle-deep into the water. At their next step, water came to their knees.

Another yard, and the bottom fell away.

Like diving in a cup of warm tea; Alan thought—the visibility was less than a couple of feet and cast with a brown murkiness at that. He felt the unseen tugs on the rope until each diver settled at the same depth. He leaned forward, having to lower his faceplate almost to the muddy bottom before it came into view.

A few feet farther and he leveled off and, moving at not much more than a crawl, inched slowly in the direction of the middle of the channel.

An eighteen-wheeler tire mostly buried in the mud materialized behind the slowly flowing, larger particles of sediment floating past his mask. The tire had been something the grappling hooks had missed. He passed over it. An out-of-sight diver to his right slowed, pulling the line in that direction, and Alan waited until the pressure eased, then inched forward again.

A glimpse of white ahead of him. He pulled himself closer to the object and found it to be a short section of plastic pipe.

He moved across it. Holding the rope in one hand, he found it easiest to progress at the slow pace forced on him by pushing off the mud with his other hand rather than using his flippers. He looked to the right and left, saw only the murky water stretching out inches from him, quickly becoming a solid brown curtain cutting off all visibility in a close-in circle all around him. It was as if he were at the center of a deep earthen well, cut off from sunlight from above, the water closest to him seeming to glow dimly with its own light. He slowly pulled his body forward.

Carolyn watched the circles of bubbles spaced a few feet apart, one circle sometimes lagging behind the others. At times a circle moved a couple of feet ahead of the line before pausing for the rest of the circles of bubbles to catch up. The men had been down for several minutes and weren't even a tenth of the way across the channel. On the river's far side, the firemen ran the bow of the *Mako* onto a mudflat. As they did, a heron suddenly flapped up from the tall water grass ahead of the boat and turned back over the marsh toward the Interstate 10 bridge in the distance.

Carolyn looked back at the bubbles. The line was stopped once more, waiting for a circle to catch up. With each of the divers having only one tank apiece she knew they weren't going to be able to cover even half the area Alan had hoped.

Alan felt the string move across his wrist before he saw it—a nylon line the same brown color as the water. A trot line—with short strings hung with sharp, barbed hooks every few inches along its length. When first set out the hooks would have been baited with balls of stinking cheese or minnows to attract the big catfish in the river.

Had the search-and-rescue divers noted it? If a swimmer hung one of the razor-sharp hooks in his leg, he couldn't break the strong nylon with his hands. The only way to escape back to the surface would be to yank the hook's barbs, flesh and all, from his leg. And if a swimmer was hooked, he wouldn't have much time to make up his mind to endure such pain before he grew dizzy from lack of oxygen and then would no longer have the strength to pull the hook through his flesh. Wondering if the line was still anchored to the far side of the channel, Alan pulled on it.

It came easily toward him. *Easily,* he thought. *No resistance from bodies hung somewhere along its length.*

Still pulling in the line, carefully avoiding each hook as it came into view, at the same time he had to keep moving forward to keep up with the other divers. Then, from out of the brown darkness one string trailed backward with something on its end. A catfish head, he saw, as it came closer to his hand, its body missing behind its ribbed, circular gills.

As the head slowly passed by his fingers, he noted its gaped mouth was large enough to place both his fists inside the jaws. The fish had been at least thirty pounds. The men who had set the line had caught it, but the turtles had reaped the benefits. The line still came easily. He released it and pulled himself forward to keep from holding the others back.

Clank!

Alan's head jerked toward the knife clanging against a scuba tank. The rope went slack in that direction.

Clank! Clank!

He kicked his flippers toward the sound. He immediately lost all bearing with his surroundings—and slowed to keep from crashing into another diver responding to the sounds.

Clank! Clank! Clank!

The sounds came from above now.

And ceased altogether.

Alan broke the surface. Four other faces already bobbed behind their face masks. One of them, the young blond named Donald, held his hand out of the water and stared at his closed fist. The rest of the divers broke the surface.

The one closest to Donald suddenly twisted his face away from the clenched fist and vomited a yellow stream of liquid into the water.

Alan saw it now.

In Donald's closed fist were two long, blue fingers extending from what was left of the hand of one of the teen-agers.

"I . . . I . . . ," Donald tried to say. "I felt it under my hand. It moved. I thought it moved. . . ." He shook his head in dismay. "I . . . God," he said.

On the bank, Carolyn's eyes had knitted at the vomiting of one of the divers. She saw Alan look in her direction and past her. Julie was coming down through the trees; Barry, holding her by the arm, appeared to be trying to stop her.

All the divers stared at the couple. The men started toward the bank. The blond kept holding his fist out of the water, as if he clutched something he didn't want to get wet.

Julie stared at the divers looking at her. "No," she said.

The divers neared the bank.

"No," Julie said again. Beside her, Barry's eyes narrowed as he tried to see.

The divers came out of the water to the bank. The young blond seemed to hesitate, lagging behind, then came up beside the others.

He looked toward Julie and Barry.

Skip's parents came a few feet behind them.

"No," Julie said.

Alan kicked his flippers off, shrugged his tank to the ground and hurried toward her. Barry suddenly collapsed to his knees, and started sobbing. Carolyn saw what the blond held. Oh, God, no!

"NO!" Julie screamed, "*NO! NO!*"

"*NOOOOOO!*"

CHAPTER 8

An ambulance backed into Carolyn's driveway for the bodies. The attendants stepped outside with body bags, but stopped as they saw Mr. Herald standing a few feet away with the partial palm and two fingers wrapped in a handkerchief. The driver went back inside the ambulance and brought out a plastic garbage bag. He inserted what there was in the bottom of the bag and gently folded it into a square.

As the ambulance drove out of the drive and Mr. Herald walked toward the house, Alan held open the front door. Mr. Herald looked at him but didn't speak as he passed him and went inside the house. Alan stepped inside, closing the door behind him. Jonas "Pop" Stark, the Jackson County Sheriff, spoke on the telephone that sat on the coffee table. A heavy man with a gruff voice, he wore gray slacks and a blue sports coat over a beige shirt unbuttoned at the collar, and kept fidgeting with the collar. He nodded at something that was said over the phone, replaced the receiver, and came across the carpet.

"So let's go over it one more time, Dr. Freeman. Am I missing anything—bull sharks, this far up in freshwater, attacking in a pack?"

That had to be the case, Alan knew, and Stark did too,

even before they had discussed it. The only other creature in the river capable of an attack was an alligator. Not only was such an attack so rare as to be almost dismissed outright, but there would have been only one victim held below the water and drowned. One of the boys would have made it back to the bank. And bull sharks were the only sharks off the American coast to venture into freshwater. "They've been spotted as far as two hundred miles up the Mississippi," Alan said.

"They've always been here," Stark said. "Lake Pontchartrain is full of 'em. A couple of people have been chewed up a little, but I never heard of nobody being killed. Hell, they're all along the coast from Texas to Florida and I've never heard of nobody being eaten before. Why now?"

The question was an expression of frustration, not meant to be answered. That bull sharks had finally killed somebody was not surprising, Alan knew. While most people thought of a great white when they thought of a shark attack, any marine expert would tell you bull sharks were much more likely to attack unprovoked. Only their size kept them from being worse than they were. The largest ones he had seen around the coast had seldom exceeded five or six feet in length.

Stark must have been thinking the same thing, for he said, "They're not big enough to take a victim in one bite. For neither Skip nor Dustin to surface after they were attacked, I . . ." He shook his head as his words trailed off. "How damn many of them were there?" Again it was a question born of frustration at bull sharks, normally solitary creatures, swimming in a pack, and what that pack might do now.

Alan answered as best as anybody could about creatures driven nearly totally by instinct. "If they've gone back out into the Sound or the Gulf, it's unlikely they'll stay together. But if they're still in the closed confines of the river and come upon some more swimmers . . . maybe."

The sheriff's gaze went toward a wide window at the front of the living room. Outside the glass on the street, a tall, attractive brunette patted powder on her face as she stood next to the WLOX-TV satellite truck. A young cameraman with salt-and-pepper hair adjusted a tripod-mounted camera near the rear of the vehicle. In front and behind the truck, vehicles of all kinds were parked bumper to bumper up and down the street.

Carolyn said, "I want to go after Paul." She was looking out the window, too. "But I don't want to bring him here in the middle of all this." As she spoke, a man and woman walked past the window, the man pointing out something of interest in front of him as they moved across the lawn.

"We'll run everybody off as soon as we talk to the media," Stark said. "So we put out the word—tell everybody not to be swimming in the river until we know for certain they're gone."

Alan nodded.

Stark added, "And be cautious in the Sound."

Alan nodded again.

A deputy speaking into a small, hand-held radio stepped from the dining room into the living room. He lowered the radio to his side and looked at Stark. "The men are out of the water," he said. "Didn't find any more body parts. They're wanting to know if you want them to refill their tanks and try again."

"No," Stark said, "they've taken enough of a chance." As his face came back around from the deputy's, he said, "Hell, Dr. Freeman, sharks shouldn't have been in a damn pack. Are you certain they won't go after somebody now—even in open water?"

"Certain?" Alan asked, and shook his head no.

"Let me go talk to the TV," Stark said, "and then I'll get these people out of here."

Mr. Herald walked toward the telephone. "I'm going to

remind Martha to be certain she doesn't let Paul watch TV.''

"She won't, Daddy.''

He lifted the telephone anyway.

"Alan," Carolyn said, "I'm sorry, but after this I really don't feel like going out.''

He nodded, then looked at the television set on the far side of the room. The volume was turned too low for what was being said to be heard, but the screen showed the brunette now speaking into the camera. The shot moved from her face and panned past the trees to the house, where the man and woman who had walked past the window now stood at the side of the yard. The man was pointing out something in the general direction of where the boys had gone into the water. He saw the camera and smiled broadly toward it.

The woman beside him smiled, too.

The television now showed a moving shot of the marshland. The shot froze in place and a graphic of a bull shark was superimposed across the tall grasses.

A warning was obviously being given.

WASHINGTON, D.C.—4:30 P.M.

Admiral Vandiver, his concentration evident in the tightness of his wide, dark face, studied an intelligence report open on his desk. He raised his eyes at the buzz of his intercom.

"Yes.''

"Sir, Admiral Kendrick, U.S. Coast Guard, is on the line.''

Vandiver smiled as he lifted the receiver to his ear. "Gus, you bastard, how are you? Your boys must have sunk a submarine for you to call me.''

"Something you'll like even more, you old warmonger. They found a megalodon tooth.''

"Found one?"

"In the waters between the Keys and the Everglades."

"Damn, Gus."

"I knew that would excite you."

"You certain it's a megalodon tooth?"

"Unless we have a hellacious-sized white shark running around down here—and needing to brush his teeth bad, they've turned dark. It measures nearly seven inches in slant-height and evidently is in pristine condition."

"Seven inches." Vandiver calculated roughly in his mind. "I have a two-and-a-half-inch tooth from an eighteen-foot white. If the tooth you're talking about is one of the larger ones from the front of the jaw, the megalodon could have been forty to fifty feet long; one of the smaller rear teeth and it could have been twice that size. Hell, maybe a hundred feet. Damn. A Miocene deposit kicked up to the surface, some deposit—how?"

"You're asking me? That's your field."

"Damn," Vandiver said for the third time. "A hundred feet."

"Manual doesn't exactly spell out standard operating procedure for what to do after finding a prehistoric tooth. I decided I could either call the black market or you. You won out since I still owe you a hundred dollars from that last poker game you conned me into."

"You can consider us even now."

"I already do. I'll get the tooth on a plane to you as soon as it gets into the station."

"Thank you, Gus. I can't wait."

After their conversation ended with both of them promising to stay in better touch, Vandiver replaced the receiver and leaned back in his chair. A smile crossed his face. While his position was Director of Naval Intelligence, his doctorate was in marine biology, and his love, too. To be able to hold in his hands a megalodon tooth that had been found exposed on the ocean floor, even if his part wasn't any more than having it pass through his hands to the Smithsonian or wherever it would end up, made him feel, he imagined, a little like an artist who was going to get to be in the chain of possession of a newly discovered Van Gogh.

What was even more exciting was that the find rekindled the fire under a thought he had carried for years. This particular tooth being exposed on the bottom would likely not pose a mystery. One of the hurricanes of the last century could conceivably have exposed it. Spanish galleons buried in the sand for hundreds of years had been uncovered that way. There was a possibility that a nearby river draining the Everglades, flooding time and time again, could have cut down through layers of sediment to where the tooth had lain for millions of years and washed it out to sea. But neither of those circumstances were possible in the case of the megalodon tooth that had first made him wonder.

It had been brought up by a dredge sampling the floor of the Marianas Trench. No rivers cut through layers of sediment at that depth. No hurricane, no matter how powerful, affected the bottoms of seas under thousands of feet of water. Yet the tooth had lain exposed or only slightly covered, allowing the dredge to scoop it up and bring it to the surface.

How was that possible? he had wondered at the time. The bottoms of the great depths were constantly being bombarded with a never-ending shower of decaying animal and plant matter floating down from the surface—what scientists termed marine snow. This was how many of the smaller bottom dwellers gained their sustenance. And this constant bombardment not only fed these creatures but also, over hundreds of thousands and millions of years, built up the floor of the seas by literally hundreds of feet. That was basically how oil and gas deposits formed under the sea, the organic material settling to the bottom, creating layers, and then having other layers deposited on top of them, the pressure caused by the ever-increasing weight of these overlapping layers eventually creating the fuels. So, again, how did a tooth from a creature extinct for some one and a half to five million years remain in a shallow enough position to have been brought up by a dredge?

He had heard one scientist quite confidently state that the tooth had obviously been buried deep at one point in time and then, through some underground anomaly such as a pocket of methane gas being released, been pushed to the top of the sea floor. Vandiver guessed any coincidence was possible. Any set of coincidences: the coincidence of that particular tooth being upthrusted, the coincidence of the dredge then sampling the particular few-square-feet area where it lay out of all the tens of thousands of square miles of the Marianas Trench. Maybe hard to believe, but possible.

But he had also continued to wonder. And, driven by that wonder, he had begun to research and found that there was much more coincidence than he would have ever dreamed. So much more it became almost a mathematical impossibility for it all to indeed by coincidence. At least that was how he started to believe.

And that had caused him to form a pet theory. Of course not one that he shared openly with most people—it was a little too far out. But, on the other hand, not any farther out than was the thinking of a handful of scientists some years before who had decided the majority of their colleagues were wrong in the decades-held philosophy that dinosaurs had been cold-blooded animals. Now enough evidence had come forward to make the warm-blooded theory the prevailing one.

And *his* conclusion was that the megalodon hadn't become extinct over a million years ago, but rather at least a number of them had lived up until the last few hundred years, maybe longer—maybe much longer.

And he knew that there was now not only coincidence

that pointed to that possibility, but, as in the case of the advocates of the warm-blooded dinosaurs, mounting evidence.

Then he thought again of the tooth Gus had called about. It *might not* have been washed out to where it lay by the action of a river or uncovered by a hurricane. It could conceivably. . . . He smiled at his thought. Surely he was grasping now. Especially with the tooth in such shallow water so far from the great depths. But then there was always a possibility, wasn't there? He spent a moment longer thinking, the idea of what could be possible growing in his mind, then he leaned forward and pressed the panel at the base of his intercom.

"Yes, sir?"

"Have Ensign Williams report in here straight away, please."

"Sorry, sir, but he's in the process of delivering Senator Lott to Andrews."

"Very well. Get word to him I want him to report in here as soon as he returns—no matter how late it is."

"She's not doing right by Paul," Mr. Herald said as he watched Carolyn in her Ranger turning out of the driveway with Paul sitting in the front seat beside her. "She ought to go ahead and take him on out to the islands like she planned, do whatever else she can think of to get him back around water before he gets scared of it. It's a horrible, horrible thing that happened to those boys, but when is the last time a shark ever attacked anyone around here, much less killed anybody? I can only remember once in my lifetime. What's happened is a terrible, terrible tragedy. More than terrible. It makes me sick to my stomach. But it's a terrible tragedy when lightning strikes somebody, too. And I've heard of lightning killing people a lot more often than once over the years. But you don't stop going outside. You use common sense. Stay under cover when it's storming and you're pretty well home free. What does she want Paul to do, never go in the water again? Maybe even never want to be around it—because she's scaring him to death telling him he can't go to the islands now.''

His wife lowered the magazine she was reading to her lap. ''She's not doing any such thing, Fred. She's his mother. When she was a little girl, would you have wanted her to go on to the islands and swim right after a shark attack?''

''Of course not. I don't want her to go into the water now, for God's sake. But she can still anchor out with him; what does she think the sharks are going to do—jump in the boat?''

''Fred, she's just too depressed to be taking the boat out for fun now. And how's Paul going to feel after he finds out what happened? You know she's going to have to tell him before he hears it from somebody else.''

''Yeah,'' he said, nodding his head. ''And telling him and then giving him the impression she's afraid to go out on the water—all she's doing is making it worse. I don't feel so hot myself, and you think I'm not going to go ahead and take my boys camping tomorrow?''

''We brought up two children, Fred. Why don't you let her bring up her child the way she wants?'' Under her breath she added, ''And I bet Calvin is tickled to death he lives in Memphis and can bring up his girl without having to listen to you.''

''What?'' her husband said, and cocked his ear in her direction.

''Nothing, Fred. I was talking to myself about the price of clothes in this magazine.''

''I thought you said something about Calvin.''

''Calvin Klein,'' she said, and turned her attention back to her reading.

But a few seconds later, with her husband still staring out the glass in the front door, she lowered the magazine again. "Now, Fred, don't you get any ideas about starting up a little game between you and Paul—working on Carolyn."

She stared a moment longer at the back of his large frame.

"You have already, haven't you?"

CHAPTER 9

Admiral Vandiver stared at the monitor of his computer terminal, linked by secure line to the megacomputers kept under around-the-clock armed guard in another section of the Pentagon. He wasn't studying any kind of intelligence information, but rather a photograph anyone connected to the Internet could view.

Displayed on the monitor was a coelacanth, a heavy-bodied, five-foot-long fish with bony, armorlike scales and rapierlike teeth. It looked for all the world like what it was, an ancient fish thought to be extinct for over seventy million years—until one was caught off the coast of South Africa in December 1938.

"By the trawler *Nerine* pulling a net in two hundred feet of water," he mumbled, voicing his thoughts aloud. It had been a hell of a shock to the scientific community. He smiled a little at that thought, then turned his face across his shoulder at the knock on his office door.

"Enter."

The door remained closed.

"*Enter,*" he said in a louder voice.

A young black ensign in a white dress uniform stepped inside, shut the door behind him and, facing the computer, came to attention, holding his cap tightly under his arm.

"Took you long enough," Vandiver said. The ensign remained rigidly at attention. "Come on, Douglas, relax. If my sister learns you stand like that when you're alone in my office she'll be all over my case. Sometimes I get the distinct impression she thinks the military silly, anyway."

The young man removed his cap from under his arm and came across the floor.

Vandiver nodded toward the photograph on the monitor. "You know what that is?"

Without waiting for an answer, Vandiver said, "A coelacanth, thought to have been extinct for over seventy million years, until one was caught off South Africa in '38." He worked his fingers across the terminal's keyboard, then leaned back in his chair as an artist's rendition of a thick-bodied shark materialized on the monitor. Facing outward and looking like it was about to swim off the screen, the shark's wide pectoral fins stuck straight out to the sides and its mouth gaped, exposing several rows of tall teeth. The artist had shaded the creature's body a dark brown color, even its teeth.

"You know what that is?"

Douglas was quicker this time: "Almost looks like a great white, but its nose is a little too blunt, not tapering down narrow enough to the front. And the color . . ."

"Carcharodon megalodon, Douglas."

"Sir?"

"Carcharodon megalodon. The giant ancestor of the great white shark of today, possibly reaching up to a hundred feet in length from the fossil evidence available. Deemed to be extinct for a million and a half to five million years, depending on which scientists you ask."

"Deemed, sir?"

"Been extinct," Vandiver said.

Douglas nodded.

Vandiver ran his tongue under his upper lip and seemed to be thinking. "I can't recall the name of the river."

"Sir?"

"The initial coelacanth was caught at the mouth of a river off the South African coast. Its name escapes me."

Douglas was surprised anything to do with the oceans escaped his uncle. There was nobody in the naval department who could even come close to matching his knowledge of the seas and their inhabitants. His doctorate not only came from that field, it was his hobby, too.

Vandiver stood and walked toward his desk. He pointed to a chair in front of it. As Vandiver settled into his seat, Douglas sat down in the chair, placing his cap across his lap and sitting so straight he almost seemed to be still at attention.

Vandiver stared at him. "You simply can't relax, can you, Douglas? Well, you come by that naturally. Our whole family's always been uptight. It's a Vandiver characteristic."

Douglas tried to sit more at ease, but actually looked more uncomfortable in doing so.

Vandiver smiled a little. "Well, I'm going to give you a little vacation—maybe that'll loosen you up. I'm going to send you down to south Florida for a couple of days."

There was the slightest wrinkling of Douglas' brow.

Vandiver felt the breast pocket of his uniform tunic. He lowered his hand to his trouser pockets. "Is my secretary still out there?"

"Sir, it's nearly eight o'clock."

"She never tells me when she leaves. Comes of working with the same person for fifteen years—they lose their fear of you."

He opened a drawer at the side of his desk. "Ah, ha," he said. He lifted a cellophane-wrapped cigar out and held it over the desk toward Douglas.

"No thank you, sir."

"Still can't think of the name of the river," Vandiver mumbled to himself. A pensive look on his face, he stripped the cigar, placed the cellophane in an ashtray, lit the cigar, and blew a thick cloud of gray smoke toward the ceiling.

He looked directly across the desk. "Let me get to the point, Douglas. I'm sending you to a site where a megalodon tooth was found today. I want you to go down and look at the bottom where it was discovered. I want to know what you think of the terrain. Specifically, whether you think there's any evidence of old volcanic activity, an upheaval in the land—anything like that. I want you to take rock samples, too, coral, anything in the area that stands out."

"Sir, my degree is in English."

"Geology would be better. But I don't have a nephew with a degree in geology. And what you're trying to find for me is some evidence that indicates whether this tooth could have been shed there say some few thousand years ago instead of a million and a half. If I told anybody else that was what was on my mind, I'm afraid I might be facing being medically boarded out."

A slight smile played over his uncle's face, but Douglas knew he had been serious in his words about the age. "Sir, why would you think—"

"Let me give you a little science lesson," his uncle said. "In fact, let me carry you a little further to make certain you do have an open mind when you're down there looking. Megalodons once roamed all of the world's oceans. Their teeth have been found in layers of sediment that show they swam tropical seas and layers of sediment that show they swam the most frigid seas during the ice ages. They swam the shallow areas that are now dry land—as far inland as central Maryland in this area, for example—and they swam the deepest trenches that have always been deep water. The Marianas Trench, for example. You know how deep it is?"

Again without waiting for a response, Vandiver said,

"Deepest spot in the world. You take Mount Everest, the highest point on earth at 29,028 feet tall, and drop it into the Marianas Trench, and the water would be over its top by a mile. The only areas on earth that basically haven't changed since time began are those deepest spots. Down there, the temperature is slightly above freezing, kept from freezing by the salinity and the pressure. During the glacial ages, like the one I mentioned, these depths remained slightly above freezing. During the temperate and tropical climates, they stayed slightly above freezing—they've always been slightly above freezing. The oxygen content that deep is basically the same as it's always been, too, somewhat less than in the shallower waters. And it's always been pitch dark down there, a black hard to imagine. The dinosaurs died out because of global temperature change, maybe gradually, or maybe rapidly from a meteor hitting the earth creating a great cloud of dust that not only caused the world's temperature to drop but killed the foliage the dinosaurs depended on for subsistence. In either case, there would have been a great environmental change from one decade to the next, or maybe from one year to the next. But the environmental conditions in the oceans' greatest depths have always remained basically the same, changing only insignificantly over time."

Vandiver leaned forward. His eyes stared directly into his nephew's. "So why, Douglas, I ask you, if any creature was originally present down there—why would he still not be there?"

Douglas didn't answer.

Vandiver, smiling, shook his head in amusement. "No, I'm not really ready to be boarded out. I'm not suggesting they are there, Douglas. With the sensing equipment we have on submarines today, with scientific vessels constantly mapping the trenches through sonar technology . . . hell, with all the people this world has flitting around now in submersibles and with robot probes, it's hard to fathom that a creature of the megalodon's size could still be alive and not have blundered into something that would have recorded its presence. What I *am* saying is that I have a theory, a hypothesis, and it's that megalodons survived a lot longer than we've previously thought.''

Vandiver paused a moment and then said, "You come back from down there and see if you can help me out on that."

"Couldn't you have the tooth dated, sir?"

"I'm going to see what I can do about that. Meanwhile I don't want a storm coming in down there and undoing something that maybe an earlier storm has done, or some kind of upheaval changing the area. That's why I want you down there as soon as you can get there. And, oh yes, I want to know how close this particular spot is to the mouth of any river running out from the Everglades."

And Vandiver left it at that, speaking no more about the tooth, but only about his sister, Douglas' mother, as he walked Douglas toward the door.

Alan reached over his head from where he was lying on his couch watching television and caught the telephone on the second ring.

"Uh-huh?"

"Alan."

"Hey," he said.

"Hey," his aunt said. "How's my favorite nephew?"

"Your only one."

"I'd sort of like to keep it that way."

"So what are you saying, that you have a sister somewhere I've never heard of, about to give birth?"

"I'm glad the fish you're around are in tanks."

"Yeah."

"You're not going diving this weekend are you?"

"Did you raise an idiot?"

"I don't know. You tried sky diving once."

"Once."

"It only takes once."

"Okay, but that was a long time ago. And, by the way, sharks don't get a taste for human blood, Rayanne. It would be safe in open water. But, in any case, I have no plans to go diving or anything else—at least for a while."

"Will you promise to tell me before you do? If you don't, then I'll be worrying every night you're going the next day. I never will get any sleep."

"Give you twenty-four hours' advance notice."

"Alan, you're the only child I have."

"I'm serious, Aunt Rayanne. And, if the real reason you called is to find out if I've bought your birthday present yet, I haven't—but I'm probably going to."

"You know what you're going to get me?"

"Wouldn't tell you if I did."

"I like candy, perfume, and pajamas—cotton ones."

"I'll think about it."

"And you're serious about the notice?"

"Twenty-four hours."

"Love you."

"Love you."

As Alan replaced the receiver, he laid his head back on the cushion propped against the arm of the couch and stared at the ceiling rather than the TV.

As terrible as it had been losing his parents, he could not have been any luckier afterwards than to have had Rayanne. She had come up into his room after the funeral and taken him in her arms and rocked him while he cried, and he had known somebody did love him.

She had brought him from Jackson to the coast to live. He couldn't remember if at nine years old he had been planning to be a fireman or a policeman, but he remembered vividly that first July he lived here when she took him to the docks to watch the boats bring in their entries for the annual fishing rodeo. He hadn't known then that he

was going to become a marine biologist, but he had known
he was going to do something having to do with the water.

Rayanne *had* cautioned him a few years before about
leaving his job with the Gulf Coast Research Lab. But when
she saw that he really wanted to try building an aquaculture
company while the industry was still in its infancy and the
major food companies didn't already control it, she not only
gave him her blessing but withdrew ten thousand dollars
from her savings account to help him get started. He kept
it safe in the bank until he saw the company was going to
make it, then gave her twice as much stock as her money
would have bought on the local market. But he could never
repay her. For a child and then later a man without a mother
or father, Rayanne came as close as possible to being a
replacement.

The telephone rang.

He smiled and reached back over his head again.

"I'm not going to tell you what I'm getting you," he
said.

"Alan, this is Carolyn."

He sat up and swung his feet to the floor.

"Alan, this is embarrassing but . . . Paul saw me putting
steaks on the grill and he realized it was after seven o'clock
and. . . .

"Alan, is there any way that you could come over here
and eat with us?"

CHAPTER 10

Paul insisted on cutting his steak into bite-size pieces himself. Carolyn then told him to cut each piece into two further small pieces. He frowned, but did as she said. She pointed to the broccoli on his plate, then came across the patio toward Alan sitting at a wicker table.

"Big boys don't have to cut their steak into tiny pieces," she said in a low voice as she settled into her chair, "that's what he's thinking. And you know what, he's right. I know I'm overprotective. I tell myself I'm going to back off, and then the next moment he's climbing a tree and I'm running outside telling him he's going to fall and break his neck. I think in some ways children are better off with parents who don't care what happens. . . ." She rolled her eyes. ". . . If the kid survives."

Alan watched Paul feed Duchess a stalk of broccoli. Duchess swallowed it whole and looked across the patio toward the table, as if she was checking to see if Carolyn was watching.

Alan smiled, then turned his eyes toward the eighteen-foot outboard sitting at a small wooden dock at the rear of the yard. "I believe you're the first woman charter-boat captain I've met."

Carolyn stopped a bite of salad on its way to her mouth

and smiled a little. "You mean, what's a nice girl like me doing in a business like this? Actually, Carl left me the *Intuitive,* too. Carl—that was his name. You notice I use *was* in the sense of 'thank God he's gone.' But then I don't guess I should be so hard on him—the *Intuitive* turned out to be the best thing that ever happened to me as far as Paul is concerned. I was going to sell it and come out with what equity I could. Then I decided that if I sold it the money would come in just once—if I charter it, it would keep coming in. So you're looking at a formerly depressed woman working in a stuffy accountant's office suddenly sailing the bounding main with her child by her side. And you'd be surprised at how much he helps out. Would you like a glass of wine?"

"That sounds fine."

After Carolyn stepped inside the house, Paul's hand started toward Duchess's mouth, until he saw Alan was looking. Alan theatrically raised his gaze to the sky. Paul smiled and lowered his entire plate to Duchess. A few seconds later he lifted it, licked clean, back onto the TV tray.

When Carolyn came outside with the wine, Paul and Duchess were playing with a Frisbee in a grassy area off to the side of the house. She looked at Paul's clean plate and came on across the patio.

Alan rose from his chair, took the glass she held out to him and, waiting for her to take her seat before he sat back down, he looked toward the river again, this time down the channel. He thought of how, after the partial hand had been found, the men had been unable to find any more body parts. They could have missed something but he doubted it.

"Alan," Carolyn said, looking up at him.

He settled into his chair, still thinking. The attack had been complete, and quick, with neither Skip nor Dustin surfacing once they had gone under the water. Bull sharks attacking in a pack?

"What are you thinking about?" Carolyn asked.

He dismissed the nagging uncertainty that played at his mind and looked toward Paul. "Does he know what really happened?"

She nodded. "He cried when I told him, but it wasn't as bad for him as I thought it would be. Nothing like yesterday when he first realized they were dead. I don't know if it's some kind of shock, or if how they died didn't make them any deader to him. I know that sounds terrible, but . . . I don't know, how do you know what anyone thinks after something like this, especially a six-year-old?"

He looked at her for a moment. "Did you ask him if he had any questions?"

"I tried to explain as best I could, but how do you explain something like that?"

He started to tell her what he meant. Then Paul stepped onto the patio. "Mr. Freeman."

"You should call him Dr. Freeman," Carolyn said.

"Alan," Alan said.

Paul smiled. "Mr. Alan, do you have a boat?"

"Yes, I do."

"Like the *Intuitive*?"

Alan smiled a little. "No, not that big. It's a Boston Whaler. Do you know what that is?"

"Is it a center console?"

Alan smiled again. "As a matter of fact it is. A center console Outrage."

"That's the best kind," Paul said. He looked toward the outboard and frowned. "I told Mother that."

Carolyn glanced at her watch. "It's bedtime."

Paul nodded and turned back to the house, opening the screen door and stepping inside. "Good night, Mr. Alan," he said before letting the screen close behind him.

Carolyn stared after him. "I'm in shock," she said. "Maybe you should come over more often." She got to her feet. "Let me get him ready for bed—it'll only take me a minute."

In Paul's room Carolyn helped him pull his pajama top down over his thick hair. "Why are you being so nice?" she asked. "Because Dr. Freeman is here?"

Paul looked up at her. "Grandpa Fred said I could go camping with the team in the morning . . . if you don't mind."

She was caught off guard. It took her a moment. "Oh, that's nice of Grandpa Fred, Paul, but those are bigger boys than you."

"They like me."

He was staring up at her.

"I know they do, Paul, but . . . maybe when you're a little older. Maybe next summer."

"He said you would have to pack my stuff tonight," Paul said, " 'cause we'll be leaving early in the morning."

"No, baby, I don't think so."

He caught his lip in his teeth and turned toward his bed.

In Pascagoula, an older, heavyset woman with her graying hair up on the back of her head in a bun, walked inside the Jackson County Sheriff's Department. She fidgeted nervously with the front of her loose print dress as she came across the dimly lit floor. The deputy she approached looked up from his desk and gave her a friendly smile.

She tried to speak in a calm voice. "My husband, Eddie. I, uh . . . I visited up at my sister's at McComb last night. Eddie, he went fishing with a friend of his named Luke. I came in and he's not back—Eddie's not. And nobody don't answer at Luke's."

Carolyn frowned into the receiver. "Daddy, I can't believe you told Paul you were going to let him go with you."

"So what's wrong with that?"

"Daddy, he's barely six."

"So, I'm not responsible enough to watch over him?"

"*Daddy.*"

"Well?"

"You're going to have your hands full with the rest of the boys."

"I have them trained like a troop of cavalry. They could take care of me."

"I wouldn't let him stay overnight in the marshes if they really were a troop of cavalry. Especially now."

"We're not going swimming, Carolyn, we're going camping. And it's almost like we'll be at your back door. You know how the boys like him, they'll be picking at him. It'll be the best thing in the world for him—help him to get his mind off what's happened, at least not have that the only thing on his mind. Martha said you were worrying about that. And if you let him go, I promise you I won't let him put his little toe in the water."

Carolyn puffed her cheeks and blew the air out in exasperation. Paul's expression after he had climbed into bed and lay looking at the ceiling had nearly killed her. But she *couldn't* let him. She would be a nervous wreck the entire time.

"Well?" her father said.

"Daddy, really, no."

"It would be the best thing for both of you. You keep sitting home thinking about those boys, it'll drive you crazy. And, Carolyn, you know I'll be watching him every minute. I'd let something happen to me before I would him."

CHAPTER 11

"I can't believe Daddy did that," Carolyn said. "Yes, I can, too."

When Alan didn't say anything, she set her wineglass back on the wicker table and looked across its top. "Are you thinking Paul should go?"

"He's your son."

"But you're thinking he should?"

"If it bothers you, you shouldn't let him."

"*Alan,* you are thinking he should. Alan, it would worry me to death."

"You want me to agree with you, or answer you?"

She frowned, but said, "Answer."

"In my opinion, if Paul is with other boys he will be pulled into what they're doing. It can't do anything but help, even if it only pulls his mind off Dustin and Skip for a couple of days."

Carolyn groaned and stared out over the marshland.

"And you know your father wouldn't even let him put his toe in the water. He'd be watching him every minute."

She looked directly into his eyes. "Have you been talking with Daddy? That's the second time you've said something like he did."

He smiled and shook his head no.

"You do sound just like him." She frowned and stared out across the marshland again. "So I'm going to be the Wicked Witch of the West."

THE PRESIDENT CASINO, BILOXI—11:00 P.M.

Leonard caught the blond staring at him out of the corner of his eyes. She was about the size he liked, not more than five-four or so if she hadn't been wearing heels—about his size. He smiled to himself and added four more hundred-dollar chips to the two he already had laying on the numbers out in front of him.

Around him several others watched his play. Spread out in every direction around the roulette table, a heavy crowd even for Friday night packed the President Casino. More than one woman had looked good in the mixture of soft and bright lights of all colors in the casino, but none quite with the upper-body structure of the blond, Leonard thought. He had first noticed her on the other side of the table. Now she stood at the end nearest him. He added a little more scent to the bait, juggling some five-hundred-dollar chips in his hand and flashing his big diamond-studded pinkie ring in her direction. She looked, too.

He smiled to himself. Years ago, when he had turned fifteen and had received his driver's license, his father had walked out of the house with him to the shiny new Mercedes sitting in the drive.

"Son," his father had said, "I want you to know that when you drive out of the driveway in this automobile, there's going to be people you never met who look on you with distaste—they don't have a shiny new Mercedes. Certainly most didn't have one when they were fifteen years old. Now their feelings don't bother me none when I been acting right. But, sometimes, when I get in a little hurry and don't treat people working in my oil company just right, I get to thinking about all those who've hit a lot of dry holes in life. Wasn't their fault, just dice didn't turn up on the right side for them when they rolled them. That certainly don't mean you treat them bad. So remember those people, be polite when you drive around them, and don't give anybody a dirty look if they're driving too slow. You get my gist?''

Leonard had been eternally grateful for that advice. Upon hearing the words he had immediately known he was *somebody*. Since then he had always thought about those people his father had talked about. Especially the women. He started noticing right away that not many of them drove Mercedeses, either. And most looked his way when he drove by.

So that is what he had been doing since then in life. Driving by in his Mercedes, so to speak. And taking full advantage of it. Without looking at the blond, he flashed his pinkie ring again.

The croupier dragged his stack of chips off the table.

Leonard put out a little more scent.

The thump-thump-thump of the rotor blades and the roar of the motor reverberated in Ensign Douglas Williams' ears. The cargo compartment vibrated as if it were about to break into pieces. He stared out the wide opening in the helicopter's side at the trees whipping past below in the increasing darkness. The craft would transfer him to an F-16 at Andrews and he would be in south Florida before dawn. Then there would be the boat ride to the spot where the tooth had been found. He had seen where a front now approached the area. If it got there before he did, he knew there would be hell to pay—even if Vandiver was his uncle.

The blond pulled off her high heels and hopped down into the sleek black speedboat berthed at the north end of the Broadwater Marina. Leonard poured her a vodka and grapefruit juice out of the jar from the cooler at the center of the boat.

"Mixed it myself," he said.

She was more interested in the ring on his pinkie held out from the bottle. That was what he was counting on—never leave them enough time to think about anything but the bait. It was like keeping the line taut after you had a fish hooked. His daddy had given him that bit of advice, too. He turned and stepped between the front seats to the ignition.

The motor roared.

He smiled at the blond.

"Get it, Leonard," she said.

He intended to.

Carolyn held her hand behind her on the doorknob. Alan stood in front of her, the moon at his back. "When am I going to get to pay you back for the steak?"

"In a few days, maybe. You know we're going to have to take Paul with us at least once after having already invited him."

"Oh, now you're planning on me taking you out more than once. Well, you are nice looking—I'll think about it."

She smiled, leaned forward, and pecked him on the cheek.

He raised his hands to the sides of her shoulders.

She shook her head.

He lowered his hands. "Thank you for going out of your way for Paul," she said.

He hoped there was more to him in her mind than only his being nice to Paul. And knowing her for only a day and a half, he was surprised he felt so strongly about it—yet he did.

He thought about that more than once on his way back to Biloxi. What attracted him so? A beautiful woman—but those could be found in a lot of places. A strong woman—in today's society many women both raised a child and held a job. And he had dated both beautiful women and those with strengths of all kinds. Yet he had never experienced the feeling he had now.

And he really couldn't believe he was thinking this way.

He smiled and thumped his fingers against the steering wheel in time with the voice of Faith Hill pouring out of the radio.

The shiny black speedboat came across the moonlit waters from the direction of Biloxi. Ahead of the craft, the blocky shape of Fort Massachusetts loomed shadowy and dark. Leonard cut the steering wheel sharply and the craft leaned on its side and raced for the east end of Ship Island— actually two separate main islands since Hurricane Camille had slashed a wide gap through the original structure's middle. They went past the gap and toward the long eastern segment, devoid of structures, deserted and dim in the moonlight.

"So this is where you wanted me," Stella shouted over the roar of the motor. "Suits the hell out of me."

Leonard liked her attitude. Feeling the vodka more than he realized, he shouted back, "You've really got balls."

Stella looked at him, and then laughed loudly.

As he slowed the boat and angled it toward shore, the craft's bow caught a wave and cold spray flew high over the windshield, soaking them both. Stella screamed her laughter and yelled, "Go, Leonard."

He yelled back, "Go, Stella."

She laughed and drank the last dregs from her glass.

Carolyn stood in her bedroom looking at the sheet of paper Paul had placed on her pillow. Right beneath the broad strokes of her father's handwriting, where he listed the items that would be needed for the camping trip, was the small printing carefully done in Paul's hand:

please. I have ben good.

CHAPTER 12

Leonard moaned a last time and rolled to his back. Stella pulled a corner of the blanket across her body. "Whewww!" she said.

"Give me a moment to rest and I'll be raring again," he said, proud of his effort so far.

She reached for the bottle of vodka at the side of the blanket and raked her arm in the sand. She sat up, holding the blanket across her heavy breasts and looked at the back of her arm. "I can't stand that gritty feel," she said. "It was on the blanket, too. You sandpapered my back." She moved her hand across her shoulder and brushed what sand she could from her skin.

"Wipe it off," she said, and turned her bare back to him. He reached up and swiped at her shoulders. "Arrrg," she said, jerking away from his touch. "You have more on your hand than I do on my back."

She came to her feet, pulling the blanket with her. He stood and pulled his pants up. He had never had the time to take them completely off. He dusted some of the sand off his belly.

Stella suddenly laughed, dropped the blanket, and ran down the beach into the water, jumping the first wave, then getting hit by the second one—up to her waist in the water one moment, then the water dropping to her knees. She waded farther out. Leonard continued to brush his stomach.

"Come on," she said, looking back at him across her shoulder and making a big sweep of her arm. "The water's fine."

A large wave burst around her chest and broke on the shore behind her, its white foam glistening in the light of the moon.

Leonard walked to the edge of the sand and looked out across the water. They were on the south side of the island fronting the Gulf, and wave after wave rolled in. Wave after wave for as far as he could see. He listened to the wind whistling, felt it blowing against his high forehead, and whipping his tousled hair at the very top of his head. A wave breaking offshore made a particularly loud crashing sound.

"Leonard."

Stella was up to her shoulders now, standing part of the time, floating when a swell passed by, lifting her and then lowering her again.

"Come on, Leonard!"

He didn't think so. In fact, it was starting to make him a little nervous that Stella was out there.

"Stella."

Stella smiled and threw back her wet hair as she rose high on a wave, higher than the beach, its brilliant white sand glistening like snow.

She went down and came up with the next wave—and the beach began to dim. She looked toward the sky and saw a thick cloud beginning to pass across the moon. The water around her began to pull gently at her legs. She looked over her shoulder into the night turning into a black void behind her. An unnerving feeling passed over her.

"Leonard."

He shouted something back, but his words were lost in

the crashing of the waves along the beach. She leaned forward and began to paddle slowly in its direction, purposely not stroking too fast, afraid too quick a pace might jolt her nervous feeling into something even stronger. But with her body flat in the water now, she no longer felt the pull at her legs and she began to relax as she stroked.

It came up behind her. If it had been daylight, the clear water would have shown its fifty-foot length, its wide pectoral fins set straight out toward the side as if for balance, and its towering dorsal fin fully three feet out of the water.

Its head remained under the surface, directly behind her and a few feet under her body.

Leonard relaxed when he caught a glimpse of Stella coming closer toward shore. He smiled and took a long drink from the vodka bottle. The moonlight began to penetrate the trailing edge of the cloud now and Stella's blond hair, even her white shoulders, began to reflect the illumination.

Behind her, something black began to rise out of the water.

Leonard's eyes widened in shock.

The bottle fell from his hand.

The shape made a sudden lunge forward. Stella was swallowed whole from the rear to the front. No sound. A last glimpse of her blond hair. The great mouth closed.

The creature, dark and glistening, lay unmoving as the waves crashed around it and against it, its black, round eyes staring directly at Leonard.

Too paralyzed to move, Leonard nearly passed out. With a superhuman effort, he took a step backward. Another step. His body trembling as if he were standing naked in a hundred-degree-below-zero wind, he finally managed to turn—and ran.

"Aaaarrrgh!"

Sprinting through the night, still screaming though he didn't realize he was, he crossed the sand. His boat was

pulled up on the beach on the island's Sound side. He
jerked the small anchor out of the sand and threw it wildly
toward the rear of the craft. He hit the bow so hard with
his shoulder he nearly dislocated it. His feet digging into
the sand, he pushed the boat backward out into the Sound.

He felt a chill as he sunk to his knees in the water, and
he vaulted into the boat. Fumbling for the ignition, he finally found it, turned the key, and slammed the gear into
reverse and jammed the throttle full forward.

The prop pulled so hard it momentarily lifted the bottom
of the motor away from the boat. Then the craft leveled
and shot backward, waves building behind it, slamming
hard against its blunt shape and pouring water over the
stern.

Leonard yanked the throttle back, jammed the gear forward, slammed the throttle forward again, turning the wheel
at the same time. The boat tilted on its side and turned in
a sharp arc. Leonard straightened the craft toward the dim
lights of Biloxi and hit the throttle with the heel of his hand,
but it wouldn't go any farther forward.

His eyes still wide with terror, his heart racing like a
machine gun, he looked over his shoulder at the island
quickly starting to fall away. The bow hit crossways on a
wave, causing the boat to yaw left and back sharply to the
right, slamming his side into the hard fiberglass, nearly
throwing him out of the craft into the water. He hung onto
the wheel so hard his hands instantly cramped.

The creature finished its run along the Gulf side of Ship
Island and turned into Camille Cut. It moved quickly at
first, then shuddered to a stop as it grounded on its belly.
With a mighty sweep of its crescent tail, it lunged forward,
scraping off the sandy bottom into deeper water.

In seconds, its body never dropping low enough for its
dorsal fin to submerge, it raced after the small boat in the
distance.

* * *

Leonard's hands, cramping, clasped the twenty-footer's steering wheel as if it was a rope to salvation. He wouldn't let go until he ran the boat up on the beach at Biloxi and sprinted over its bow onto the sand. He looked back across his shoulder. The stretch of water between him and Ship Island was bright now, with the moon totally free of the obstructing cloud. With his path directly behind Ship Island and the island's long bulk preventing any of the waves from the Gulf to come farther, the water was perfectly smooth.

He saw the fin.

Two hundred feet back, like the tall, thick periscope of a submarine, it split the surface, throwing a shower of water reflecting in the moonlight to each side. Leonard didn't realize how much his heart had slowed until he felt the blood rushing through his veins again. He looked at the speedometer. He was at thirty-eight knots. He pressed hard on the throttle, then jerked his hand away, suddenly afraid that any more strain on it might break the cable. He looked forward past the bow at the lights of Biloxi, growing brighter—but still so far away. He looked past the stern again. Saw nothing but the smooth water.

There it was.

Off to the side of where he had first seen the fin.

The shower of water was higher now.

He looked at the speedometer. He looked back at the fin. He felt again like he was going to pass out. There was no doubt it was gaining. But it couldn't be. He closed his eyes, looked at the mirrorlike surface of the water ahead of him, the lights still miles away. He looked back at Ship Island— much closer. He bit his lip, felt the whipping of the wind freezing the sweat running down his round face and dripping off his chin to be blown backwards toward the wide wake trailing the boat.

He looked at Biloxi again. He looked back at Ship Island again. *My God,* he thought, *what did I ever leave the island for?* He could have huddled in the center of the sand until the bright morning when he could be seen. Somebody would have come to help. Somebody in something much bigger than a twenty-foot boat setting so low in the water. The terrible picture had never fully left his mind—the great wide head of the creature. The body had to be fifty feet long. At that, another thought nearly caused his heart to stop. A determined effort of a creature that big swimming hard into the side of the boat, even a bump at this speed, he thought, and the boat could flip, flying upside down into the water. *Sending him into the water.*

He started shuddering so hard he was afraid the vibration of his hands was going to cause the wheel to break. He looked back across his shoulder.

The creature, with great steady swipes of its huge crescent tail, continued to close the distance. Its head completely underwater, its eyes unable to see far in the murky darkness, it nevertheless knew exactly where the boat was, the sensitive, wide lateral line canals running along each side of its length picking up the boat's vibration, pinpointing the roar of the prop and the slashing of the boat's bow through the water more accurately than any towed sonar array of a submarine. The creature's only handicap was the shallowness of the Sound. Not more than twelve to fourteen feet deep at any spot and only ten and eleven feet in places, the water was almost too shallow for its great bulk to navigate. Had it been low tide the creature couldn't have come as far into the Sound as it had, but it was high tide, at its peak. Still, its belly was scraping bottom in the soft mud at times and the sweeps of its tail were casting up great clouds of silt. Had the boat turned only a little more east toward the waters directly between Horn Island and Biloxi the craft would have crossed into even shallower waters and the creature couldn't have come any farther. But the craft suddenly turned hard back to its left, west, away from the shallower water, and came around in a wide circle, and the beast shifted its angle towards the boat.

Leonard realized his only chance was to make it back to Ship Island, to the safety of being huddled in the sand in the very center of the place. He saw the fin and spray of water angle to cut off the boat. He looked at the throttle, pressed all the way forward. He closed his eyes.

The boat now headed directly toward the island. The tall fin came toward him from a corner angle off his bow. He refused to look. The sand on Ship Island glistened in the moonlight.

The fin kept coming, still toward the bow, closing the distance.

The bow went past the line where it would intersect with the fin. Leonard looked toward Ship Island a few hundred yards away and closing rapidly. He had the advantage. He stared as the fin turned sharply, throwing a tall spray out to the side like a slalom skier, and moved in a line toward the boat again.

Leonard looked at the island.

The fin straightened now, the showers out to each of its sides beginning to mount.

Two hundred yards to the island.

The gap between his boat and the island narrowed.

The gap between the fin and the boat narrowed.

He looked at the island. He looked back at the fin. The showers to each side of the fin were so high now they resembled sprays coming from firehoses—and so close.

And closer.

His eyes locked on the thick, dark protrusion, he watched it angle out toward the left of the boat. Tears started running down his cheeks. He watched the fin as it drew even with the boat. He watched it as it began to draw slightly ahead of the boat, the spray from the fin falling across the motor. Into the rear of the boat. Across him. "Get away. Get away!

"*Get away!*"

The fin suddenly angled, leaned slightly to the side. The head angled under the front of the boat.

It happened almost exactly the way he had feared, him screaming, the motor roaring, the creature's head nudging under the bow, and then rising hard, lifting the boat, where, aided by the thrust of its own propeller, it climbed into the air, starting to revolve, went higher, turned almost completely upside down, and then crashed back into the water like a submarine on an emergency dive.

Leonard, thrown clear, was running in the air, his arms flailing, his feet hitting the water and seeming to start to walk across it, and then he splashed hard against the surface, flipped, skidded across the water, and disappeared under it.

Ensign Douglas Williams looked from the rear seat of the F-16 Fighting Falcon as it neared touchdown. He could see the orange-striped Coast Guard helicopter that was to be his next ride, setting off to the side, its rotor blades spinning. The night sky was already growing darker with clouds rolling across the face of the moon. He shook his head and looked in the direction of the water off the Everglades.

CHAPTER 13

Taking advantage of a high tide, the charter fishing boat, returning from an all-night fishing trip at the oil rigs south of the Chandeleur chain, headed toward the short cut through Camille Cut rather than the longer route around the western tip of Ship Island into the Sound. The captain, a barrel-chested, bearded man in his early forties looked from the flying bridge toward the faint glow of light in the eastern sky. In the rear of the boat, three middle-aged couples from Chicago carried on a conversation too low for him to hear over the hum of the boat's twin diesel engines.

"Kevin," his wife called from the bottom of the ladder leading up to the bridge. She held a plate of sandwiches in her hands and lifted it in a gesture asking if he wanted one. He shook his head and she turned toward their passengers. Kevin looked past the dark shape of Fort Massachusetts toward the lights of the freighter making its way past the end of the island along the deep-water ship channel leading toward Gulfport. The Russian national flag whipped at the vessel's stern. The freighter rode high in the water, meaning it had delivered its original cargo elsewhere and was now making the passage into Gulfport to load cargo for its return trip. Most likely frozen Mississippi chickens. Vessels from

the old Soviet Union and its client states often arrived there
for that cargo.

Aboard the freighter, the stocky captain standing at the
bridge yawned. His mouth froze open when he glanced at
the depth sounder.

"Vladimir! Glubina!"

The first mate stared at the depth sounder. Four meters
under the keel. Three meters. Two. Holding at two.

Still holding. Three. Four. Five—and the depth under the
vessel dropped back to a normal reading.

The captain released the bulkhead he had grabbed to
brace himself for the grounding that hadn't come.

"*Myelkie vody ili zdyes' shto-to zatonulo. Soobshchite
amerikanskoi pribrezhnoi okhrane.*"

The first mate lifted the mike from the Single-Side-Band
radio and spoke in perfect English.

"U.S. Coast Guard. This is the Russian freighter *Sho-
lokbov.*"

Then he repeated what the captain had ordered him to
say:

"The channel is shoal or something is sunk here."

A hundred yards behind the freighter's churning wake, and
moving with the tip of its thick dorsal fin barely beneath
the surface, the long, dark shape passed Ship Island into
the Gulf. From out of the deep blackness a quarter mile off
to its side came faint vibrations of another large creature
passing under the water, moving in the opposite direction.
But the vibrations were familiar and comfortable, and the
long creature didn't vary from its course or change its
speed, already fast, though its great crescent-shaped tail un-
dulated and swept sideways only once every minute or so.

The bow of the charter boat bumped with a loud thump.
Something scraped along its bottom as Kevin grabbed for

the throttles, jerked them back, and pulled the engines out
of gear. His wife braced her feet at the sudden slowing and
looked up at him. She hurried up the ladder to the flying
bridge.

"What was it?"

Kevin shook his head. He looked back past the stern.
Then he cut the wheel toward the left, engaged the gears,
and edged the throttles forward, turning the boat in a slow
circle.

He peered forward off the port side of the vessel, and
eased the throttles back a little. His wife stepped across the
bridge and stared off the starboard bow. The couples in the
fishing cockpit stood at its sides now, looking at the water.

The oldest man among them said, "I see it. It's . . . I lost
it. Something black and about five or six feet across. It was
right under the water." He leaned his thin frame way out
over the rail and stared back toward the rear of the boat.

Kevin pulled the throttles the rest of the way back and
took the engines out of gear. He pulled a flashlight from
the control panel and shined it over the side of the craft
into the water close to the stern. His wife shook her head.
"I didn't see anything," she said. "There!"

He centered where she pointed with his light. The up-
side-down stern of a speedboat missing its motor and bobbing only inches under the surface slowly passed behind
his craft. His light had penetrated far enough through the
water to read the name across the stern. He reached to the
VHF radio, turned it to channel sixteen, and lifted its mike.

"Coast Guard," he said, and gave his vessel's name,
then said, "there's a small boat sunk just north of Camille
Cut, nearest the eastern section of Ship Island—maybe a
hundred feet from shore."

He waited a moment. "Coast Guard, do you read me?
This is the charter fishing—"

*"This is Coast Guard station Gulfport. Go ahead, Cap-
tain."*

"I've come upon a speedboat sunk north of Camille Cut. The stern is buoyant right under the surface. I scraped it with my keel. It's too dark to see much. It's name is *Scent*. I know it. It's berthed at the Broadwater. Guy that owns it has a Bertram, too, called *Bigger Scent*—an oilman from New Orleans. A short, nice little guy."

There were sections in the Pentagon that never closed down. Admiral Vandiver's office was not among them, but he was at his desk despite the early morning hour and the fact that he had not gone home until well after midnight the night before. He blew a cloud of gray cigar smoke across his desk and glanced at his watch. He had met the courier with the package from south Florida over an hour before. It should almost be at the laboratory now—a laboratory where he could rely on an old acquaintance to give him the facts the way they were and not the way somebody with a preset opinion might think they should be.

But then there were so many variables in the testing—in dating anything. He thought of the example currently making the rounds in the nation's newspapers. The Shroud of Turin, an ancient fourteen-foot three-inch burial linen somehow imprinted with the image of a man who had been crucified, who wore a crown of thorns and who greatly resembled the earliest artists' depiction of Jesus, had been thought when first discovered to possibly be the shroud in which Jesus' body had been wrapped. Then carbon dating indicated the cloth had been woven after the year 1200. Now, a team of scientists from the University of Texas Health Science Center in San Antonio had, upon subsequent testing, concluded that a layer of bacteria and fungi had contaminated the earlier test. The Shroud could indeed be what many thought it to be from the beginning. Both groups of scientists stuck to their results.

Then there was also the story of the ancient map containing the outline of continents generally thought to have been unknown to Europeans at the time the map was said to have been drafted. Dating of the ink used on the map showed the map couldn't possibly be as old as claimed. Subsequent dating by other scientists indicated it could be. Again, both sides stuck to the results they had obtained.

Classic examples of different groups of highly educated professionals, both using the latest technology available, coming to diametrically opposed conclusions—and the Shroud and the ancient map weren't the only examples of this. Far from it. Contamination, advanced aging caused by association with certain elements, the retardation of aging caused by other elements, what had originally lain in association with the object to be tested, even how long it had or had not been exposed to the simple rays of the sun—all of these circumstances and a multitude more could throw off various tests used to determine an object's age.

But one thing the testing *could* do, Vandiver thought. It would be able to determine if the tooth was only a mere few years old, or less. He glanced at his watch again, then rose and walked toward his computer terminal. He pulled back a chair and turned the terminal on.

It instantly posed the request for a password. He typed it in and began stroking a series of keys.

Seconds later, a shark's tooth appeared in the center of the screen.

The voice that emanated from the terminal's speakers was that of a woman, her articulation of each word done precisely and in a pleasant tone as she spelled out the details pertinent to the tooth:

". . . from Carcharodon megalodon. Probability: ninety-nine point ninety-nine percent certainty.

Slant-height, eight point one eight seven inches, with a corresponding width as seen by the ruler superimposed next to the tooth." The ruler flashed twice.

"Dimensions confirmed. If tooth is presupposed to be one of the larger teeth as are commonly found in front of

jaw of modern sharks, then megalodon from which it came is estimated to be from fifty to sixty feet in length, with a possible error of twenty percent either plus or minus. If tooth is presupposed to be one of the smaller teeth as are commonly found in rear of jaw of modern sharks, then megalodon from which it came is estimated to be from seventy-five to ninety feet in length, with a possible error of twenty percent either plus or minus. Key feature: color beige. Confirmed. Conclusion . . .''

The tooth shrank and became enclosed in a square, which moved to the top left corner of the screen, and flashed. The center of the screen now displayed a depiction of a bulky, thick-bodied shark with much the same mouth and fin structure of a great white shark, but with a blunter, less pointed head.

'' . . . Carcharodon megalodon. Prevalent in all oceans during Triassic through early Pleistocene Epoch. Probability: ninety-nine point ninety-nine percent certainty.''

The shark shrank and became enclosed in a square, which moved to the top-right corner of the screen and flashed. The center of the screen now displayed a map of the South Pacific Ocean. A small circle appeared in the center of the ocean, and enlarged, bringing that particular section of the South Pacific to the full size of the screen. The picture changed to a topographical layout of the bottom of the area, complete with ridges and peaks depicting a mountain range, and a deep valley running to a side of the range.

''Tooth was raised by robot dredge sampling area of Marianas Trench at twenty-six thousand feet on June fifteen, nineteen hundred eighty-two. Depth confirmed.

''Overall conclusion: Carcharodon megalodon tooth: reconfirmed. Probability: ninety-nine point ninety-nine percent certainty.

''Extinct for one and a half million to five million years.

''Variable conditions: Tooth's dating inconclusive.

"Tests conducted by qualified European laboratories and Russian research institution indicated lack of evidence of carbonization, amino-acid racemization, or other obvious fossilization.

"Overall conclusion: Unknown action, possibly chemical in nature, in close association with deposit where tooth was found, retarded fossilization, or original apparent and real age tests were faulty.

"Probability; seventy-five percent."

Vandiver sat for a moment in thought, then reached for the telephone next to the terminal and lifted the receiver.

The number he called didn't answer, though Dr. Tegtmier had said he would be at the laboratory waiting for the tooth.

Vandiver frowned, replaced the receiver, looked back at the screen, and started thinking again.

A Coast Guard forty-one from the Gulfport Station sat close to the *Scent,* its stern barely visible under the surface in the light of the rising sun.

Bos'n Mate Third Class Beverly Cowart, her hands on the hips of her dark-blue trousers and her blond hair cut short above the collar of a crisply pressed short-sleeve shirt, stared down at the vessel. "We'll mark it with a buoy," she said, "and then see about getting somebody out here to move it out of the way of the pass."

The Coast Guardsman next to her nodded.

The diver down near the bow of the sunken boat had been there for only seconds, but he was suddenly coming up.

His head broke the surface of the water with a splash.

"Sir . . . Ma'am, there's a foot down there."

There were eight boys in all. They had on bright orange life preservers and were standing next to a pair of eighteen-foot aluminum boats pulled up alongside the bank. Carolyn parked the Ranger and reached into its backseat for Paul's tightly rolled sleeping bag as he hopped outside with his backpack and hurried toward the craft.

She pushed open the door and stepped to the ground as her father came toward Paul.

"Boy," he said, "do *men* let *women* carry their equipment for them?"

Paul came to a sudden halt and dashed back toward the Ranger. He stopped in front of Carolyn and reached for the sleeping bag.

"Daddy," she said, as Paul tugged the bag from her, "it doesn't weigh anything."

Paul, balancing his backpack on his shoulders where you couldn't see his head, held the sleeping bag in his other hand as he ran back toward the boats.

Mr. Herald placed his hands on his hips and stared toward the children. "Look at them work without me saying a word," he said.

San-hi and Armon were carefully checking each of the boys' life preservers to make certain they were fastened properly, and then letting the boys step into the boats one at a time, each of them immediately going to the craft's middle seats and sitting down, their backpacks held in their laps. San-hi handed Paul a preserver, watched him put it on, then pointed to the lead boat. Paul stepped into the craft and sat down next to the shortest boy on the team, a dark-skinned muscular boy with his hair cropped so close he appeared nearly bald. San-hi moved to the other boat and settled at the stern seat in front of the small outboard motor. Armon moved to the bow and looked back toward Mr. Herald.

"See," her father said. He leaned forward and pecked her on the cheek. "See you tomorrow afternoon . . . late."

"Daddy, if you knew how much this worried me. . . ."

"I'm not taking any liability on myself. You're the one who decided you wanted him to go."

"Daddy, this is your daughter you're speaking to—I know you planned this whole thing."

He kissed her cheek again. "The team's away," he said. Then in a softer voice, "Carolyn, what you should do is come with us, have a good time yourself. I'd like that."

"A girl with the men?" she said in a deep voice. "Heaven forbid, Captain." Then, her voice lower, she said, "Do keep an eye on him."

Her father winked and nodded. Then he walked toward the boys patiently waiting in the boats.

"Ready, men?" he said as he stopped at the edge of the bank.

"*Yes, sir,*" the boys came back as one.

"Yes, sir," Paul said.

"Good." Mr. Herald stepped into the lead boat and settled into its stern seat. In a moment, the outboard motor roared to life and he used its steering arm to guide the boat away from the bank. San-hi started the other boat's motor and guided the craft out toward the center of the channel.

Moving slowly, the water behind the boats barely churning with the slow speed of their props, they headed toward the long Interstate 10 bridge, shimmering and blurred in the humidity-created haze in the distance.

Her father looked back over his shoulder and waved.

Paul's face came around for a moment. Then he looked back up the river, as the other boys were doing.

Ensign Douglas Williams stared over the forty-one's rail at the bright water zipping past the craft. He was thinking about sharks. Not the kind his uncle thought about, but real live sharks. Specifically, deep-ocean sharks. The species that stayed in deep water, or in shallow waters not far from the deeper ones—like shallow water around islands formed by seamounts, volcanic projections that over time had risen from miles below and now formed such places as Hawaii and the many other islands in the mostly deep Pacific.

Sharks like the oceanic white-tip and the mako, the kinds of sharks that, along with the far-ranging tiger sharks, were responsible for far more deaths than the more publicized but less numerous white sharks, the kinds of sharks that yanked thousands of sailors from floating debris· during World War I and II—although this almost always occurred in deep water.

But was that going to continue to be the case? The world's commercial fishing fleets, forced far offshore by countries all over the world trying to protect their inshore waters, had congregated in the deep ocean the last couple of decades. Giant, super-efficient fishing vessels from the more technologically advanced countries such as Japan, pulling nets up to forty miles long, had wiped out entire schools of fish that had once swum these waters, not only taking them from the food chain but also any young they might have produced. With these fishes' dramatic decline, he knew that the great ocean predators that had depended on them for subsistence since time began had started moving into the shallower waters of the continental shelves in search of prey. Sharks never before seen close to shore or only seen there once in a great while were starting to be seen frequently in shallower waters.

He was a witness to that. He had been assigned to the Pentagon for only the last few months. Before that he had been a junior officer on a destroyer. Only two months prior to being transferred from that vessel, he had been on its deck as it made its way up the eastern side of the Gulf of Mexico and had looked down over the rail to see a twelve-foot deep-water mako staring back at him.

He thought of the perception people had of a shark attack—a person struggling, yelling for help. But the general public really didn't know. Maybe that scenario was true of what happened during an attack by some of the smaller, shallow-water sharks common to the American coasts. But it was not the case with the great giant creatures from the open seas—some of them reaching fifteen to eighteen feet in length and weighing two to three tons. When they attacked it was swift—no struggle, a swimmer often swallowed nearly whole, or bitten completely in half. He had a shipmate on the destroyer who had been present at such an attack. Swimming off a beach in the Philippines with a friend, the shipmate had looked away from his friend for a moment, and then looked back to see nothing but open water. Seconds later he had glimpsed the top of a thick dorsal fin momentarily breaking the surface, moving away from him—and nothing more.

And now I'm going to dive in waters not all that far from where I saw the Mako, Douglas thought. He knew that, despite the almost universal misconception of a shark's poor vision, such creatures in reality could see half again farther than a man could underwater, and several times farther than a man in poor light or murky water. So watching carefully did no good—a person would never see a shark before it saw him. And even if sharks were blind, the advantage would still be overwhelmingly theirs. They could hear and feel vibrations for over a mile. The predominant portion of their brains was devoted to olfaction. They could often smell prey farther even than they could hear or feel it. There was no possible way a swimmer could enter the water and stay very long and that presence not be known to every shark for miles in every direction.

And even if somehow an intended victim sensed an attack coming, to flee was useless, even when relatively close to a place of safety. Makos like the one he had seen had been clocked swimming at speeds in excess of thirty miles an hour—and that when they were not even up to attacking speed.

Douglas closed his eyes at the thought of his upcoming dive. He had actually wanted to be an English professor, teaching at some small college where he could spend a great deal of time involved with his interest in poetry. But his uncle was an admiral. So despite his mother maybe thinking the military silly, as his uncle had stated, she had directed him that way. And he had acquiesced. Her advice had always proved wise in the past.

Man, he thought, *why did I listen to her?*

And he cursed his uncle silently under his breath—almost meaning it.

"Sir," the Coast Guardsman behind him said.

Douglas turned to face the shorter man.

"Sir, did you bring swim trunks?"

Douglas nodded.

"We have your scuba equipment ready inside," the man said.

Douglas stared toward the center of the boat.

And then, a somber expression across his face, he followed the man down the deck.

CHAPTER 14

"How many of you have seen a beaver dam before?"

Paul raised his hand. "I have," he said. Fred cut the outboard's throttle. The boat glided broadside against the bank. San-hi guided the trailing boat in behind him and Armon stepped off its bow onto the soft ground.

"Easy, men," Fred said as the boys in front of him began rising. Paul stood in the rocking boat. His backpack in one arm, his rolled sleeping bag in the other, he wobbled to the side of the craft. Put in motion by the feet pushing off of its side as the other boys stepped to the bank, the boat began to swing out into the water.

"Grab it, Armon," Fred said.

At that moment Paul stepped out of the boat into knee-deep water, stumbled at the unexpected depth of the step, and splashed forward onto his stomach at the edge of the bank.

Armon smiled as he caught the side of the boat.

Fred stared at him.

Armon shrugged, but couldn't help but continue to smile.

San-hi caught Paul by the shoulder and pulled him to his feet. His jeans and shirt and preserver soaked, his backpack dripping, his sleeping roll soggy, even his thick, dark hair hanging wet down across his forehead, Paul came up on the bank and grinned.

"Whew," Armon said, wiggling his nose. Paul looked in the direction of the strong stench coming from the trees off to the side as the rest of the boys started unloading the trailing boat.

Except for the pair of blond-haired brothers in the group. Ten and twelve years old, and almost identical in looks except for a slight difference in their heights, they slipped their life preservers off, lifted their backpacks over their shoulders, and stepped back to the boat for the cane fishing poles lying lengthwise along its center. In a moment they were walking around the edge of the slough.

"Don't overload yourself," San-hi called after them.

The older blond suddenly began to struggle with the weight of the few poles he carried across his front. Staggering awkwardly back and forth beside his smiling brother, he continued toward the mouth of the creek at the end of the slough.

San-hi stepped to Paul and took the sleeping bag and backpack from his arms. Unbuckling the top of the backpack he slid the soggy sleeping bag under the flap, pulled the straps back through the buckles and pushed the backpack into Paul's hands. Paul smiled and slipped it around his shoulder.

Armon stared at the two. "When you finish baby-sitting . . . ," he said. He stood beside the trailing boat, unloaded now except for the boxing equipment.

As San-hi walked toward him, Armon placed one foot over inside the craft to hold it steady against the bank. He began to stack San-hi's arms with tubes of tape, small boxes of gauze, jumping ropes, and headgear. The last thing the stocky youth lifted from the boat was the heavy-bag, big around as a tree trunk and heavy as a bag of cement.

Balancing the bag on its flat end on the bank, he looked toward the other boys. It took two of the smaller ones, one at each end of the bag, to carry it toward the creek.

Armon stared into the trees and wiggled his nose again.

"Something big," Fred said.

He stared at the smallest boy on the team, up on top of the dam and disappearing over the jumble of protruding logs and limbs into the gap at its center.

"Come on, Edward, get out of there."

The boy didn't answer.

Fred waited a moment. Edward was the only boy on the team who couldn't swim.

"Edward!"

The boy's head reappeared.

A moment later he came back along the top of the dam. He carried a bill cap and a rod and reel in his hands.

Admiral Vandiver had a thought. He had several thoughts, actually, all of them leading toward the same possibility.

He had said to his nephew, *So why, Douglas, I ask you, if any creature was originally present down there—why would he not still be there?* He had quickly made light of his question by saying he wasn't suggesting the possibility that megalodons might actually still be present, but only that they lived a lot longer than was popularly thought. What else could he say and keep any credibility with a nephew he wanted to be especially observant when he studied the bottom where the Coast Guard had found the tooth? To emphasize to Douglas how much he *didn't* believe megalodons still existed, he had stated that with the modern technology now probing the seas in the form of submarines, submersibles, and robot probes, it was hard to fathom that the giant creatures could still be alive and not have blundered into something that would have recorded their presence. Certainly a full-grown megalodon, not only alive but moving into water as shallow as that between the Keys and the Everglades, would have likely been seen somewhere during the many days and nights it would have taken for it to travel from the nearest great depths. There was one possible explanation.

The white shark was the only shark that marine biologists credited with intelligence—not simply instinct. Whites were known to stand up with their heads out of water and look around, observing what was outside their kingdom as well as within it. Other sharks had that physical ability, but they didn't do it. Whites obviously distinguished between boats and the people within them. There were several cases in particular when whites had tried to come up over the sides of boats after the occupants. And whites, when attacked, would almost always come after the attacker. The tiger shark, the hammerhead, the oceanic white-tip, and the other giant so-called man-eaters usually fled when injured, unless already engaged in a feeding frenzy or an attack they had launched themselves. It was instinctive to flee when injured.

But what Vandiver thought most about was the notion held by some experts that whites were possibly even capable of planning.

If nothing else, the white's preferred method of attack suggested this. While other sharks were generally known to attack their victims from whatever angle they originally spotted them, or circle in clear view of the victim before attacking, whites, when given the opportunity, preferred to dive deep after spotting a victim and come up under them, unseen. More than one swimmer, treading water, had been jerked under the surface by his legs. More than one surfer had fallen prey to an attack after first being bounced into the water by a white slamming into the bottom of the surfboard to dislodge him.

But there were also a number of other, more dramatic instances of the white's actions which led to the speculation that they could plan. Probably the most dramatic was the story of the English sloop *Byrum* in the late 1800's.

A white shark followed the sailing vessel for days, eating

the garbage the cook threw overboard every night. During the day the white stayed next to the ship. Day after day. The crew became accustomed to seeing the great fish. Sailors on the vessel swore afterwards that they had noticed the white's eye rolling up to follow them when they passed along the rail. But, in any case, they became comfortable with the creature's presence. One day one of the men went around the outside of the rail to work on some lines to the rigging. The white, witnesses say, swimming some thirty feet from the vessel's side at the time, suddenly veered hard toward the hull and came up out of the water and snatched the man off the rail—almost as if the shark had been waiting for that moment.

Planning? Waiting patiently for days to execute that plan? Or simply an easy meal presenting itself to the white? Who would ever know with certainty? But even putting that action aside, there was still the evidence of intelligence in the mere fact of the white rising to look around and in not reacting to a base survival instinct and fleeing when under attack, but rather responding—turning on its attackers.

Was the megalodon, the direct ancestor of the white shark, as intelligent as the white of today? Or more intelligent? In either case, was it possible that the megalodon had enough reasoning ability to simply avoid being seen if it didn't wish to be seen . . . for whatever the reason?

The blond-haired brothers stared at the fishing pole, its butt pushed down into the soft ground at the edge of the bank and the line hanging limp from its end into the water.

Fred stopped behind them.

Three bass, their bodies swollen and blue, floated on their sides a couple of feet out in the water. A stringer ran through their gills and back to the bank where a branch pressed down into the soft ground held the line secure close to a minnow bucket, with its lid half off.

"Snake got them," one of the brothers said, looking at

the round, dark fang marks easy to see against the pale blue color of the bass's bloated stomachs. Edward looked at the minnows floating in the bucket and twisted his face at the smell. Fred stared at the pole a moment more, and then over his shoulder in the direction of the stench that had been plain at the dam.

"Wait here for a minute," he said.

"I'll go with you," Armon said.

Fred nodded. "Keep the other boys here, San-hi," he said.

The stench came back as Fred and Armon neared the trees. It became stronger as they walked between the thick trunks. A few steps farther, it became nearly overpowering. A sound like the buzzing of a beehive came from behind the trunk of a wide oak a few feet ahead of them. Fred stepped around the tree to see the swollen carcass of a large boar lying on its side, its thick forelegs held stiff out in the air. Its right rear leg was missing where it had joined the hip. Bloated blue flies buzzed loudly as they swarmed the cleanly severed wound, the boar's fixed eyes, and its gaped mouth where sharp tusks eight inches long curved out and up into the air.

"You thought it was a body?" Armon asked.

Fred nodded. "Could have been."

"An alligator got him?"

Fred nodded again. "Must have grabbed him when he was at the bank drinking." He looked at the ground where the boar had plowed deep ruts with its tusks in its dying agony. In the soil off to their side he saw where the hog had fallen and dragged the stub of its hind quarter, leaving a wide strip of soil darker than the surrounding ground. More flies swarmed a smear of blood low on the trunk of a gum tree a few feet farther back toward the slough.

"Would think the alligator would have at least smelled him and come after him," Armon said, "wouldn't you?"

"Something will," Fred said, and turned back in the direction of the slough.

When they stepped out of the woods, Armon looked toward Paul standing in the middle of the line of boys staring toward the trees.

Armon shook his head in a seemingly worried manner as he neared the group. "Two big old bull alligators fought and killed each other. You never can tell what they're gonna do when they get like they are this time of year—mating season. Guess someone's gonna have to stand guard out by the water tonight to keep them from getting into the tents."

He looked directly at Paul.

Paul grinned. He had been in the marshlands and up and down the river more than any of the others.

Fred knelt at his backpack and pulled its top flap back. He pushed aside a light blanket and felt down past a flashlight and a bottle of Maalox to a cellular phone. Lifting it in front of him, he punched in a number.

As he waited he stared toward the cane pole, stuck in the mud, its thin end bending toward the water and the bass floating tethered beyond the bank.

"This is Fred Herald. I'm on the Pascagoula, a few miles above the Interstate bridge at what's left of a beaver dam. There was a rod and reel and a cap hung on a limb near its bottom. Didn't think too much about that—people always losing something. But now there's a cane pole stuck in the ground back off a slough here, hook still hanging in the water, a bucket of minnows, some dead fish on a stringer. Like somebody just up and vanished—maybe two somebodies."

Paul didn't grin this time.

Fred's call was relayed from the Jackson County Sheriff's Department to a young, dark-haired deputy standing at the bottom of a narrow dirt landing leading into the river. He looked up the landing at Eddie Fuller's old Ford pickup. "Might know where they went now," he said.

The older, gray-haired deputy next to the truck looked down at the younger man and walked toward him.

Their boat sat tied to a tree branch off to his side.

CHAPTER 15

The heavy-bag hung from a limb of a cedar. The limb was springy, and every time Armon pounded his tight, gauze-wrapped fists into the bag, it bounced. He came with an uppercut and the bag sprang several inches into the air.

"Got 'em good that time," Armon panted, sweat dripping from his dark face. "That's how I'm going to do it, put them up into the air and catch 'em coming down."

Fred stared at his stopwatch. "Not with you at only ten minutes and starting to breathe hard already."

"Rounds are only two minutes," Armon said, glancing over the shoulder of his T-shirt, continuing to dance back and forth in front of the bag. "Man, I'm working hard, Mr. Herald."

A few feet away, Edward, not quite six inches taller than Paul, wrapped San-hi's hand with gauze. He stopped wrapping and stared up at San-hi. "How am I going to get this right if you don't keep your fingers spread?"

"Shut up, Edward, and wrap."

"Thirty seconds left," Fred called out.

Armon dropped lower, squared his muscular shoulders evenly with the bag, and started pounding it with sharp, hard punches.

"Fifteen," Fred said.

Armon's fists became a blur.

"Ten."

The smacks into the bag became one long staccato sound. Paul's eyes widened.

"Time," Mr. Herald said.

Armon stepped back from the bag. "He's dead," he said. "He should have never climbed in the ring with the Biloxi Pounder." He raised the back of his hand to wipe the sweat from his forehead and looked up into the blazing sun. Paul handed him a plastic squirt bottle full of Gatorade.

"Thanks, man." Armon leaned his head back and squirted the solution into his wide mouth.

San-hi stepped to the bag.

"Time," Mr. Herald said.

San-hi started hitting the bag, his blows more crisp jabs from afar than the way Armon had worked.

"Hey!" the older deputy exclaimed.

The younger deputy looked in the same direction and spun the wheel of the eighteen-foot boat. The craft leaned up on its side toward the small aluminum boat, floating partially submerged and nearly hidden from sight in a stand of tall water grass growing in the shadows of a line of tall oaks leaning out over the river.

Paul handed San-hi the squirt bottle. Edward pounded the heavy-bag. Paul was surprised at how hard the small boy's smacks sounded. Paul looked at his own hand, and clenched it into a fist. San-hi reached down and pulled Paul's thumb from inside his fingers. "You pop somebody that way," the thin Vietnamese said, "and you'll break your thumb. Keep the thumb tucked down in front of the fingers." Paul moved his thumb down to the first joint of his forefinger and clenched his fist tighter. San-hi nodded and raised the squirt bottle back to his mouth.

Smacksmacksmacksmacksmack.

Edward's shoulders were following each punch. He looked like some kind of four-and-a-half-foot puppet being thumped rapidly back and forth. Paul started moving his shoulders. His head moving back and forth in rhythm with his body and Edward's punches.

Smacksmacksmacksmacksmack.

"Time," Mr. Herald called. "Okay, work's over; get the tents up, fires started, we'll cook dinner, and then go fishing—and somebody get rid of those dead bass."

The boys hurried to do his bidding.

The young deputy slapped at a mosquito on his neck as he leaned from his craft to hold the bow rope of the half-submerged aluminum boat.

The older deputy leaned from the other end of the craft as he stared at the line of jagged rips angling across the bottom of the aluminum boat's stern. The line curved slightly as if somebody had hit the craft repeatedly with a sharp ax every few inches for a distance of three feet, changing the angle of the blows only minutely, but evenly, with each stroke.

"Who in hell would do that?" the younger deputy asked. "You can't sink a boat with flotation seats by knocking holes in its bottom."

"It's like a giant old-fashioned bear trap," the older deputy mumbled to himself.

"What?"

"I said it looks like the tooth marks from an old bear trap my granddaddy kept in front of his fireplace. In one way bigger than that in fact—one bigger than they ever made. And look how the punctures are damn near exactly the same distance apart. It's as if somebody measured each blow with a ruler. Beats hell out of me, is what it does. And that's with a big question mark."

He reached for the cellular phone at his feet.

*   *   *

The foot, still in the expensive Ferragamo shoe, its laces still tied, sat on the stainless-steel table in the corner of the morgue.

"Mr. Leonard Fraizer the Third," the medical examiner said. "Positive identification."

Harrison County Sheriff Bobby Broussard, his thick frame in a pair of brown slacks and a blue sports coat that fit too tightly, stared at the shoe. He had a strange look on his face. "You put the shoe back on after you took the prints?"

"Didn't take any prints," the medical examiner said. He was a short, thin man with glasses that magnified his eyes to twice their normal size. "Called the shoe store in New Orleans where the captain of his Bertram said he shopped. It's the kind he bought, the same size, and the color of the last pair he bought."

"He ain't gonna be buying any more," the little man next to the sheriff said. He was even shorter and thinner than the medical examiner. The morgue's all-around assistant. Dropped out of middle school in the eighth grade. Been irritated with everyone who didn't ever since. He had been especially irritated when he had learned Leonard owned a Mercedes. He nodded his head at the justice of it all.

The door to the front office opened and Jackson County Sheriff Jonas "Pop" Stark strode inside the room. He looked at the foot while still walking toward Sheriff Broussard. He shook his head as he stopped in front of the medical examiner.

"There's something not right about this."

Broussard held out his hand. "Hi, Jonas," he said.

Stark shook Broussard's hand without looking away from the table. "Three bodies in three days. All that's left is this and a piece of a hand. A pack of bull sharks? A school of piranha would have left more."

"Was a hell of a lot bigger than a piranha," the medical

examiner said. "Look closely at the cut. It's clean, one fell swoop at the bottom of the ankle—like a giant scalpel. When I was in med school in California, I saw a seal that a great white had killed—carcass washed up on the beach. There were big jagged chunks out of it. If you checked close you could see where each tooth cut cleanly—the jagged edges resulted from where the points of the teeth went deeper into the carcass than the body of the tooth, leaving a serrated effect. The shark that bit through this ankle had such big teeth that one tooth did this. Couldn't be anything I know of other than a great white—a big one."

Before either Stark or Broussard could respond, the doctor added, "I know there's never been a white shark around here. Wasn't before I moved down here, and never heard of one being anywhere up and down the coast since I moved here. But I'll bet my Aunt Laura's skinny butt we have one now."

The Coast Guard forty-one cleaved the water rapidly, its bow throwing spray wide to its sides. Droplets of moisture blew back across Douglas and he turned his face away. Wearing a pair of flowered shorts hanging past his knees, his long legs bent cushioning his bouncing, his hands gripped the rail. Behind him his flippers, face mask, and double air tanks vibrated on the deck. Ahead of the boat the sky continued to darken.

He looked down at the side of the boat at the porpoise thrusting up out of the water and cleaving the next big wave easily. Another of the big animals, preferring a smoother ride under the troubled surface, continued to race in a blurred shape, knot-for-knot with the speeding boat, its throttles pushed all the way forward in an attempt to reach the site where the tooth had been found and, hopefully, back again, Douglas thought, before the torrential rains and lightning began.

His eyes caught the dark shadow out from the side of

the boat as they raced past. His head jerked back in the shadow's direction as it disappeared into the rolling wake behind the craft.

A big sea turtle?

A large ray near the surface?

He shook his head, took a deep breath, and, rubbing the back of his neck, stared up at the clouds racing toward the boat.

On the Pascagoula there was movement in the trees behind the riverbank. Nothing more could be seen for a few seconds. The deer's head stuck around a gum trunk. A moment later the animal's shoulder showed. It was a small doe. She stepped out from behind the trunk into the open. A fawn stepped around her. Born late enough in the spring to still carry pale spots against its brown coat, the baby's movements were nevertheless agile, springy. A male, he came ahead of his mother to the edge of the river. As she lowered her neck to drink, he stepped past her into the water. His hooves sunk in the soft mud, his head tilted forward splashing the water, and he twisted and lunged backward onto the bank.

He stared at the water, then took a careful step forward, again moving into the water, but now only went a few inches past the edge of the bank. He extended his neck forward and began drinking. The mother's head suddenly lifted.

Her front legs stiffening, she stared into the water a few feet in front of the fawn.

The mother's movements were warning enough. The young male backed quickly to her side. The mother whirled. The fawn wheeled and dashed ahead of her, the two quickly disappearing into the thick trees.

In the water, the top few inches of a thick fin slowly surfaced, turned, swirling the water gently, and sank from view.

CHAPTER 16

Alan stood next to the fingerling tank. Ho had a big grin across his face. He patted the surface of the water gently. "Me and little woman do it again," he said. The red snapper hatchlings were too small to be visible in the churning light-green water blurred with algae, but they were there. "She tired, I'm sure," Ho added. "But I tell her Chang call this morning and say he has relief on way. She be friends with me again."

Alan pulled the sleeve of his sports coat back and glanced at his watch. "Rayanne's not going to be pleased with me unless I get her presents." He ran them off in his mind: candy, perfume, and pajamas—cotton. And something to surprise her with. "I'm going to go now before I get tied up and forget."

Ho nodded. "Good to not make her angry. She make good roast beef and carrots. And fried cucumbers—never heard that until I met Rayanne."

Sheriff Stark tried to look through the big magnifying glass the medical examiner held over the round stub of the ankle. He finally took it from the doctor's hand and held it down close to the cut, where the ankle had been severed close above the top of the shoe.

"See the fibers," the doctor said. "Smooth, slick, like a serial section in a lab; even the talus and the calcaneus, one clean cut did that, one tooth, sharp as a scalpel and as wide as the ankle."

Stark straightened and held his thumb and forefinger about three inches apart.

The doctor nodded. "At least," he said.

Alan slid behind the steering wheel. He slipped his cellular phone from inside his coat as he backed the Jeep toward the street. A couple of minutes later, the phone at his ear, he turned off Bayview Drive toward Highway 90 and the beach area running alongside the twin cities of Biloxi and Gulfport.

In the morgue, Sheriff Stark listened on the telephone as Mrs. Hsiao gave him Alan's cellular number.

He quickly punched in the digits, listened to the receiver for a couple of seconds, then replaced the phone on its cradle.

"Busy," he said, and looked back at Leonard's foot in the Ferragamo shoe.

"A helluva big shark," Sheriff Broussard said.

Stark looked in the direction of the doctor standing next to the door on the far end of the morgue as a body was wheeled inside. "If he knows what he's talking about," Stark said in a low voice.

"You saw the fibers yourself," Broussard said.

"And what did that tell me?" Stark came back. "That I thought I was seeing what he told me I was supposed to be seeing." He reached for the telephone and punched Alan's number in again.

"Still busy," he said a moment later.

"Coffee?" the doctor asked from the side of the room, and held a steaming cup in their direction.

Stark stared at the cup a moment. It certainly wasn't a

Folgers morning in the morgue with the sharp smell of the antiseptic in the air and the stench of something else, pungent and . . . well, dead. But coffee did *sound* good. He walked across the room, at the same time suddenly deciding he would take his black when he saw the doctor lift an uncovered sugar bowl off a shelf stacked with gallon bottles of preserved organs, some of them with their lids ajar, and the spot where the bowl had sat, stained where liquids had sloshed.

Alan finished his conversation, slipped his phone back inside his sports coat, and turned the Jeep west down Highway 90 toward the Edgewater Mall. Out in the Sound, a fifty-three-foot Hatteras made its way in the direction of Pascagoula. There was a stiff wind from the north, and a darkly tanned young girl with blond hair rode a sailboard slashing rapidly across the dark water beyond the shallow-water markers. A small Coast Guard boat came toward her so fast it appeared it might run her over. The boat slowed and cut out to her side, stopping as it came up beside her. Alan stopped for a red light. His telephone rang.

It was Rayanne.

"I already told you Happy Birthday," he said, "so that can only mean you're checking on me."

"Would I do that?"

"Or else wanting to know what I'm buying you."

"No, actually I'm getting ready to step inside the supermarket and I wanted to know what you would like me to fix you for *my* birthday dinner."

"Bribery."

"Call it what you will."

"Just some simple steaks and a baked potato."

"Simple? At what steaks cost?"

"I'll grill them for you."

A pickup made a U-turn at an intersection just ahead of him, cutting across the Jeep's front, and he had to slow to keep from clipping the truck's rear. He frowned, then saw who drove it and smiled. It pulled into a service station and he turned off the pavement behind it.

"Happy birthday again," he said into the phone. "I'll see you around eight."

Stark replaced the receiver on its cradle in the morgue and shook his head. Broussard sipped from his coffee. Another body came in through the door at the far end of the tile.

"Fun place," Stark said.

When Ronnie Khulman stepped from his pickup in front of the gas pumps, he saw Alan's Jeep stopping behind him and smiled. Friends since high school, they had played junior college football together, then gone to separate universities, Alan to USM and Khulman to Ole Miss. They shook hands at the rear of the pickup.

"In town for the weekend to see Mother," Khulman said, "and then back out to the big D again. She tells me you're getting ready to break ground on a new plant—an entrepreneur headed to the top. You going to loan me some money when I need it?"

Alan smiled. "What does a plastic surgeon make nowadays?"

"I thought enough, until my accountant told me what I owed Uncle Sam. But they left me barely enough to buy an old roommate a beer—if you still drink beer."

"Fine, let me park my Jeep out of the way and then you can get the DUI."

"You know," Khulman said, squinting his eyes up into the sky, "I believe it is hotter here than in Dallas."

Alan looked at the blazing sun and began slipping off his coat as he walked toward his Jeep.

The younger deputy shook Fred's hand. "Jim Fairley," he said.

"Fred Herald."

Edward handed Fairley the rod and reel and bill cap he had found on the dam. "The pole's back by the creek," Fred said. "I left everything just the way it was."

They started around the edge of the slough.

The boys waited by the boats.

A mile downstream, on the same side of the channel as the boys, the blunt, rounded nose of the creature silently broke the surface of the river. The mouth gaped slightly as it rose quietly out of the water. The shark continued to rise until five feet of its thick body poised above the surface. A few feet in front of the shark, the trees grew thick along the bank, allowing only the barest glimpse of anything behind them.

Movement. The lean, low shape of the small doe could be seen for a brief moment. A prancing movement beside her, near her stomach. The fawn's pale white-on-brown coating allowed only a blurred glimpse of the animal's thin body. Continuing behind the trees, they vanished again.

The shark slowly sank back into the water. A slight rippling of the brown surface as it closed over the wide head. Another narrow, longer ripple created a line moving down-river in the same direction as the deer.

The ringing sound came for the second time. The attendant filling a car with gas realized it wasn't the telephone inside the station ringing. He looked toward the Jeep parked in the space in front of the rest rooms.

In the Jeep, the ring sounded again. It came from the locked glove compartment. On the floorboard beneath the glove compartment, Alan's sport coat, folded, was slid back far enough under the seat that it was almost hidden from view.

The ringing stopped.

A few seconds later it began again.

* * *

Douglas pushed off the ladder at the rear of the Coast Guard forty-one. A watertight camera hanging from its strap around his neck, a net-bag trailing from the hip of his flowered shorts, and the Coast Guard diver assigned as his diving partner following along behind him, he glided toward the doctors' craft, turned upside down on the sandy bottom. The damage caused by whatever the boat hit was obvious from one end of the hull to the other. The tooth had been found about forty feet away from the craft, close to the remnants of the dead reef off to his side. Everything about the bottom appeared normal—it seemed.

But how in the hell would I know? he thought.

A frown tightening his face around his mouthpiece, he kicked his flippers and glided out farther from the Coast Guard craft. His head moved slowly from side to side as he tried to spot something that would catch even his untrained eye, anything that looked like it might be caused by some kind of upheaval.

Yet the sandy bottom stretched flat in every direction. The reef, while dead, was like a solid, molded piece of concrete, no crack or other sign that the ground under it had moved.

He kicked his flippers and glided over the wide top of the reef.

Its other side was the same, no sign of a crack anywhere.

He turned over onto his back and, kicking his flippers slowly, moved away from the reef, getting a perspective from one end to the other. Except for the normal up-and-down flows of what had once been living organisms, there was no sign of any of its length being thrust higher or sunken in a spot.

The sand on that side was the same, too.

He glanced up at the shadowy hull of the forty-one as a four-foot barracuda swam under the keel. His eyes narrowing behind his face mask, he watched the thin fish with the ugly smile until it passed out of sight into the green veil in the distance, and then he looked back at the sunken boat.

It rocked slowly with the force of a wave rolling over-head. Above it the forty-one's keel rose and fell. Douglas could see the white foam breaking on the opposite side of the craft. The increasing waves on the surface were strong enough to be felt now.

He looked at the sand below him.

Though the sea grass moved in rhythm with the rolling backwash from above, the sand barely stirred at all, only a slight rising and then resettling of the finest particles—the actions of waves wouldn't have uncovered something as deep as the tooth should have been buried.

Now he felt his body pushed to the side and noticed a particularly large swell moving across the surface above him. The forty-one's hull rose and fell sharply. The water around him grew dimmer. He turned his gaze back to the bottom and, kicking his flippers, swam farther out from the reef.

Could an upheaval have happened some distance away and then a resulting strong storm have swept the tooth to where it had been found?

How would he know?

A few moments later, far enough away from the reef that it was only the barest, hazy figure in the distance, and the forty-one's hull couldn't be seen at all, he began the start of a long circle, the other diver following along a few feet behind him.

CHAPTER 17

Douglas stopped kicking his flippers. He stared through his faceplate at the depression running from below him out into the distance like a shallow V-ditch cut across a sandy beach.

He refocused his eyes to be certain he wasn't viewing some kind of distortion caused by the mask's glass or an optical illusion caused by the water. He wasn't. It *was* like a shallow V-ditch, but more rounded than a V. A wave above caused sand to slide down the gentle slope at a side of the sunken area.

Not realizing he had stopped breathing from the instant he had seen the depression, he suddenly felt the need for a breath. He took in a great gulp of the cool air, self-consciously glanced back at the diver behind him, and settled closer to the bottom.

The depression ran into the distance, so shallow it lost its shape in the haze of water and the surrounding sand and patches of sea grasses to its sides. A wave's backwash caused more sand to crumble below him.

He kicked his flippers softly, starting along the sunken area. Its length clicked off in his mind.

Thirty-five to forty feet later the depression ended, narrowing to a rounded point. But he could see another depression eight to ten feet beyond the point, this area more easily discernible because it was deeper, maybe a full foot deeper. It ran in a different direction, at an angle directly across the sunken area he was above—like the line topping a T.

A swell sweeping the surface suddenly thrust him downward, then lifted him. A large section of sand at the end of the sunken area crumpled and ran like a miniature avalanche toward the center of the depression under him.

It was quickly filling in.

He stared at the newly formed loose pile of sand. The storm above, though kicking up waves high enough to have made him uneasy when he had prepared to enter the water, was nothing compared to some of the storms that would have regularly swept the area. The depression couldn't have been here long or its trace would have already been obliterated.

He let his body settle lower, his flippers gently touching the sand at the center of the sunken area.

And his mind went to a new thought: *If there was this place, sunken, would there be another place somewhere else, thrust upward?* Upward enough, and from a deep enough depth to have pushed a tooth up from several feet below the bottom? A million years or more his uncle had said the megalodon had been extinct. Maybe the upthrust would have had to push up from several hundred feet below the bottom. He looked around him into the green veil of water, the color thickening into the distance until a dark curtain of green cut off all farther view. If a mountain range rose only a few hundred feet away he wouldn't have been able to see it.

He looked down at his feet.

The toes of his flippers barely touched the sand. He kicked them gently. As he rose a couple of feet from the motion, the sand disturbed by the flippers swirled into a tiny dust cloud and settled back into the center of the trench.

Did there have to be a protrusion somewhere of great magnitude, or was he, untrained and unknowing, looking at something that already portended a much greater disturbance than he could guess?

His uncle was crazy to have sent him. Here he was looking at *something*. By the time he could get somebody else back to the area who might know what it might represent, the depression might already be gone, swept smooth once again.

He looked at the sand, still crumpling in rhythm with the swells passing overhead.

He looked back past the diver behind him in the direction of the reef, unseen from his distance.

Could the reef being dead have anything to do with something that might have taken place here years before? Corrosive agents brought up from deep in the earth by an upheaval that had settled now but left the tooth?

He shook his head in disgust. *How would he know?* Irritated, he caught his camera, turned where he faced back down the long depression, and raised the camera to his faceplate. A large swell rolling across the surface above caused his body to be pushed down once more. Another mini-avalanche slid down the slope to his side.

Something dark, barely visible, showed in the sand.

Black. Thin filaments.

He reached out his hand.

The thin pieces came easily loose from the sand. *Decaying plant matter.* Buried sea grasses. He dug his hand into the sand. More of the black matter was exposed, still held together in its former living fashion, but crumbling as it was exposed. He dug in another spot. More of the dead grasses.

He looked ahead of him along the trench. To each side the grasses that ran above the depression weaved with the action of the waves, but the depression itself was devoid of living matter.

But the grasses had grown there not long ago. He had no idea exactly how long—he wasn't a marine botanist either. He had no idea how long it would take for buried grasses to completely disintegrate and disappear. But once—days, weeks, maybe months—they had grown there. And then been wallowed beneath the sand.

Wallowed, he thought.

He looked at the long depression stretching ahead of him. Behind him was the smooth, flat area of undisturbed sand, and then the other depression, crossing the first at a right angle.

Wallowed?

He suddenly visualized a long, bulky shape lying breathing on the bottom, its body wallowing out a trench. The trench ending where the rear part of the thick body curved upward from the sand in a curve toward the tail—the tail sweeping slowly back and forth, digging a trench.

Now he did know.

And his heart raced. He suddenly became disoriented, looking around wildly for the direction of the forty-one. Just as quickly he reoriented himself and, barely taking time to motion to the Coast Guard diver that he was sur-facing, he kicked his flippers hard and swam rapidly in the boat's direction.

CHAPTER 18

At the point where the tree-lined, east bank of the Pascagoula gave way to the vast expanse of marshland curving back into the distance, the small doe fed on a clump of tender grass growing in the sunlight at the edge of the water. Her fawn stepped into the water and reached his head around in front of her to get at the grass. Pushing against the side of her face to move her head out of the way, the fawn stiffened his legs, and his front hooves sunk into the mud. Rearing to jerk them loose, his rear hooves slipped out from under him and he splashed sideways into the water. He kicked his legs into the air and his back submerged. Jerking his head back toward his mother, stepping out into the water after him, the fawn slid farther away from the bank. He submerged completely for a brief instant, splashed upright on his knees, his head straining toward the bank, his chin held up, and caught the slippery mud under his body with his hooves. They slipped again. He slid backward down the slope angling toward the center of the channel. The doe stepped farther out into the water and reached her muzzle toward him.

He was jerked backward under the water.

The mother's forelegs stiffened. She tried to whirl toward the bank, but her hind legs slipped from under her and she sat sideways into the water. As she lunged forward, stretching her neck out for the bank, the mouth came out of the water behind her and grabbed her hips. Her thin forelegs kicking into the air, her head thrashing wildly, she vanished backward under the water.

A few feet from the bank the water boiled.

Bubbles rose.

In a moment the surface began to calm once again.

Why would the megalodons, known by fossil evidence to have once roamed all the world's seas, have retreated to the deepest trenches and remained there ever since? Vandiver wondered. For that's what they would have to have done; the only place possible they could have remained alive and their presence not be known.

Something chasing them from the shallower waters? It was unlikely that there was ever a creature that swam the seas that was so fearsome that the megalodon had run in fright. Maybe not a creature at all, he thought. Perhaps in the world changing from glacial to tropical climates a hole unimaginable today had appeared in the ozone layer. Maybe somehow the megalodons were sensitive to that. The last dim rays of the light spectrum could penetrate to around fifteen hundred feet in water—that might have driven them at least to those depths. Or perhaps a switching of global temperatures created something on the order of an all-encompassing, worldwide poisoning of the shallow waters in the same manner that weather triggered what would be termed a red tide today. Or maybe climatic changes caused great winds, creating huge worldwide dust storms to pollute the ocean's shallower waters, sending the megalodon to the trenches where the deep waters alone would serve to dissipate the settling dust. Vandiver smiled at that thought—was the megalodon moving to the depths simply no more mysterious than an asthma patient moving to Arizona?

Then his expression became serious once again. To try to guess what caused the migration was useless. He knew that even if he guessed correctly he would never be able to confirm it. And it would be even more difficult to guess why the megalodon, after retreating to the depths, would have stayed there. Maybe it was better for him to concentrate his efforts on coming up with the reason why one might have suddenly moved up from the depths now. That it had happened before, and more than once over the last few hundred years, he would bet his life on. A buzz from his intercom brought him out of his thoughts.

"Dr. Tegtmier on line one, sir."

It's about damn time, Vandiver thought, and took a deep breath as he reached for the phone.

"Admiral Vandiver here."

"Admiral, the preliminary tests are inconclusive. I expected them to be. These kind of solitary items are nearly impossible to date with any great degree of accuracy without knowing the layer of sediment they came from. Often, in fact, when you hear of anything as old as a megalodon tooth being dated, the scientist in reality often dated the layer of sediment associated with the find. We're sending the tooth to Massachusetts for radiocarbon dating, but that isn't always conclusive on phosphatic samples like shark teeth. I'm only speaking preliminarily at this stage, of course, but there appears there is an outside chance that there is a degree of retardation of aging due to prior association with some unknown gas or element in the location where the tooth was—"

"What does it look like to you, doctor?"

"Sir? Look like? I mentioned we're going to have to send it out for further evaluation before we can—"

"No, doctor. Look like—with your eyes."

"You didn't observe it before you sent it over here?"

"Of course I did. I want to hear what it looks like to you."

"Well, it's laying on the counter right over here. But you know as well as I do that there are all kinds of reasons why one tooth will look one way and another—"

"Answer me, damn it, Kurt—look at it."

There was a moment of silence.

"It shows no obvious sign of pitting, Admiral. No sea organisms have penetrated the enamel that we have been able to determine with the preliminary testing. It's not crusted or brittle in any way."

Vandiver nodded. "Kurt, it's as smooth and silky as I remember a little cheerleader's stomach many years back, isn't it?"

"Well, I don't know about that, Admiral."

"I do. Couldn't be any smoother if it dropped out of a megalodon's mouth in the last few weeks."

His intercom buzzed.

"Sir, Ensign Williams is on line two. He told me to break in on your call."

Vandiver cut Tegtmier off without saying a word.

"Douglas."

"Sir, you're not going to believe this." His voice sounded high-pitched. "There's a depression not far from the remnants of an old reef, sir. It's as if it were made by something lying on the bottom. You can see where it wallowed grass under the sand. It's several feet wide. And there's another depression. . . ."

"Sir, I think it was made by the tail."

Vandiver's pulse surged.

"Sir, there's nothing else that would make a long depression, is there? Do whales ever lie on the bottom, sir?"

"How long a depression, Douglas?"

"Counting the . . . if it were a tail . . . over fifty feet. Sir, at the same place the longer depression ends and the gap starts, to each side of the depression, at that spot I found a barely detectable disturbed area out to the sides—as if something similar to the rungs of a ladder, several ladders,

pressed down in the sand at an angle leaning back toward
the trench. Doesn't a shark . . . a white shark . . . have some
small fins coming from his lower body there?"

"A depression over fifty rungs long," Vandiver mumbled to himself.

"Sir, does a shark have—"

"Yes. Yes. What about the slashes on the boat?"

"I have someone coming to check on it."

"Who?"

"A forensic specialist."

"A forensic specialist?"

"In teeth marks, sir—in rape cases."

The two boats drifted sideways down the river. The four
youngest boys on the team sat back-to-back straddling the
lead boat's center seats, their life preservers lying beside
them and their fishing poles held straight out from the sides
of the craft, their corks trailing in the brown water passing
alongside the boat. Armon sat at the bow, the only one not
fishing, his pole leaned against his shoulder.

Fred looked back over the outboard motor to the second
boat trailing twenty feet behind and off to the side. San-hi
sat in its stern seat with his elbow resting on the throttle
arm of the motor and one hand holding his fishing pole out
over the side. Paul, after asking if he could ride in the same
boat with Edward, sat back-to-back with his newfound
friend on the seat in front of San-hi. The remaining member
of the team, the older blond brother, sat in the seat past
theirs, beyond Fred's backpack that lay in the bottom of
the boat between them, and the cooler of sandwiches and
Cokes. Nobody was moving around; everybody sitting still
like he had told them. Nevertheless, he cautioned them
again: "Be careful now about yanking any of those hooks
back in the boat. They'll snatch an eye out in a second."

The boats drifted slowly forward.

The sun had already dropped behind the trees on the west bank.

A cork jerked under the water.

Edward yanked up on his pole. A bare hook jumped into the air and plopped back into the water. He said something under his breath and Paul looked over his shoulder and grinned.

"Give them time to take the bait," Fred called.

Edward lifted his pole and caught the hook swinging back toward him.

A few seconds later, baited again with a minnow, the hook disappeared into the water. The cork ran out away from the side of the boat, tugged twice, then slowly came back in line with the others.

Alan, a pair of cotton pajamas under his arm, a bottle of perfume in one hand and a box of candy in the other, stopped at the glass counter and looked over its top at a woman with blond hair who appeared to be in her early fifties.

"Do you wrap things?" he asked.

She nodded and held her hands out for the items. He handed her the candy and perfume and slipped the pajamas out from under his arm, laying them on the glass. "For a birthday," he said.

The woman looked at the pajamas. She noticed he didn't wear a wedding ring. "Not for a wife?" she said.

"No, ma'am."

She looked at the perfume and box of candy. "I think lingerie might go better with those than pajamas," she said.

"Not in this case," he answered, and looked down through the glass. "I need something else special, too."

She waited.

"For an aunt."

"Oh." The woman nodded. "What kind of special?"

"I don't know. Something nice."

"But for an aunt—how old?"

"Sixty-two today."

"Let's see," she said, "Perfume, candy, and pajamas—what about some houseshoes?"

He nodded. "And a robe—cotton. Do you have any long earrings—silver that sparkles a lot?"

Ten minutes later, Alan stepped from the front entrance of the Edgewater Mall and walked toward his Jeep. In addition to the gaily wrapped packages, he also carried a thick book on gardening he had bought in the Bookland store. His phone rang as he piled the items on the Jeep's backseat. He reached to the glove compartment.

"Uh-huh."

"Sheriff Stark here. I've been trying for . . . never mind. You've heard about the latest attack."

"Sharks?"

"Or one damn big one. In the Sound this time. Not far from Ship Island. Coast Guard found the body. What was left of it—the foot. Medical examiner said it was severed at the ankle by one tooth."

"Tooth?"

"The shark was that big, he said. He said it had to be a white. I know he's not a marine expert, but he seemed pretty damn certain of what he was talking about. But whites don't go up rivers. So do we have bull sharks *and* a white?"

"I want to see the foot."

"It's over at the morgue. And, Alan, deputies called in from the Pascagoula. They've been out there looking for an Eddie Fuller and Luke Crenshaw, missing after a fishing trip a couple of nights ago. I haven't talked to the deputies yet. My dispatcher says they're on the way in. But they found Fuller's boat and they told the dispatcher it had a line of punctures across its stern. The way he described them I wouldn't bet they're not teeth marks. And, Alan, if it is teeth marks, then whites do go up rivers. The way the dispatcher repeated what they said, the marks would have had to come from something with a mouth big enough to swallow an eighteen-wheeler tire whole—bigger.''

"Can you get them on the radio?''

"Hell, I'm not on my radio. I'm at my house. Stopped by to get a hot dog. Hang up and let me get out to the car and I'll patch us together. Hell, I can't do that either. The boat they used needed a trailer one of my deputies owned. He's in his truck. He has a cellular phone with him but I don't have his number. Hell, hang up and I'll get it from the dispatcher and have him call you and you can meet me down at the morgue.''

Alan had been so taken aback by the news of another attack and what the sheriff had been saying that he hadn't taken time to think. But he did now.

"Jonas.''

"Yeah, Alan, I'm getting ready to call him right now.''

"No. Tell him to not worry about calling me. Tell him to get his boat back in the river and find Carolyn's father. He's camping out there with a bunch of kids tonight—and they're going fishing.''

Fifteen minutes later Alan turned his Jeep off the interstate onto the frontage road leading toward the blacktop in front of Carolyn's house.

His phone rang.

"They were in a frigging Quick Stop drinking coffee!'' Stark exclaimed. "Left the phone in the truck. They said they know right where Herald and the kids are. At an old beaver dam about two miles upriver from Carolyn's. They're on their way. It will take them about fifteen or twenty minutes to get back to the landing and get the boat in the water. Another ten minutes or so to the dam. They should have them on their way out of there in a half hour or so.''

Alan shook his head. "Call your deputies back and tell them to stay where they are. I'm not five minutes from Carolyn's now. She has a boat. I can be to them in ten minutes. There's no reason to have anybody else out on the water. You need to get everybody off the water. Don't ask—order them if you have to."

"I did that a couple of hours ago. I hate it, but I didn't even know Mr. Herald was at the dam until Fairley just told me they found some poles there."

"Poles?"

"There was a rod and reel and a fishing pole left there. Probably belonged to the missing men because Fairley said Fuller's wife told him her husband fished with a cane pole and the other man with a rod and reel."

Stark paused a moment.

"Alan, I was thinking they were fishing and the boat capsized and they went into the water and maybe the sharks got them. But they wouldn't get back in the boat to fish the river, and leave their rod and reel and pole . . . would they?"

CHAPTER 19

Fred looked at the lights shining from the rear windows of his daughter's house. If it had been any other time he would have had the boys join with him in serenading her loudly as they drifted past, bringing her laughing outside the house. But he didn't want to embarrass Paul.

He looked at his grandson, sitting with his back against Edward's, ignoring the house as it began to pass out of sight behind them. Paul had looked at it only once, and then with his face down toward the water and only his eyes rotating up toward the bank. And then he had looked across his shoulders to make certain none of the boys had noticed.

Fred smiled and flicked the switch that turned on the red stern light mounted on a short aluminum shaft at the rear of the boat. Behind him, San-hi flicked on the stern light of the other craft. A mile back, they had left the part of the river where trees rose from each side of the channel, and now to their east the marshland stretched out seemingly endlessly to their side in the moonlight.

"Can we go into the channels, Papaw Fred?"

Fred looked toward the tall grass. The brackish water in the narrow passageways winding through the marsh did provide the ideal nesting spot for freshwater shrimp, and they in turn attracted everything from bass to saltwater fish, and the large predators like the gar and the alligator who fed equally on the shrimp and the fish attracted by them. It was a place where it was hard not to catch something. But there were problems in fishing there, especially with a bunch of young boys. Fred looked back at them. "I guess we can, if everybody will be careful about not hanging their hooks in the grass. You'll be jerking them around trying to get them loose and the next thing you know we'll have a hook stuck in somebody's ear. Maybe mine.

"And," Fred added, "if everybody keeps sitting quietly like they're supposed to. If not, then I'm going to make you put your life preservers back on—whether it's hot or not."

Alan forced himself to sit a brief moment in the Jeep after he stopped it in Carolyn's driveway. He didn't want to scare her to death. It would be so rare for something big enough to leave teeth marks that size to swim up rivers that an attack could almost be ruled out. The boat had become hung on something that had caused the damage. Something. He stepped out of the Jeep to the pavement and walked toward the front of the house.

Carolyn smiled when she opened the door. She said in a slow voice: "I hope you're happy . . . and Daddy, too. I know Paul is—I let him go."

A nervous sensation passed through his stomach.

Carolyn's expression changed. "What?"

"It's nothing to worry about, but—"

"*What*, Alan?"

"There's been another attack."

Her face turned ashen.

"Not in the river," he quickly said. "Out in the Sound. But to be safe I'm going to get Fred to bring the boys back in. I need to use your boat."

She turned and walked hurriedly toward the telephone at the bookcase. At his questioning expression she said, "I'm going to call him and make sure they're not already fishing.''

He walked up beside her as she punched in a number. ''He keeps his cellular phone with him when he takes the boys camping in case there's an emergency,'' she said.

She lifted the receiver to her ear, listened a moment, and frowned. She lowered it and began rapidly punching in the number again. Alan noticed her hand tremble, but she finished the number and lifted the phone back to her ear. A moment later she lowered it again and shook her head.

''It keeps saying it's not in use.''

He took the receiver from her. ''What's the number?'' She told him and he punched it in, taking care to go slower than she had with each digit.

''We're sorry, the cellular customer you are attempting to reach is either not available or not in the service area. Please try your call again later.''

''You certain that's the right number?''

She nodded. ''Let me call Mother.''

In a moment Carolyn had her on the line. ''Mother''— she closed her eyes as she forced her tone to sound normal—''did Daddy take his phone with him this time?''

It was several seconds before her mother finished with her answer. Carolyn said, ''No, I thought I might call and check on Paul. Yes, Mother, I let him go. No, I'm not worried, I . . . Mother, a friend of mine is at the door. I'll call you back later.'' She replaced the receiver without waiting for a response.

''Mother said he leaves it off unless he has to use it,'' she said, starting toward the back door as she spoke. ''She said he'll call before they go to bed tonight. She obviously hasn't heard about the attack today.'' She shook her head as she pushed the screen door open and started out into the yard. ''I've been catching up on my bookwork all day. I usually have the TV on but I . . .'' She was walking so fast she was nearly running. "How are we going to know which way they went?"

"They're upriver, camping next to an old beaver dam."

"How do you know that?"

He stepped out onto the small wooden dock and undid the boat's stern line. Carolyn pitched the bow line over the boat's windshield. "Maybe you should stay here," he said. "It's only a couple of miles. I'll be back with them in a few minutes."

"Are you crazy?" she said, dropping into the craft. She slid behind the steering wheel and turned the ignition key.

The motor roared to life.

At the sound of the outboard motor starting, Fred looked across his shoulder in the direction of his daughter's house. He was far enough downriver that he couldn't see even a faint glimmer of lights now, but the motor sounded as if it had started right behind the house.

Now the motor opened wide. Even at its distance, the whine as it wound to full power came clearly through the dark.

Paul looked up the river toward the sound.

Carolyn's dark hair whipped in the wind streaming past the craft. "I asked you how you knew where they were?" she said over the roar of the motor.

He stood next to her, his hands on the top of the windshield. "Some deputies saw them earlier today. The deputies didn't know about the attack in the Sound. They'd been on the river all morning."

"What were they looking for?"

When he didn't answer immediately she looked at him. "Alan."

"Two fishermen disappeared a couple of nights ago."

She looked at the throttle, but it was leaned forward as far as it would go. Behind them a wide wake rolled out to

crash into the bank on one side of the channel and cause
the tall water grass on the other side to weave back and
forth like it was dancing.

Ahead of them trees rose from both sides of the river. A
minute later they passed in between them.

"They said only a couple of miles," he repeated. "We'll
be there in a minute."

Ahead of them the wide beam of the bow light brightly
illuminated the center of the channel and reflected out
against the trees to each side.

Behind them the boat continued to form a wide wake,
now spreading out to crash into the banks to each side of
the river and slosh back toward the center of the channel.

A bug glanced off Alan's cheek and ricocheted to the
side.

"There," he said.

Carolyn pulled the throttle back.

A small wave building in front of its bow, the boat settled lower in the water and coasted toward the gap in the
dam.

Carolyn edged the throttle forward and turned the wheel,
lining up the boat perfectly and passing through the gap
with inches to spare on each side.

Dark outlines of three tents could be seen to one side of
the slough. No fires burned. No one moved about.

"*Daddy!*" she called.

"They're fishing," he said.

She spun the wheel, turning the boat sharply, and pushed
the throttle forward. Branches protruding from the dam
brushed roughly against the boat's side as it sped though
the gap toward the center of the channel.

Carolyn shook her head.

"Which way?"

CHAPTER 20

"Hang on!" Armon yelled and laughed loudly.

San-hi's long arms yanked back and forth spasmodically with the darting motions of the big fish he had on the line.

Paul leaned out over the side of the boat as he looked back at the jerking line.

"Not too far out, Paul," Fred called from the other boat.

"You're not keeping the line tight," Paul said to San-hi.

"Paul," Fred called, "I'm going to make you put on your preserver."

Paul eased his upper body back inside the boat, but kept his head and neck extended out over the water, dimly glowing red from the craft's stern light.

San-hi lost the fish.

Armon roared his laughter.

The Vietnamese stared across the water at his friend.

Paul nodded knowingly. "I told you," he said.

San-hi stared at him.

Armon laughed again.

Fred smiled.

The water swirled several feet out past the side of the trailing boat.

"A big one," Paul said. He lifted his cork from the water. Leaning forward, he flicked the end of his pole, flipping the baited hook out as far as he could. It landed several feet short of where he'd seen the swirl.

He frowned. Behind him, Edward yanked his pole, and his hook popped clear of the water.

"I'm glad Martha fixed a lot of sandwiches," Fred called from the other boat.

The water out in front of Edward swirled, and a big bass came half out of the water after a dragonfly.

"Read it and weep, Edward," Armon called from the other boat. "That's the one you lost."

Then a rapid swirl in the water a few feet to the side of where the bass had disappeared, followed by a long ripple running several feet across the surface pulled Armon's eyes to the spot.

San-hi stared, too. "I think an alligator just got your bass, Edward," he said.

The spotlight on the bow cast a wide beam of bright light in front of the speeding boat. Carolyn shut the spotlight off and stared ahead of them down the channel in the dark.

She couldn't see any lights at all.

The two small stern lights raised on short shafts at the aluminum boats' rear illuminated the boys in the craft in a red glow and cast a circle out over the water.

Armon slapped at a mosquito on his broad forehead. The young blond on the seat in front of him passed him a can of insect repellant.

Armon sprayed it liberally up and down his arms, around his tennis shoes, and onto his palms, then rubbed his hands around his face. In the other boat, Paul's cork jerked under the water. He yanked up on the line to set the hook.

The end of the pole suddenly bent into a sharp curve. The line sped toward the front of the boat. The older blond ducked as Paul's pole swung over his head.

"What'n hell?" Armon said as he looked across the water.

The line circled the bow, straightening the pole toward the water. The fish rippled alongside the boat. Edward ducked as the pole came around over his head.

The fish splashed near the stern and its thin body, four feet long and spinning, jumped clear of the water.

"A gar," Armon said. He laughed. *"Catch it, Paul."*

Paul's arms strained as the fish dove deep, pulling the tip of the pole underneath the water, clanging the side of the pole against the edge of the boat.

The fish splashed clear of the surface again, dove . . .

And the line snapped. . . .

The tip of the pole popped into the air and vibrated.

Paul frowned.

Carolyn caught the faint glow of the red lights ahead of them. She switched off the bow light to cut its reflection off the water.

"Is it them?" she asked above the roar of the motor.

"It's two boats."

Carolyn looked at the water flying past the speedboat's side. It had never seemed so black to her before. She looked across the windshield again and caught her lip in her teeth. Ahead of them, the red lights moved slowly toward the edge of the marshland.

Somebody slapped at a mosquito.

Fred used a paddle to guide the boat toward the narrow channel running off the river into the marsh grasses.

Armon turned the other boat with him.

The sound of a speedboat approaching from the rear grew quickly louder. A bright spotlight glowed from its bow.

There was an audible plop.

"Son of a bitch!"

"Armon!"

"Sir, the little bas . . . he hit me with a water balloon."

Holding his arms out, Armon looked down at the water soaking the front of his T-shirt and jeans. The younger blond brother stared out across the water.

"Milton," Fred said.

The boy kept his stare out over the water.

"Milton."

The boy's face slowly came around.

Fred didn't say anything.

Slowly, the boy slipped two water-filled balloons out from behind his hips and placed them in the bottom of the boat at his feet.

"Milton," Fred said again.

A half dozen still-unused balloons came from behind the boy this time. Armon leaned forward, grabbed them and stuffed them into his jeans pocket.

The light behind them became blinding and the speeding craft coming downriver turned directly toward them and slowed.

Paul raised his hand in front of his face and looked back into the light.

"*Daddy,*" Carolyn called.

Paul frowned.

Carolyn guided the speedboat between the two smaller boats.

"Daddy, there's been another attack—in the Sound. There might have been another one here on the river. There's two men missing and deputies found their boat and said it has teeth marks across its stern."

Paul's face tightened.

Fred's face had a questioning expression across it.

Alan nodded. "I know it sounds crazy. I haven't seen the boat. But the deputies told Jonas that's what it looks like."

The boat paddled by San-hi came around the right of the

speedboat. Fred's boat, rocking gently on the small waves created by his daughter's boat, drifted on toward the shallow channel running through the marsh grasses.

"Tie the boats here," Alan said, "and we'll take you back."

Fred looked across the width of the river toward its far bank. "Okay, you take the boys and let me take the boats over there. I can bring my pickup down the street and load them in the morning."

"Daddy, no. We'll worry about getting the boats later."

"Okay, we'll tie 'em together and anchor them in the grass. Armon, paddle us over there." Fred pointed to the water grass to his right. Armon lifted a paddle from the bottom of the boat and leaned over the bow.

"You need to call Mother, too," Carolyn said. "She's going to see the news, if she hasn't already—she'll be panicking."

Fred's boat was half within the entrance to the narrow channel now. San-hi's was still out in the river, but right behind them. Fred looked toward the cooler and his backpack lying in San-hi's boat in the space between its middle seats.

"Mack, my phone."

The older blond brother leaned forward, but Paul's hands reached quicker. He pulled the backpack's flap open, felt inside the pack, found the phone and battery pack and pulled them out. San-hi used his paddle to guide the bow of the craft toward the left of Fred's boat.

Paul stood. The boat rocked slightly under his feet.

"Paul," Carolyn said.

"Careful, son," Fred said.

Paul nodded and waited for the two craft to come together.

A wide head burst through the surface in an explosion of water between them. The mouth gaped wide toward Fred. The bow of San-hi's boat ran into the creature's back and lifted. Paul, still clutching the telephone and battery pack, fell sideways into the water. Carolyn screamed. The shark turned partially in the direction of what struck him and splashed back under the water. San-hi's boat, pushed to the side by the wave created by the splash, hit the side of the speedboat and tilted. Edward rolled over its side into the river.

Fred dove from the other boat into the water. Alan was trapped from entering the water by San-hi's boat directly beside him. He vaulted over the seat to the rear of the speedboat, came up on its stern with one foot on the motor, and dove in a flat racing dive for the water.

Paul paddled as hard as he could for the speedboat. Edward's head came up in front of him, and went under again. Paul stopped swimming and grabbed for him. Paul sunk under the water. Fred and Alan reached the spot together. Paul's head came up. He sputtered and pulled hard with his arm. Edward came up, Paul's fingers twisted tightly in the neck of the boy's T-shirt. Alan grabbed Paul. Fred grabbed Edward. The speedboat's motor roared as Carolyn backed toward them, hitting the aluminum boat with San-hi and the older blond and spinning it around.

"*Watch out!*" Carolyn screamed as she jerked the gear into neutral and the boat continued coasting backward. The stern slammed hard into Alan's ribs as he reached up for its top, but he was able to grasp the rim and hang on. Fred's big hand grabbed next to his. Carolyn jammed the gear forward and pushed on the throttle.

The prop spun close to Alan's leg. San-hi's boat, slowing its spin, still sat partially out in the river. Edward clung to Fred's neck as Fred, holding the speedboat with one hand, reached out with his other hand and grabbed the aluminum boat. His arms stretched painfully. He grimaced, but held on. Alan pushed Paul over the rear of the speedboat, where he went sprawling into its bottom as its bow slammed into the other small boat in front of them, knocking it and the wide-eyed boys within it farther into the shallow channel between the marsh grasses. Fred's hand slipped loose from the speedboat as it sped into the channel. Burdened by Edward's weight, he disappeared under the water.

His arm rose up through the surface, splashed, and grabbed the side of the aluminum boat. His head and shoulders popped above the water, Edward clinging to his neck. The shark's head rose up out of the water behind him. Fred dove under the small boat. The blond vaulted over its side onto a small, triangular-shaped wedge of marsh grasses. He sunk in water to his ankles. San-hi splashed into the grass beside him. The shark's wide head crashed down on the boat, submerging it under its thick body.

Fred's head popped to the surface. He pushed Edward ahead of him, and scrambled up onto the small section of grass.

CHAPTER 21

Four bright orange preservers floated on the water. The cooler bubbled and sank beneath the surface of the river. Fred, San-hi, the older blond-haired brother, and Edward stood on the spongy, triangular-shaped section of ground not much larger than a dining room table. The last boy from the other aluminum boat scrambled over the side of the speedboat and rolled into its bottom. Their small boat drifted backward past Alan, standing in water up to his mid-thighs next to the speedboat's stern.

"Come this way," he said. "It's too shallow for it to come in here."

Out in the river, San-hi's boat suddenly shot bow-first up through the surface and splashed back onto the water upside down.

"Come on," Alan said.

The blond and San-hi looked at Fred, as if waiting for what he was going to say, then stepped toward the edge of the grass, but stopped and stared at the thirty feet of brown water between them and the speedboat. Suddenly the blond dove as far out in the water as he could. He splashed on the surface and never went under as he race-stroked toward Alan's waiting hands. Alan caught him and pulled him toward the side of the speedboat.

San-hi stared at the water, out at the river, and back at the water. Edward was clinging to Fred and shaking his head no.

"Wait," Alan said. He grabbed the side of the aluminum boat drifting behind him. He worked his hands down its side to its bow, pulled on the boat, twisting it at the same time, swinging the other end in a sweeping curve toward the section of grass, and gave it a push.

Fred edged forward and reached out his hand as the boat neared the grass. Behind him, San-hi and Edward, bathed in the dim red glow of the craft's stern light, looked toward the dark river again.

A few feet from the edge of the grass, a thick dark fin rose a foot out of the water. They backed to the very edge of the section of ground.

"Daddy!" Carolyn said.

The fin was edging toward the shallow channel. Fred stepped back into the center of the grass.

The wide head broke the surface and nudged against the grass with its nose. Paul held tighter to his mother's arm. Fred backed closer to San-hi and Edward standing at the very rear of the grass. Behind them the dark water was part of the river, curving into a cut sweeping several feet back into the marsh area where thick grass began again.

The head sunk from sight. The fin, its tip glowing a dark red from the illumination given off by the stern light of the drifting aluminum boat, turned toward the rear edge of the small section of grass.

And disappeared.

Fred looked over his shoulder and stepped forward to the center of the grass, pushing Edward ahead of him and holding San-hi by his shirt. They huddled tightly in the center of the grass, watching the second aluminum boat float out toward the one overturned in the river.

"Fred," Alan said in a low voice, "the water here is too

shallow for it to get in the channel. Just come forward to us."

Fred pushed Edward forward. Edward pushed back against him.

"Go on, boy—you have to. I'm not going to let you go under." Fred glanced over his shoulder again.

San-hi looked at the edge of the river a few feet to their side, then back at the speedboat, and stepped around Edward. Alan held his hand out. Carolyn looked where the river water met the entrance to the channel.

"Wait!" she screamed.

The fin rose quickly, the head rose in front of it and the creature lunged forward into the channel entrance.

San-hi stumbled backward. Edward was pushing against Fred, nearly driving him backward into the river cut.

The shark lunged again, came a few feet farther into the channel. Alan backpedaled through the water and reached for the side of the speedboat. Its motor was still running. Carolyn reached for the throttle.

The creature lunged once more. The upper half of its body was out of the water now, its mouth gaping, its teeth reflecting a shiny brown in the moonlight. Its body stretched back a full twenty-five feet to the top of its tail rising out of the river.

With a sudden violent twisting, the creature slid backward, floated with its top half above the surface, then sank from view in a swirling suction of water.

"Fred," Alan said.

"No!" Carolyn said.

They all stared toward the river.

A few seconds passed.

The fin broke the surface a hundred feet out in the river, coming fast toward them, a spray of water mounting to each side of the dark protuberance.

"Back up, Daddy!"

Alan vaulted up out of the water into the speedboat.

The blunt head broke the surface, water streaming around it like a sea rushing around the bow of a submarine moving at flank speed on the surface.

The black eyes emerged.

The body rose.

The water sprayed higher.

The shark slammed into the entrance of the shallow channel, abruptly rose higher, came forward. Carolyn hit the throttle of the speedboat. The shark threw its head to the side of the channel, its body partially around the small section of spongy ground, cutting off Fred, San-hi, and Edward from the speedboat. Its dark eye stared at the three forms clustered at the very rear of the tall grass, their heels at the edge of the river. The shark began to roll side to side, wallowing out the mud beneath its great bulk.

Suddenly the shark rolled its body hard to the side, lifting another couple of feet of its bulk from the water and crushing the tall grass to its side. Its head twisted, trying to come up on the spongy section of ground.

Fred took a quick step to the rear, found his footing gone and, holding Edward, sat backward into the river. His arms thrashing forward wildly, pushing Edward in front of him, his knee caught the spongy ground. He pushed Edward before him, and came up onto the grass.

The shark rocked its body back and forth, compressing the muddy ground and slipping to the side a couple of feet more.

"Alan," Carolyn cried. The back of her hand was at her mouth. Paul twisted his face into her stomach. The other boys, crouched down in the boat, stared in horror. Alan vaulted over the seat to the steering wheel. He threw the motor into gear.

"Lay down!" he yelled and jammed the throttle forward.

The speedboat shot backward. The boys dove to the bottom of the boat. The edge of the stern slammed hard into the creature's side. The head jerked around toward the boat as the craft rebounded and came back again, smashing into the body once more. The shark twisted, trying to turn toward the attacking boat. Alan ran the craft forward twenty feet, jerked the gear into reverse, and backed hard again.

This time the stern crashed hard into the creature's body with the metallic sound of the prop disintegrating and the lower unit locking.

The boat rebounded forward down the narrow channel.

The shark rolled. Its head lunged partially toward the speedboat, one eye staring in that direction. Blood stained the water at the creature's side.

The head slowly pulled back toward the spongy section of ground. And began rolling again.

Half the ground had been compressed now—half the grass lay on its side under the water. Only half of a section originally but a few feet wide was left now.

The bow of the speedboat grounded in the grass on the far side of the channel. Armon knelt at the rear of the boat next to the motor, dead now and silent. His hands worked at the gas tank.

The shark rolled its body and tried again to turn its head toward the three figures only five to six feet away.

Armon came to his feet.

Facing the shark he came up on the rear of the stern and drew his arm back.

He held one of the balloons, full of liquid and drooping to each side of his hand.

He threw it hard at the wide head.

It splashed squarely between the creature's eyes and ran down toward its mouth.

A lighter flared in Armon's hand. *"Watch out!"* he screamed. His arm burst into flame as he pitched the lighter out past the rear of the boat.

The shark's head burst into a wide ball of fire. The three in the grass ducked and threw their hands in front of their faces. The shark's mouth gaped open. Flames trickled inside around its teeth. The head twisted. The body rolled from side to side. The thick bulk moved backward. The flames burned higher. The head pulled back from the entrance to the channel.

Its black eyes seeming to stare directly at Armon, flames jumping higher above its head, the creature submerged beneath the water, leaving small patches of burning gasoline rocking above it.

Smoke rose above the surface.

Two of the boys wrapped a wet towel around Armon's smoking arm.

Fred grabbed Edward behind his shoulders and pushed him toward the front of the grass.

"Come on, San-hi." Fred pushed Edward to the edge of the water. *"Go!"* he yelled at San-hi.

San-hi dove head first toward the speedboat, splashed into the water, and stroked frantically. Fred looked across his shoulder.

"Hurry, Daddy!"

Fred grabbed Edward, lunged forward into water to his thighs, and kicked his way toward the boat.

The fin rose at the entrance to the narrow channel and surged forward.

Alan grabbed San-hi and pulled the boy up into the boat.

"Daddy!" Carolyn screamed.

"Papaw!" Paul screamed.

Fred fought forward.

The blackened head rose ten feet to his side, lunged forward, but only moved inches. It lunged again. Again only inches. Fred reached the boat's side and lifted Edward up toward the other boys reaching for him.

The great fish, its black eyes staring, twisted in the water, raising its head, trying to fight its way to the boat.

San-hi leaned over the side with a paddle and stroked it hard into the water. Alan vaulted over the side of the boat into the water and began to push on the craft's side. Fred pushed from the rear. The shark stopped twisting. Its eyes still seeming to stare, it slowly began to back from the channel.

A moment later it sunk below the river's surface.

Armon moaned in pain.

Paul began crying.

Rayanne reached for the telephone, hesitated, and dropped her hand back into her lap. Behind her the dining room table was set with plates and silverware. In the kitchen the steaks still sat on the cutting board.

Outside on her small patio the charcoal began to lose its glow.

She sighed, picked up the remote control, and turned on the TV.

CHAPTER 22

Armon lay with his legs along the speedboat's front seats, his muscular shoulders propped against the side of the boat. Carolyn had made him as comfortable as possible by stuffing a life preserver behind his back. His arm, wrapped from hand to elbow in one of the boys' T-shirts, was cradled in his lap. His face was tight with pain, but he hadn't said anything since they had helped him to the seats. Paul fumbled in his jeans pocket and pulled out a partially filled pack of spearmint. He slipped out a stick of the gum and held it toward Armon. The boy took it, unwrapped it with his good hand, and moved it to his mouth. Paul stripped a second piece of its wrapper and held it across the seat. Armon shook his head. Paul moved the stick into his own mouth. Carolyn stared down at Armon.

The rest of the boys, except San-hi, sat without speaking in the bottom of the boat, their shoulders leaning back against its sides. San-hi stood next to Alan and Fred near the motor.

Alan spoke in a low voice. "He's burned bad enough he's seeping fluid." He looked toward the river, a hundred feet away back toward the entrance of the shallow channel. How long after the sun rose would it take for a boat to come by, if one would come by at all with Sheriff Stark having ordered everyone to stay off the water? He didn't know how many hours a burn like Armon's could go untreated without it endangering his life or reaching the point where the arm would have to be removed.

Then his gaze went across the expanse of tall water grass stretching out toward the long Interstate 10 bridge covered with the tiny lights of vehicles moving along its surface. Back to the left of the bridge were the trees that marked the high ground, at least two miles away. There was no way to paddle the speedboat as big as it was.

"I'm going to wade out."

"I'll go with you," Fred said.

"I can probably make it faster by myself."

"And break a leg, or pull a muscle, or anything else—and we'll all be waiting here for nothing."

There was nothing more said. Carolyn handed them a pair of life preservers. Alan moved his leg over the side of the boat and dropped into water to his mid-thighs. Fred splashed down beside him. San-hi plopped down next to them. They didn't say anything then, either. Carolyn handed another life preserver over the side.

"Let's push the boat as far up in the grass as we can get it," Fred said.

The other boys came over the side to help.

Rayanne looked at her birthday cake, with six candles set into the icing on one side, two on the other.

She looked at the phone mounted on the wall next to the refrigerator, and walked toward it.

In Carolyn's driveway, the cellular telephone lying on the Jeep's seat rang. It rang a second time, and then a third.

A minute later, the telephone in Alan's apartment rang. It rang again. Then several times more.

*   *   *

They had found the quickest way to move along the shallow channel was by placing the preservers under their stomachs and lying forward on them as they paddled. It had been an hour. Ahead of them the narrow strip of water curved back in another direction once again. Their idea of wading out to the trees and dry land had quickly dissipated when, as the channel had weaved back to their right, away from the direction of the trees, they had left it and moved into the grass. It was two or three inches deep in water, with another foot or so of mud so liquefied it might as well have been water, and then an almost bottomless sucking, thicker mud underneath that. San-hi lost both his tennis shoes on his first steps. By the time they had started breathing hard, they had barely moved ten feet. The only way out was to follow the channel to the interstate bridge, and then hope they could attract someone's attention or, somehow, scale the thick concrete pilings up to the structure's surface.

Fred's deep voice trailed back to San-hi, floating behind him: "Son."

"Sir?"

"Armon's started smoking again is why he had that lighter, isn't it?"

San-hi didn't answer.

"Thought so," Fred said. "That's why he was breathing hard on the heavy-bag—after only ten minutes."

San-hi still didn't speak.

"Well, wish you smoked, too," Fred said. "Wish all of you smoked and had lighters, matches, a whole pile of matches. Smoked like an old train engine. I'd take your matches and your lighters and your cigarettes and build the biggest, nastiest, smoking signal fire you ever saw."

San-hi smiled.

The expression left his face at the sudden splashing sound.

Alan slipped backward from his preserver and stood in water to his waist. Fred held his preserver in front of him. San-hi stared ahead of them.

It came again: *Splash-splash, splash-splash, splash, splash.*

It wasn't ahead of them. It was in the tall grass off to their right.

Alan moved away from the grass toward Fred. San-hi edged behind them.

The hiss came short and deep.

"Get up in the grass," Alan said in a low voice, pushing on Fred's shoulder. "Hurry."

Fred sloshed to the side, pulling his feet as quickly as he could out of the mud that sucked at his shoes. San-hi was quicker, reaching the grass, faltering a moment as he tried to move his feet up the mushy bank, and then pulling himself into the thick growth.

Across the channel, two quick splashes, and an alligator stuck its broad snout into the open. Its forelegs parted the grass, and took two more quick, choppy steps. The reptile hissed again.

Alan pushed Fred farther into the grass. He felt a shoe suck from his foot. San-hi splashed forward rapidly for a couple of steps, and his feet sinking again, tilted forward. He tried to catch himself by wrapping his arms around a clump of the grass, but pushed it down with him as he splashed face-first into the water.

Alan glanced back over his shoulder as the alligator's head disappeared. He slowed, caught Fred's shirt, said in a low voice, "She's not coming after us."

A *she* because it was obvious. If it had been a male, he would have swum off at the first sound of the three of them talking, coming in his direction. A female would have, too, if she wasn't guarding a nesting ground she had fashioned on a high damp spot hidden somewhere behind her.

San-hi was shaking the mud off his hands. At Alan's

next step his leg sunk into what almost seemed to be a hole dug by a posthole digger. He went to his side, his arm down in the water, trying to get his balance. Fred caught him until he could regain his feet.

San-hi seemed to be stuck. His eyes widened in the moment it took him to move his feet again.

Parting the tall grass before them with their forearms, they struggled around the side of the channel.

The speedboat was pushed half into the tall grass to the side of the channel, the rear of the craft projecting back into the open water. Armon's cheeks glistened with his silent tears. Gnats swarmed the fluid-soaked T-shirt wrapped around his arm. Mosquitoes buzzed around the craft, lighting on the boys leaning back against its sides, causing hands to slap constantly against skin. Every time something splashed in the dark it made Carolyn nervous. Paul stood by the motor, looking up the narrow channel in the direction Alan and the others had gone. As he continued to stare, his eyes began to tighten. To Carolyn or any other adult there would be nothing to see but the long, thin strip of brown water fading into the distant night. But until a child approaches ten years of age, his eyes retain a greater ability to see in the dark than those only slightly more advanced in age. It was that ability that Paul used now.

"Mother."

His tone caused her head to come around quickly.

She stepped to his side and clasped his arm.

The blond brothers lifted their heads over the side of the craft and looked in the direction he stared.

It was almost a full minute before Carolyn made out a long, thick shape moving toward them in the middle of the channel. By then, Paul and the younger blond could see it clearly.

"An alligator gar," Paul said, his tone showing his relief. The eight-foot-long fish continued slowly along the chan-

nel. Unlike the thin, needle-nosed gar that had been hooked
in the river, the fish he looked at now had a wide, thick
body. Anybody at first glance might think they were actually viewing an alligator. To people not accustomed to the
creatures of the marshlands, rivers, and sloughs of the lower
Mississippi Valley, the confusion might remain even after
a longer look. The gar's head was flat, stretched out long
and rounded like an alligator's snout. Even its markings
were similar to the thick scales of the reptile, and its lower
fins greatly resembled four stubby legs. The fish, relatively
unchanged from its prehistoric ancestors who moved
through the same kind of wetlands, swam slowly by the
boat toward the river. The blonds' heads disappeared back
below the boat's side, and Paul looked up the channel
again.

A loud splash in the tall grass in front of the craft caused
Carolyn to jump.

Alan floated in front. Fred was off to the side, his large
form mashing a preserver deep into the water. San-hi
floated at their rear. Another intersecting channel lay ahead,
this one much wider than the ones they had passed before.

Alan pushed his arms out in front of him and pulled his
hands back through the water in a slow breaststroke. Fred
kicked his feet rhythmically. They entered the intersection.

San-hi moved backward off his preserver, and his head
went under. It immediately surfaced. He sputtered and spit
the brown water from his mouth.

Fred looked across his shoulder at the boy. Alan slipped
backward off his preserver and tried to touch the bottom
with his feet. He held his breath and, keeping his hands on
his preserver, slowly sunk underneath the water. His feet
still didn't touch. It was the first time since they had started
traversing the narrow channel that they couldn't stand with
their faces above the surface. He looked down the intersecting channel stretching wide back to their left and dis-

appearing around a bend in the direction of the river. Fred kicked his feet harder, and was using his hands again now. San-hi splashed even with him. Alan quickly followed, swimming with one arm extending out in a sidestroke, pulling his preserver along behind him.

It was a hundred yards before their feet could once again touch the bottom.

It was still a mile to the bridge.

CHAPTER 23

James L. Broderick III was famous in southern Florida law-enforcement circles. At fifty-five, with a sharply receding hairline and wearing baggy swim trunks and a too-short T-shirt that left a strip of skin exposed around his wide middle, he didn't cut that impressive a figure as he stood at the forty-one's rail, being soaked by showers of spray arching back from the bow every time the boat crashed through a wave. "Gets me used to the water," he said.

To Douglas, standing nearer the center of the deck on the lunging craft, it didn't make much sense. But Broderick should know. A former Navy Seal in Vietnam, and then a hard-hat salvage diver for several years before he suddenly went into law enforcement, few people could claim more hours under water. Then Broderick had suddenly started doing something else, attending night school until he earned a master's in forensic science. He could have a job anywhere, he had told Douglas. Several universities had courted him, and he might go into that someday. But for the moment he remained one of the most knowledgeable, highly educated police detectives that ever continued to serve in law enforcement.

Bite marks were his self-proclaimed specialty, and genuinely so—he had solved untold cases where such imprints had been left behind on victims' bodies, and written more than one paper on the subject. "But this is a first," he said, thinking aloud as much as addressing the remark to Douglas. "Across the bottom of the hull. How large did you say the slashes were again?"

"Large enough to stick your arm through," Douglas answered.

Broderick shook his head in awe, but his thoughts were that he had a highly imaginative, basically undereducated young navy officer on his hands. Yet the trip to examine the doctors' sunken speedboat would be well worth the time spent, Broderick thought. Proving somebody wrong was in many ways as exciting as proving something correct.

He nodded knowingly to himself—he had a habit of doing that when he was certain of something. Then he looked through the night at the lightning flashing in front of the forty-one. In its quivering illumination a black line of rain moved rapidly toward him.

He never left the deck through the ensuing torrential downpour and booming thunder. He had a flair for the dramatic.

The Vice Chief of Naval Operations was a short, heavyset man with graying, brown hair and a perpetual squint. Vandiver had done all of the talking so far, explaining about the discovery of the tooth by the Coast Guard and about the subsequent discovery of the trenches by a highly talented young officer he had sent to the area. Vandiver still didn't feel free enough to openly express his long-held theory, only what possibly had taken place. He did, however, lay the groundwork for what he was wanting to put into operation by reminding the Vice Chief that there had already been one other species of shark that, after remaining hidden at the bottom of the depths and having never been seen by man, had suddenly come up into the shallows—a huge shark now commonly known as the megamouth. In fact, the megamouth's emergence had, in one sense, surprised scientists more than they would have been if a hundred megalodons had suddenly emerged from the depths. For, unlike the megalodons that through their teeth had at least left evidence of their existence at one time in the oceans, there had been absolutely no prior knowledge of the megamouth having ever existed, with no fossilized evidence of any kind having ever been found, the giant shark spanning its hundreds of thousands, even millions of years in complete anonymity. Until 1976, when in November one had been snared off Hawaii. Now the species, for reasons still not even to be guessed at by scientists, had surfaced en masse, becoming widespread throughout the relatively shallow waters of the world.

"It could be coincidence," the Vice Chief said.

"Sir?"

"A depression in the vicinity where the tooth was found could be coincidence."

Vandiver nodded. "Yes, sir."

"Where is the tooth now, Admiral?"

Vandiver told him.

"And you say that you have an officer trying to confirm the possibility that this tooth is from a . . . living shark?"

"Evidence that might tend to confirm the possibility. Yes, sir."

"You'll let me know if any evidence points in that direction."

He sounded almost unconcerned, certainly not like a man who thought the world might be facing the reemergence of the most fearsome creature to ever swim the seas. Vandiver went to the next step in his plan, lifting a book he had retrieved from the bookcase off to the side of his office, and handing it across the desk.

"You might take this with you to glance through. You can make of it what you will, but I'm certain you'll find it interesting."

The Vice Chief looked at the cover photograph of a shark. The book was a nonfiction work by Theo Brown, a prominent Australian marine researcher and naturalist. Its title was *SHARKS, The Silent Savages,* published by Little, Brown & Company of Boston, and it could be found in any major library. In the work, Brown cited eyewitness reports ranging from a captain of a vessel who told him in 1963 that a shark at least as long as eighty-five feet had drifted beneath his boat when they were stopped and making repairs in the Central Pacific, to the well-known story first reported in 1918 by naturalist David G. Stead of a giant shark possibly over a hundred and fifteen feet long appearing off New South Wales. Dozens of fishermen who were said to have witnessed the creature and who refused to go back to sea for some days afterwards, though their livelihood depended on their fishing, swore to seeing this shark surface and swallow whole a long line of lobster pots nearly four feet in diameter and filled with catches. And these reports only mirrored similar tales that went back as far as the ancient Polynesians moving across the Pacific in their dugouts. This wasn't going to be the first time a megalodon had moved, Vandiver knew. But he also knew the fish might go back to the depths as quickly as it had risen, without leaving a scintilla more evidence—and he couldn't take the chance of going too far out on a limb. But if it didn't go back, he wanted to be ready for that, too. And now his plan:

"If the officer now at the site finds enough evidence to confirm the, uh, at least the possibility of such a shark still existing," he said, "then I think we should have a contingency plan."

"Such as?"

"There isn't a great deal we could do, sir—except maybe alert the fleet to the possibility."

"Alert the fleet?"

"Yes, sir. Put into action a detailed search. Unpublicized

of course. But at least not risk having one of our officers dismiss a sighting as being a whale.''

''A whale with a dorsal fin, Admiral?''

''Sir, it would take a very brave officer to report that he thought he saw a fifty-foot-long prehistoric shark without being aware of the possibility there was such a creature out there. Most career officers I know would blink, rub their eyes, go down and take a drink, and never mention it to anyone. Maybe it would be wise to discreetly reposition some of our submarines in, let's say, a thousand-mile circle around where the tooth was found. Do some sonar and laser soundings with surface vessels. A few other things I could think of.'' It was his dream—a concentrated, concerted search for such a creature. He was almost certain if that happened there would be results *now*.

The Vice Chief shook his head slightly. There still remained the relaxed air of his not being very interested in the meeting. In fact, he now looked at his watch and yawned. Coincidence was still much more likely.

As far as the Vice Chief was concerned.

San-hi dug his fingernails and toes into the rough face of the slanted, concrete piling. Above him vehicles roared across the bridge. His hands slipped, he grabbed at the concrete, and fell ten feet to splash into the water. He went completely under and had to tread water when he came up. It was several feet over their heads now. Fred looked at the life preserver he laid across. He slipped backward off of it, and sweeping one hand back and forth to stay afloat, raised the preserver with his other hand and tried to throw it straight up in the air. It went ten feet and fell back across his head.

Alan stroked toward the nearest water grass. He dug his toes into the silt sloping upward, sank to his ankle with one step and to his knee with his next, struggled to pull loose from the suction, and came up into the thick growth. His next steps went to his knees in mud again. Pulling one leg loose and twisting the other around, he squared with the top of the bridge, thirty to thirty-five feet above. He leaned backward, holding his preserver, heavy with water, almost down to the liquefied mud, then whipped it up into the air as hard as he could. It climbed to within a few feet of the bridge railing and then came back down to splash in the water under the wide structure. San-hi swam toward it.

Coming toward its other side in the dim moonlight was a nine- to ten-foot water snake ringed with brightly colored bands, slithering in a jagged line through the brown water.

San-hi saw the snake and broke off his stroke toward the preserver, abruptly swimming out to the side.

The snake made an equally abrupt turn toward the opposite side of the preserver, and submerged. San-hi waited a full minute before again beginning to stroke slowly toward the preserver.

Moments later, he kneed his way into the grass, pitching both the preserver he had retrieved and his to Alan.

Leaving one laying at his feet, Alan leaned back again and threw the other preserver as hard as he could. It climbed to where the last one had, seemed to hang momentarily in the soft, hot breeze blowing under the bridge, and spun backward to land in the grass a few feet behind him.

He threw the second preserver, and it reached the height of the first two. It took him nearly five minutes to travel the few feet to where they lay. San-hi came up into the grass. Fred stood on one foot sunk in the mud and his knee at the edge of the grass and pitched his preserver to the boy. San-hi caught it by its edge and started spinning it above his head like a lariat. The spins became wider and wider and faster and faster, San-hi's body leaning from side to side with each revolution, and he took one last great swing with his arm and sent the preserver sailing sideways up into the air. It climbed almost to the top of the bridge rail, hung there for a moment, then spun back down toward the channel.

San-hi lifted a stick from the grass. It was water-logged and heavy, about two inches in diameter and two and a half to three feet long. He stared toward the top of the bridge for a moment, then drew his long arm back, hesitated a second until he saw a vehicle's lights nearing them, and whipped the stick upward as hard as he could. It went straight into the air like a rocket, arched, seemed to hang a moment, and disappeared over the rail.

Fred and Alan cheered.

The pickup truck coming along the bridge caught the thick stick in its headlights as it flew over the rail and bounced across the pavement. The old black man driving the truck stared at the rail as he passed the place where the projectile had come from the darkness, but kept driving, staying ahead of the eighteen-wheeler roaring at his rear bumper.

San-hi looked for another stick. He saw one and stepped to it, but as he lifted it from the mud and water it crumbled in his hands.

"Alan." Fred's voice was almost a-whisper.

The shape came around a bend past the far side of the bridge. Dark, low in the water, it came silently toward them. Fred scrambled out of the channel. San-hi stepped rapidly to the rear. The mud sucked at his heels and he splashed backward onto his hips. He turned while still on the ground and scurried deeper into the grass on his hands and knees. Fred passed Alan.

Silently, into the dark shadows under the bridge, it came.

"It's a boat," Fred cried out.

The scream came toward them, short and abrupt.

Alan heard Fred fall backward into the water behind him. A light flashed on, blinding them.

"It's friggin' people," an amazed voice said. "What'n

hell?'' The light cut off. "You damn near scared me to death,'' the voice added. The boat glided out of the shadows beneath the bridge. "What'n hell are you all doing, anyway?''

As Alan's eyes adjusted rapidly back to the dark he saw that the man speaking was short and stocky and stood at the bow of the boat. In the stern, a thinner man lowered the shotgun he had pointed toward the grass.

San-hi splashed into the water and thrashed toward the boat. In a moment he was lunging up over its side. "Easy, boy,'' the stocky man said as the boat rocked violently, "you'll turn us over. What'n hell happened to your all's boat?''

"My daughter's back behind us,'' Fred said as he sloshed toward the boat.

The man flashed his light up the channel. "Near the river,'' Fred said. "We have to get back to her.''

Alan reached the bow. "Where's the landing where you came in?'' he asked.

"A mile back.''

"We have to get to a telephone.''

Sheriff Stark's graying brown hair whipped in the wind. Mosquitoes, gnats, and a constantly varying variety of water bugs burst against the boat's windshield.

Deputy Fairley suddenly pulled the throttle back and turned the bow of the boat toward the aluminum craft floating upside down at the side of the river.

As they drew alongside it, Stark saw the other small boat, floating a few feet behind the first one. They both had circular lines of indentations dug into their metal.

Stark shook his head. "How many kids did you say Mr. Herald had with him?''

"Do you mind if we go back in now, Sheriff?'' Fairley asked. "I . . . uh, my wife didn't like me coming out here.

With, uh . . . you know, with this thing. . . ." He smiled feebly. "You know how scared women get."

The younger blond slapped at a mosquito. A large flying insect, humming as loud as a horsefly, kept flitting around Edward's head, causing him to duck back and forth as if he were slipping punches. Out of the tall grass a hundred feet to the boat's side, a shrill shriek, turned ragged and dying at its end, caused Carolyn's blood to rush cold. She took a deep breath. It was silly, she knew, but what had scared her most since Alan and her father had pushed the boat into the grass was the short, thick water moccasin that had swum past in the channel behind the craft. One thing she liked about being a charter-boat captain was that you could be any place on saltwater and know it was unlikely you would ever see snakes. That was the one thing that had scared her ever since she was a little child and been lying back in the bathtub at her grandmother's house in Laurel and had looked up to see a snake draped across the top of the curtain rod. She shivered at remembering the incident.

A splash sounded behind the rear of the boat.

"Mrs. Haines," the older blond said, looking across his shoulder. "You hear that?"

She tried to force a comforting smile, and nodded.

Then she *did* hear it, a faint sound coming from the direction of the river. The blond stood and looked out over the side of the boat. The other boys were coming to their feet.

A motor.

The sound steadily grew louder, an outboard motor revved to full power.

Down the channel they saw the light sweeping past on the river.

"*Hey!*" Carolyn shouted as loud as she could. "*Here!*"

The boys started yelling at the top of their lungs. They were jumping up and down and waving their arms.

"Look this way, damn it," she said under her breath.

But what good would it do if they did? With her boat a hundred yards from the river, if it could be seen at all in the dark it would only look like a clump of grass sticking out in the narrow channel, or a drift hung on the bank. She was angry for a moment, feeling intentionally hurt by those speeding past and not coming her way. Then she thought about the shark in the river with the boat, its occupants completely unaware. And she was suddenly angry with them no more.

Douglas directed the watertight flood lamp's broad beam on the upturned hull of the doctors' boat as Broderick floated prone above it. They both wore helmetlike face-masks now, complete with microphones and earphones. Broderick lowered his head for a closer look, and ran his hand down through one of the long slashes.

A small brightly colored fish swam by Broderick's face-plate as he raised his head to look at an even bigger slash a couple of feet from his hand.

"Er," was all he said. It came out metallic sounding through his mouthpiece.

"Errr," again.

Then he began talking to himself: *"An incomplete semi-circular pattern of linear slashes with irregularities measuring up to zero point eight. . . . And I mean zero point eight feet, not centimeters. . . . Feet, that's right."* And he nodded his head knowingly to himself. It had to be to himself because he wasn't looking at Douglas.

"Suggestive of angled tooth imprints from maxillary ridge . . . ," he started again, and nodded knowingly once more.

"Suggestive, hell," he suddenly said.

And without ever looking at Douglas, Broderick turned and swam up out of the light, kicking his flippers rapidly.

* * *

Sheriff Stark stared at the small dock behind Carolyn's house. A black Labrador stood in the yard a few feet short of the water.

"They haven't come back, either," he said.

Deputy Fairley swallowed to clear his dry throat. "Sheriff, my wife is really going to be worried."

He smiled feebly as Stark looked at him. "Okay," Stark said, "go ahead, get out." He jabbed his index finger toward the dock. "Go on," he said.

"No, that's okay, Sheriff, we'll be going in now and—"

"Go on," Stark repeated. "I have enough on my mind without worrying about you."

Fairley appeared reluctant from the look on his face, but he nevertheless hopped over the side of the boat onto the rough cypress boards of the dock. He smiled feebly again at Stark. "I'm, uh . . . going to get her straightened out," he said. "This won't happen again."

The Labrador barked.

Fairley looked over his shoulder at the dog, but the animal wasn't looking at him. Instead she was staring out at the water past Stark and the boat.

Stark turned the wheel away from the dock and pushed the throttle forward.

The Labrador's now frenetic barking was lost in the sound of the boat speeding upriver in the direction of the beaver dam.

The two men hopped out of their boat onto the bank and ran after Alan, sprinting barefooted toward their pickup. He swung into the passenger seat as the stocky man slid behind the steering wheel. San-hi, Fred, and the other man jumped into the truck bed. Its wheels throwing mud out behind it, the truck spun away from the water and up a narrow gravel road.

*　　*　　*

Nearly thirty minutes had passed since they had last heard the sound of the motorboat, but now it was coming back down the river. "Mrs. Haines," the older blond said in a low voice.

Moments later the craft's light came into view.

"Mrs. Haines," the older blond said again.

The light was turning in their direction.

The boys started jumping up and down and cheering.

The boat came rapidly toward them, then Sheriff Stark cut the throttle back and the boat coasted slowly in their direction.

"I'm there," he said over his radio. Now he counted the children standing looking back at him. "Tell Alan and Mr. Herald they're all okay. I'm . . ."

Then he had to stop speaking to keep from crying.

CHAPTER 24

Carolyn felt a chill sweep across her back as Sheriff Stark's boat sped out of the narrow channel running through the marsh grass and turned up the river. Paul pushed closer to her side. She tightened her arm around his shoulder and felt herself subconsciously leaning away from the side of the craft.

Its big motor revved to full speed, they raced up the channel toward her house.

The deputy's cruiser, its blue lights flashing, braked to a stop in Carolyn's drive. Alan sprang out of the car and hurried ahead of Fred and San-hi toward the side of the house.

Deputy Fairley had come out of the wicker chair on the patio at the sound of the Sheriff's boat roaring up the river. A cruiser had braked to a stop in front of the house. Now an ambulance, the glow from its flashing red lights reflecting through the trees along the river, sped up the street, and Alan and the others hurried into the backyard.

Stark didn't pull back on the speedboat's throttle until he was within thirty feet of the dock. The craft settled into the water at the last moment and, its bow pushing a rolling wave of water out in front of it, scraped hard against the side of the dock.

Fairley saw the children and smiled in relief. And then the boys were scrambling over the boat's side onto the bobbing cypress.

Alan and San-hi reached for Armon at the same time, but the stocky boy hopped from the boat and, holding his burned arm against his chest, hurried past them onto the grass. Fred took Paul from Carolyn's arms and she came out of the boat behind them. Stark turned toward Alan.

"I said only bull sharks come up into freshwater, Alan, and you agreed with me. White sharks don't."

"That's right," Alan said. "They don't." He walked to Armon and San-hi, looked at the fluid-soaked T-shirt wrapped around Armon's burned hand and forearm, and slipped his arm around the boy's shoulders. "Come on," he said, nodding toward the two ambulance attendants coming down across the yard toward the water.

Two more deputy's cruisers were stopping in front of the house now. Fairley looked at Stark, and the Sheriff frowned, and Fairley dropped his gaze to the ground.

Stark hurried past Fairley to catch up to Alan and walked by his side. "Alan, what do you mean, 'That's right?' Carolyn said it was a white. What else could it be but a white and be twenty-five feet long?"

"There might be a precedent."

"Precedent, hell, what do you mean?"

The attendants took charge of Armon, leading him toward the corner of the house. Alan looked at the deputies and Fred walking with the other boys in that direction. The younger blond suddenly started crying. Paul, walking across the patio toward the kitchen door, looked at the boy and back at Alan, then stepped inside the house ahead of Carolyn.

"Alan," Stark said, "will you answer my damn question—what precedent?"

Alan looked toward Stark as they walked toward the house. "I don't remember the exact date, Jonas. It was around 1916 or '17. A white took two victims off the coast of New Jersey, but it also traveled twenty miles up a creek. Around South Amboy. It killed a ten-year-old and a young man and mangled a third boy before it went back into the ocean. Everyone then was wondering about a white coming up into freshwater, too. But it was July, the same as now. It had been especially dry. The creek would have been low. From rainfall records back then, scientists now think it's likely the ocean had run inland, leaving the creek highly brackish, maybe even containing more saltwater than fresh."

Stark looked toward the river as he stopped on the patio. "Okay," he said. "It's brackish up into the marshes, as far as the Interstate bridge at least. But not more saltwater than fresh. And not brackish past here to the dam, anyway. But I believe it got those two fishermen. It damn sure got their boat. After it ran out of brackish water, could it have just kept going upriver? I mean it's not like freshwater's poisonous or something to it—it just doesn't prefer it, does it? Right?"

"That's all I can tell you, Jonas. Other than for that one incident I don't know of any other time a white has come up a river, brackish or otherwise." Alan opened the door and stepped into the kitchen, and Stark came in behind him.

"Could there be two of them, Alan? Because if there isn't, you not only have a white coming up the river, but leaving the river to attack Mr. Fraizer in the Sound and then coming back here again."

Before Alan could respond, Stark said, "But it couldn't be two, because if it was it would not only be *just* two, but two *big* ones. But, hell, there can't be two that size. Both of them here at the same time. It has to be just the one. Right?''

"You want another guess?'' Alan asked.

"There couldn't be,'' Stark repeated. "Not two here at the same time when there hasn't even been one in years. Damn sure not two of them twenty-five feet long. It's just that the son of a bitch is roaming.''

Stark looked back toward the kitchen door, as if he could see through it to the river. "And now we have the problem of finding it in this crap you can't see through. If it was outside the Barrier Islands. . . . Hell, about anywhere else anywhere along the Gulf Coast its size would play against it. We could spot it with a plane. Hell, from a boat that got within a hundred feet of it as big a shadow as it would leave. But even if it goes back out of the river again, the Sound is so damn silted, too, that you can't see a couple of feet through it. . . . Hell, it could be four or five feet under the surface and we wouldn't be able to see it.''

As Stark quit talking he looked up at the kitchen cabinets. "You think she'd mind?'' he asked in a calmer voice than he had been using.

Alan shook his head and Stark opened a cabinet and then a second one, finding the glasses he was looking for and lifting one from the shelf.

"Twenty-five feet,'' he mused as he stepped to the sink. He filled the glass with water, drank half of it at one time, then looked back at Alan.

"Twenty-five feet?'' he said again.

Though the size *was* unusual when compared to the normal size of whites seen off the coasts of North America, one that size wasn't out of the question, Alan knew. The biggest white ever caught off North America was thirty feet long, caught off California in the late 1800's. And, more recently, in Cuba, not that far away from the Gulf in particular, a twenty-one-foot specimen had not only been caught but photographed and weighed as well, topping out at over three and a half tons.

What did make Alan wonder, though, was the white's rolling in the shallow channel, obviously trying to push away the small section of grass to get to Fred and the kids. The only similarity he could think of were the killer whales that had been seen using the weight of their great bodies to come up up on the edges of sections of floating ice and tip them to slide their helpless prey into the water. But a shark?

"I need to call the Coast Guard," Stark said, and walked toward the living room. "All they'll do, though, is warn boaters. If it's going to be caught, it'll be up to us. And when you stop and think about it, we're going to have to do it the same way they did in the Middle Ages, with a long line, a big hook, and a chunk of meat. That's modern technology for you, isn't it? And what if the son of a bitch decides he doesn't want to bite?"

Alan walked to the front of the living room and looked out a window as the ambulance drove out of the driveway. A deputy's cruiser, the children filling its seats, pulled out onto the street behind the ambulance. Fairley walked toward the house and Alan opened the door for him.

"Mr. Herald said to tell his daughter he was going in the ambulance with the boy who was burned," Fairley said.

Alan nodded. Fairley looked toward the Sheriff, speaking on the telephone to the Coast Guard. Stark looked back at him then turned his face back into the receiver.

Fairley turned back toward the last cruiser parked in the drive. Alan shut the door as Carolyn came out of the hallway. "Paul went to sleep almost as soon as his head hit the pillow," she said.

Stark replaced the telephone receiver and walked toward them. "If we're going to have a chance to catch it, we're going to need all the boats we can get," he said.

Carolyn nodded. "I'll have the *Intuitive* here in the morning."

"I'll get something for bait tonight," Stark said. "Somewhere." He glanced at his watch and walked toward the door. When he opened it, he looked back at Carolyn. "The earlier the better."

She nodded.

"I'll get ahold of the other captains tonight, too," he said. He stood there a moment longer, seemed to be thinking about something. He looked back at them. "Hell, I hated *Jaws* anyway," he said, and stepped outside.

Alan walked to the window and watched Stark walk toward the cruiser with Fairley standing by the driver's door. As they backed out of the driveway, the cruiser's lights shined on the Jeep, illuminating the gaily wrapped presents sitting on the rear seat.

"I'm going to get her a present, too," Carolyn said as she stepped up beside him. "If she hadn't started calling around about you and let Stark know we hadn't come back from the dam yet, I would have been out there for another hour before you could have found a boat and gotten back to us. I don't think I could have taken five more minutes."

She glanced at her watch. "I'm going to call Mother and have her come stay with Paul. I might as well go after the *Intuitive* now. By the time I would get to sleep it would be time to get up and go after it, anyway. Alan . . ." She looked a little sheepish. "I know this is silly, but would you mind going with me? Bringing it back by myself is going to make me . . ." She shrugged.

He smiled and nodded.

She looked directly into his eyes now. "I couldn't move when Paul fell out of the boat," she said. "Thank you for what you did." A tear welled in the corner of her eye. As it started down her cheek, he kissed her softly on the forehead.

She leaned her face against his chest. He moved his arms

around her back and cupped the back of her head with his hand. Her tears started coming freely now, and she shook her head. "It's crazy to cry now that it's all over," she said, "with it all over."

CHAPTER 25

Dawn broke over a thin layer of mist suspended above the marshes and a half-dozen charter fishing boats moving slowly along the river. Each of them pulled lines running to a chain leader and big hooks baited with large pieces of meat. Floats the size of small buoys, hooked to the lines near their ends, kept the bait at the proper depth. Two smaller boats moved along the shallow passageways winding through the tall grasses, using their depth sounders to see if there might be a channel deep enough for a twenty-five-foot white shark to use. One of the boats coasted to a stop and started backing out of a channel too shallow to navigate any farther. Carolyn steered the *Intuitive* from its canopy-covered flying bridge. Fred stood in the fishing cockpit as he stared out past the line trailing the boat. Alan and the Sheriff rested their hands on the bow rail, just past the small, black, hard-rubber Zodiac inflatable boat secured to the forward deck.

"Look at those crazy bastards," Stark said, staring at a small ski boat coming slowly up the river. One of the two men in the craft's front seats waved at a captain of one of the charter boats passing it in the opposite direction. The captain stared back without returning the greeting.

"Carolyn," Stark called toward the flying bridge. "Can you cut them off?"

She turned the wheel in their direction.

The stocky man in T-shirt and swim trunks pulled the throttle of the ski boat back when he couldn't determine on which side the charter boat was going to pass him. The *Intuitive* coasted to a stop across the small boat's bow.

The skinny man in a windbreaker and trunks in the passenger seat smiled when he saw who guided the *Intuitive*. "Morning," he called, still looking at Carolyn.

"You all planning on skiing?" Stark asked.

The men laughed at the joke. They both had a beer in their hands. The skinny one reached behind him over the seat and lifted a stick of dynamite into the air.

"Planning on making shark soup," he said and laughed.

"Where did you get that?" Stark asked. He wasn't in his uniform, wearing only khakis and T-shirt and a pair of deck shoes.

"There's places," the man said. "You want a few sticks? Do a helluva lot better job than that line you're towing."

"No, I think I'll just confiscate it all."

The man still grinned, but it was artificial now. "Come again?" he said.

"I said I'll just take it all."

The grin was completely gone now. "That's what I thought you said." The man looked at his heavily built partner.

He was dark-skinned with wide shoulders, thick arms, and an old-fashioned flattop. He slid up from under the wheel to sit on top of his seat. Carolyn put the *Intuitive*'s gears into reverse and touched the throttles lightly, stopping the craft's drift toward the bank. The heavily built man watched her until she cut the throttles again, and then he looked back at Stark.

Stark's badge glinted from his billfold, held open out

over the rail. "You're in violation of Mississippi Code Section Ninety-seven dash Thirty-seven dash Twenty-three—unlawful possession of explosives meant to be used in the commission of a crime."

"Crime? We're going to blow up a damn shark."

"Exactly—using explosives to kill fish. In addition to the Mississippi code, a violation of numerous federal statutes, not to mention pissing off the Wildlife and Fisheries Department."

"Aw, Deputy, come—"

"Sheriff," Stark said.

"Okay, Sheriff, we're just trying to help out. You know that thing ate a couple of kids."

"I appreciate your thoughts, and that's why I'm not going to arrest you right now. Unless I see you out on the water again."

The men looked at each other. The skinny one grinned. "You mean you think he might come up and snatch us outta here? I heard he smashed one of those little ole aluminum jon boats. That for real?"

"That's just exactly what happened. But I'm not thinking about it coming up in a boat the size of yours. I'm thinking I have a couple of boys getting drunk and whipping in and out of the charter boats. You'll end up fouling one of their lines. Or be throwing those sticks around at something you think you see."

"We wouldn't be throwing them around at nothing but the shark," the stocky man said. "And I wasn't whipping in and out of nothing, Sheriff. Didn't I come up the side of the river careful-like?"

"You're not all the way drunk yet," Stark said, looking at the two cases of beer sitting in the rear of the boat.

"No, and we ain't gonna be either with that little bit. What do you say that—"

"Hey," Stark said in a suddenly sharp tone, cutting the stocky man off. "Enough talking. Bring the dynamite around to the stern and then get on back to where you came from. Watch you don't foul the line."

A couple of minutes later, Fred looked at the cardboard box of dynamite lying near his feet. The box had a waxy-looking film impregnated into its surface. Written across its top in big, black letters were the words RED DIAMOND BRAND, DITCHING DYNAMITE, 50% STRENGTH.

"It's not dangerous," Stark said.

Fred looked at him with an uncertain expression.

"It's not," Stark repeated, "as long as you keep these away from it." He handed Fred the small box of percussion caps and the length of orange-colored coiled fuse he had taken from the men. Then he looked at their ski boat speeding back down the river in the direction it had come. "You have some dumb asses in the world—but most of them mean well."

"Your men are back," Carolyn called from the flying bridge.

Deputy Fairley and an older, gray-haired deputy in a wide-beamed steel-hulled workboat of the kind that serviced the offshore oilrigs motored past the skiboat and came toward them. The rear of the boat was stacked with a half-dozen forty-gallon drums. In a few moments the craft slowed and pulled alongside the *Intuitive*.

"You know how much a slaughterhouse stinks, Sheriff?" the older deputy said.

Stark smiled. "Get it dumped out down the center of the channel."

The deputy nodded. Fairley looked up over the rail at Stark. "Sheriff, about last night. It wasn't really my wife doing the worrying. I was thinking about my children and something happening to me where—"

Stark held up his hand, stopping the deputy's words. "If it were me, Jim, and I was the deputy and you were the Sheriff, I'd probably would have figured the same way you did."

"No, you wouldn't have, Sheriff, but I appreciate your saying so anyway. You won't have a problem again."

Stark raised his face at the sound of the helicopter sweeping up the river toward them. It flew so low he could see the face of the brunette from WLOX through its Plexiglas front.

The Sound bristled with charter boats, too. Anyone driving along Highway 90 between Bay St. Louis and Pascagoula and looking out over the beach would think it was one of those times when speckled trout or redfish swarmed the Sound, except for the fact that all of the boats were empty of paying passengers and were pulling thick single or double lines behind their sterns, instead of having fishing lines running from the ends of rods and reels.

The Gulfport Coast Guard Station also had their boats out. One of their forty-ones came slowly around the western tip of Ship Island. As Fort Massachusetts moved back to the boat's left, Bos'n Mate Third Class Beverly Cowart looked past the blocky structure to a small sailboat, its canvas down and two little children in orange life preservers splashing in the shallow water between the craft and the island. They weren't over a couple of hundred meters from where the foot had been found. Though the ferry from Biloxi was tied against the narrow, wooden dock extending out from the island and tourists walked in and out of Fort Massachusetts, the glistening white sands on the Gulf side of the island had been completely devoid of swimmers, only one couple, fully dressed, sitting in deck chairs under the shade of an umbrella and reading. But there was always somebody who didn't get the word. Maybe transients on their way between anchorages who hadn't heard any of the warnings broadcast by the radio and TV stations up and down the Coast. Cowart raised the forty-one's loud hailer microphone to her lips.

"*Attention, sailboat dead ahead. There was a shark at-*

*tack in the immediate vicinity night before last, and there
is reason to believe the shark is still in the area.''*

The bronzed young man and the blond-haired woman, in
bathing suits and lying on a blanket at the bow of the craft,
looked her way. The man raised up on his elbow and waved
with his other hand and nodded, then lay back against the
blanket.

Beverly stared in disbelief.

The man turned his face towards the blond and said
something, making a shrugging motion in the air with his
arm, obviously discounting the danger. The blond glanced
toward the children and then nestled her head against the
man's shoulder.

Beverly stared in sudden anger now, mixed with disgust.
She jerked the mike back to her mouth.

*''Mister and Miss whoever in the hell you are, if you're
not going to remove your children from danger, I suggest
you at least get in the water with them and give them a
fifty-fifty chance that the shark might rip your heads off
instead of theirs.''*

The two Coast Guardsmen on the bow stared back at
Beverly. Several tourists coming down the walkway from
Fort Massachusetts were now talking rapidly with each
other and pointing in the forty-one's direction. An old man
at the end of the ferry landing nodded his head and stared
at the sailboat.

The couple got the children out of the water.

''Broderick said the pressure was consistent with teeth
marks,'' Douglas said. He sat in a chair across the desk
from his uncle. Now he held up his hand with his fingers
spread and cupped like a claw. ''He said when a bite closes
it's like your fingers come down and your thumb comes
up—the pressure is exerted toward the center of the bite.
But after he calmed down, he started backing off some. He
said there were so many slashes on the hull that the semi-

circular patterns he thought he saw could have been formed by chance. He's not going to go out on a limb for you, sir.''

"I didn't expect him to. I knew we were basically on our own, that somehow we were almost going to have to be able to point the megalodon out before we could get anybody to believe. And, you know what, I think we have a shot at it."

Douglas' eyebrows knitted questioningly.

"Okay, Douglas, what's the one thing we can say we know for certain? It's that the doctors called their wives one night, then didn't reach their destination the next night. From that approximate spot to where the boat is off the Everglades is about seventy miles."

"Yes, sir, it had to be carrying the boat with it, playing with it like it was a toy."

"Seventy miles," Vandiver repeated. "On a north, northwest course. If instead of seventy miles we had a track of a few hundred miles in one direction we could get some general idea where we might look to try to find it. That's why where it came from is important. The longer the distance it has come in one general direction, the more likely it is we'd know which way it's headed. Isn't that right?"

Douglas nodded.

"So I kept thinking about that—where would it have come from, why would it have left there in the first place? Something had to cause that. Are you familiar with subduction zones?"

"No, sir."

"Picture the world as a soccer ball with its outside layered with plates."

"Yes, sir, I know that."

"Okay, there are places where matter is coming up out of the mantle to form new plates, and other places where matter on the surface is going into the mantle. Now, for instance, it's coming up in the middle of the Atlantic

Ocean. It's called the mid-Atlantic Ridge. And it's called ocean floor spreading. So the floor of the Atlantic gets wider and wider, spreading both east and west. So if it's getting wider someplace, it has to get narrower someplace else. Well, that's a subduction zone. That's where a plate has collided with and is going under another plate, the crust going down into the mantle. The Marianas Trench, for example, is a subduction zone, where the ocean floor is depressed by the plate collision. The collision can cause earthquakes. So I was wondering if some of our seismic studies might give me an idea where there might have been some catastrophic activity that might have spooked a megalodon in the last few months. A longshot. But I realized a long time ago that if you start your mind working on something, sometimes it sparks a thought from out of nowhere. It did. I thought of another quite different kind of disturbance in the South Pacific—the French tests—and suddenly I remember one of my people talking about it scaring the hell out of a whale. You *are* familiar with the French tests?''

''Yes, sir. Generally.''

''They originally scheduled eight, but there was such hell raised around the world about the resumption of nuclear testing that they finally announced they were cutting the tests back to six. They detonated the last one this past January twenty-seventh. What they didn't announce was that to make up for cutting the overall number of tests back, they jumped that one up to a hundred twenty kilotons in order to learn as much as they could. This was four times the power of their fifth test only the month prior. The end result was that they fractured the atoll where they conducted the test. That could be our big problem eventually. If the atoll continues to deteriorate, as some scientists forecast it will, and it eventually fractures into the sea, you could possibly have radioactive contamination of the entire fish stocks in the Pacific. Plutonium 239 can remain radioactive for nearly a quarter of a million years. Can you even comprehend that? The starvation around the Pacific Rim would be unbelievable—and essentially forever.

"But that's for worrying about later. For our purposes now, the important thing is that the test not only fractured the atoll, but generally knocked the hell out of the floor of the Pacific surrounding the atoll. We recorded fractures in the sea floor as much as twenty thousand feet deep and several miles in length. And then one of my people talking about the whale. I went to the files and ... Do you have security clearance for ... Never mind. We had submarines there. Most of the world did. We might have bitched about the tests, but we would have been foolish not to take advantage of them to learn as much as we could."

He lifted a tape recorder from his desk and depressed the play button. "Listen."

There was a faint roaring noise, punctuated by what could best be described as dull thumps.

"This is a muted tape," Vandiver said. "It would blow out your eardrums if it wasn't. Did you hear that quick, shrill sound?"

Douglas shook his head no.

"It doesn't matter. Nobody else did either at first. You'll hear it again in a minute. What you're getting ready to hear is the voice communication in one of our subs."

"Still sounds like the world's ending."

Vandiver said, "That's the sonarman on station."

Several seconds of silence passed.

"What in ..."

"Sonarman again," Vandiver said.

"Like a ... like a screech, Captain. Bearing two-five-zero. A few miles from the atoll, in front of the range of peaks there. Moving, sir. But I can't pick up a screw, reactor plant, engine noises. . . . Yet something barely perceptible—high-pitched."

"A whale?"

"That's the duty officer next to him," Vandiver said. "I think he's pissed off the sonarman by insinuating that he wouldn't recognize a whale. The sonarman doesn't answer the question."

There were a few more seconds of silence. Except Douglas could hear a faint breathing sound in the background.

"Russian, British, Israeli, no telling who else. Take us all together, we probably look like a school of sharks lying around the test site. Go to active sonar. Give her a ping. Let her know we saw her first."

"The captain speaking to the sonarman," Vandiver said.

A few more seconds of silence.

"Permission for continuous pinging, sir." There was a different tone to the sonarman's voice.

"Permission granted."

The surges could be heard, one right after the other:

Ping. Ping. Ping.

"Target's running at . . . I lost her, Captain. She went behind the peaks. Slipped through a gap at full bore. I mean real speed . . . top end speed of an Alfa at full power. And, sir . . . still no sound of a drive."

"A whale?" It was the young duty officer's voice again.

"Not with the damn echo we got back . . . , sir."

"Listen, now," Vandiver said. "It's computer-enhanced."

A moment later there came a high-pitched squeal—a sound almost like a baby's shrill scream of pain.

CHAPTER 26

Douglas felt the chill still tingling across his shoulders as his uncle laid the tape player back on his desk. "This one recording wouldn't be very definitive in and of itself, Douglas. There are people in this section who think it *was* a whale—that the shock waves reverberating through the water from the test distorted what was fed back to the submarine—even the reading of the speed. But I've been running my computer through every search I could think of. And I think I found where it happened again—sort of—a month later off the tip of South America. One of our submarines picked up the same real-time swimming motions, the same rapid cutting motions when the target turned in the water and disappeared in the distance. You're not entitled to know how, but I can tell you the reflection wasn't off steel, titanium, anything like that. And the reflection was the perfect size as far as I'm concerned. But there's a caveat again as far as my people are concerned. I see it as an angled reflection off something fifty feet long or longer. They see it as a broadside shot of something around thirty feet—and are certain it's a small whale. And I have to admit I have people a lot more attuned to the reflections than I am. But I can't help it—I come up with what I come up with."

Vandiver leaned back in his chair. "So if I'm not just wanting to believe so badly as to be seeing ghosts, we have a shot of a megalodon off the atoll, another shot off the tip of South America, and, we know for certain, a stop off in the Everglades. It looks for all the world like it's been headed here from the beginning, and that it's gone on into the Gulf now. If I had my say, I'd start an all-out search for it there right this moment. But I don't have my say, and I'm not going to unless I can come up with something more than sonar and laser reflections no one can agree on. Short of it popping up in clear view of some freighter or fishing trawler, we're going to have to come up with something else before I can go to the head of the Joint Chiefs and say, 'It's real.' "

Vandiver slipped a cigar from inside his tunic, began speaking again as he stripped it of its cellophane wrapper: "I think there's at least a chance we *can* find that something else. I have to believe that the megalodon has been kingpin no matter what else is in the depths. It gets hungry, it eats. And I think that other big fish and people would appear to him to be more the size of lunch than a school of redfish. That's what I think happened to the doctors. And I don't see it stopping with them. What I want you to do is start making some calls. The computer can only spit out what it's been fed. We know about the doctors' boat, but we don't log every Tom, Dick, and Harry who's drowned or every boat that's disappeared under mysterious circumstances in the Gulf. Sheriff's departments along the Coast would. I want you to check on that."

"Along the Coast?" Douglas asked in a tentative tone. "Sir, do you have any idea how many counties are along the Gulf Coast? You're speaking of Florida through Texas."

Vandiver nodded as he slipped the cigar in his mouth. "Florida, Alabama, Mississippi, Louisiana, and Texas. No

telling how many counties, and that's before you cross over
to the Spanish-speaking sheriffs.''

Deputy Fairley dipped a bucket into one of the rusty forty-
gallon drums and lifted it out. He hefted the bucket to the
rail of the workboat and dumped the thick blood and con-
gealed matter into the water. Behind the wide craft, alter-
nating dark stains of the beef parts and blood spread in a
V-shaped trail.

"What we are really doing," he said, "is probably at-
tracting what bull sharks that *aren't* here for sure now."

"Naw," the older deputy said as he dumped a bucket
over the stern of the craft. "River current will wash it out."

"Yeah, guess so, down to the Sound where they can all
eat up somebody there."

"Anybody dumb enough to be in the water right now
needs to be eaten up. Save us having to mess with them
later when they do something else crazy—like those nuts
with the dynamite."

"No," Fairley said. "Nuts that crazy don't get eat up or
blowed up."

"That's what I'm telling you, Fairley, be better if—"
The deputy suddenly ducked his head. There had been the
sound of a shot. He looked over his shoulder toward the
bank. "What are those crazy bastards doing?"

Standing in the trees near the edge of the water, a tall
man in a jumpsuit raised his rifle back to his shoulder,
sighted down its barrel for a moment, then lowered the
weapon. The shorter man next to him laughed wildly,
slapped the thighs of his overalls and raised his hands high
in the air, laughing again.

Carolyn turned the *Intuitive*'s wheel in the men's direction as Stark and Alan walked to the bow rail.

"Hey!" Stark shouted.

The shorter man looked toward the *Intuitive*, but the one

with the rifle kept looking out toward the water. He raised his rifle again and stared down its sights.

"*Damn it, you hear me!*" Stark yelled.

The rifle slowly lowered. The *Intuitive* neared the bank.

"What in hell are you doing?" Stark asked.

"Thought I saw the shark," the man with the rifle said.

Alan looked toward the center of the river.

"Saw an alligator gar is what he saw," the short man said, and laughed.

The taller man stared at his companion.

Stark shook his head in irritation. "It occur to you we have people out here—and you're shooting a damn rifle off around them?"

"I know which way I'm shooting," the taller man said.

Stark's billfold came out again. He flashed the badge. "Get your ass somewhere else, okay?"

"Deputy, I was born and raised around guns."

"Yeah, buddy, and an experienced idiot is still an idiot."

"That so?" the man said, staring his displeasure at Stark's remark. "What's your name?"

"Jonas Stark."

"And that's a Sheriff's Department badge you're flashing around?"

"That's right, sure is."

"Maybe the Sheriff would be interested in how you're talking to voters in this county. What's the Sheriff's name?"

"Jonas Stark."

The shorter man turned silently and started toward the street beyond the trees. The taller man still stared. "Okay," he finally said, "I can remember that."

As the man turned and walked after his companion, Alan smiled. "That's two sets of voters in a couple of hours."

Stark said, "Son of a bitch didn't even know my name; he didn't vote for me."

At the sound of the motors, they looked toward the two

small helicopters sweeping toward them above the river. The one with the brunette from WLOX swept overhead. The other craft stopped, tilted slightly to its side, and a man leaned out the passenger-side opening and pointed a television camera down toward them.

Carolyn turned the *Intuitive*'s wheel, guiding the boat back into the middle of the channel. Fred glanced at the dynamite setting just inside the cabin, then looked at the line trailing taut down into the water behind the boat. Deputy Fairley threw the last bucketful of chum out into the water, and the older deputy spun the wheel, turning the workboat around and starting it back down the river.

The sun was beginning to set.

Empty wrappers from a pair of Big Macs sat on Douglas's desk along with a large plastic cup containing nothing but ice. He slipped the last french fry into his mouth as he cradled the telephone receiver on his shoulder.

"Sarasota County Sheriff's Department."

"I'm calling about any unexplained drownings or boat accidents you have had in the county since January."

"Do what?"

And Douglas started his spiel once more. "This is Ensign Douglas Williams, I'm calling from Washington, D.C., the Office of Naval Intelligence. We are seeking information on any unexplained drowning or disappearance of . . ."

Vandiver looked at the red light on his telephone, indicating that his nephew was making another call. Douglas was going through them at a rate of about one every five or six minutes. Vandiver hoped he wasn't passing over them too quickly. He looked back at the terminal screen. All that had been on it for the last ten minutes was the artist's rendition of a megalodon, the thick-bodied creature facing outward and looking as if it were about to swim off the screen. The depiction was meant to jar his mind, help him to think what else could be done to locate the creature. But nothing new had passed through his thoughts. He continued to stare. An artist's rendition, he thought. If technology had progressed only a little bit more, he knew he might be staring at a picture of the real thing. But it hadn't, at least not enough for even computer enhancement to show what didn't register on the videotape—you had to have at least something fuzzy and registering before it could be enhanced.

It had been the lack of light. And maybe, somehow, possibly the megalodon's intelligence.

It had happened only four years before—the image caught on the now famous videotape had initiated endless speculation among marine scientists the world over. The robot camera equipped with several-hundred-thousand-candlewatt flood lamps had been lowered thirteen thousand feet to a distant bottom in the South Pacific.

The experiment was conducted in the hopes that the lights would draw some of the strange bottom dwellers at that depth into view, allowing the camera to photograph them for future study. But even with the great candlewatt of the flood lamps, they illuminated only a few feet, before the water at that depth, blacker than the darkest night, absorbed all their power. A creature would have to come very close.

A few had. A three-foot-long yellow-brown gulper, with its mouth extending back nearly the full length of its body, which is how the fish derived its name, had come slowly into view. Tiny, flashing yellow-greenish lights in the sand off to the right of the field of view indicated small deep-water shrimp, directing their mating signals toward the light.

Suddenly the gulper had spurted to the side and disappeared. Out in front of the camera, at the very periphery of the light, a huge shadow against a blacker background moved slowly through the field of view. A full fifteen seconds passed before it seemed that the camera was again photographing only the black water. Then another almost imperceptible movement began and lasted for thirty more seconds.

Scientists had been able to calculate the speed the creatures swam by comparing their barely visible movement against the movement of the sediment drifting slowly across the sand floor. One of the creatures had been approximately twenty feet long. There had been a gap of about thirty to thirty-five feet between that creature and the one trailing it. And then the trailing one had been calculated to be nearer forty feet in length. The scientists, aware of the recently discovered giant deep-water megamouth shark, had decided that the camera must have picked up a pair of those large creatures moving in the dark.

Vandiver wasn't so certain. There was no way anyone could be certain that there had in fact been two different creatures. As far as he was concerned, a single creature passing near the camera's periphery, then drifting slightly farther away as it proceeded, then nearer again, could have easily been viewed as two separate creatures.

The twenty-foot length of the so-called first creature, plus the thirty- to thirty-five-foot gap while the creature drifted farther from the camera, and the forty-foot length of the so-called second creature, added up to ninety to ninety-five feet—if it had been one creature.

And one thing that made that even more possible in his mind had been that when each creature passed, its top-to-bottom thickness had completely filled the field of view. A megamouth even forty feet long couldn't have been as thick from top to bottom as the twenty-foot minimum that would have been needed to completely obliterate the field of view.

He had seen two scientific explanations regarding that.

Both of them basically had to do with a play of shadows.

"More than likely," one of the scientists had stated.

The other one had said, "Or something similar."
Learned opinions.

"Have a shark-attack fatality off Tampa, sir," Douglas shouted from the outer office. "Male, age twenty, wind-surfing, hemorrhaged to death after they got him to shore."

Vandiver ignored him. There wouldn't be anything to bring back to shore after a megalodon attack.

"Everybody is getting tired," Stark said as he stepped next to Alan and Carolyn illuminated in the *Intuitive*'s running lights as they stood at the flying bridge. "We don't know how long this is going to last. I'm going to ask half of the boats to go in and some of them to come back in eight hours, the rest eight hours after that." He looked at the Bertram passing them going in the opposite direction. "I called the county supervisors. I told them these captains all lost charters, that we needed to at least reimburse the boats' running expenses. But I'm not counting on that happening. I know you two have to be worn out. You want to go in first?"

Carolyn nodded. "I would like to take a shower and see Paul before he goes to bed. Then I'll come back. There's a bunk below. Daddy and Alan and I can take turns getting some rest."

Stark looked ahead of them upriver and then down the channel. "I haven't seen Fairley in an hour or two. If you will, call him on the radio and tell him to bring the boat by to pick me up."

Fairley arrived as they reached Carolyn's dock. The half-dozen drums in the workboat were filled again, the thick mixture of blood sloshing out of one with its top ajar as Fairley slowed the craft and came alongside the *Intuitive*. The stench was terrible. Fairley's and the older deputy's clothes were soaked red.

Stark shook his head as he climbed from the *Intuitive*

down into the workboat. "Your wife wouldn't have wanted you home last night if you smelled like this," he said.

Fairley frowned. "Now, Sheriff, I told you I was sorry about that."

Stark smiled as he slipped behind the boat's steering wheel. A moment later its engine coughed, began to putter, and the boat pulled away from the *Intuitive*.

Fred finished pulling in the long line with its big stain-less-steel hook baited with a several-pound section of meat cut from a beef quarter. He coiled the line and chain leader in the cockpit, set the buoy on top of the coil, and left the meat balanced on a rear corner of the cockpit.

A strip of skin hung down nearly to the water. The meat, softened by being in the warm river for hours, oozed red juices that seeped down the strip and fell drop by drop into the brown water.

CHAPTER 27

Carolyn's mother looked from the kitchen toward the back door as it opened. "I was just getting ready to call you," she said. On the counter behind her there were four plates covered in aluminum foil. A two-liter bottle of Coke and a thermos sat next to the plates. She looked at the door when Fred closed it behind him.

"The Sheriff's not with you?" she asked.

"We're going back out in a while," Carolyn said. "I'll take his plate then.".

"Your Aunt Rayanne came by and got her presents, Alan. She left you a change of clothes and a shaving kit."

Paul stepped into the kitchen.

"Hey, baby," Carolyn said.

"Did you get him?" he asked.

"Not yet."

"You will," he said and nodded.

"Darn sure right," Fred said. He looked at the plates.

"Be about fifteen more minutes," Martha said. "I put the cornbread in late."

"I can eat it without cornbread," Fred said.

"You can wait like everybody else," his wife said.

He frowned and walked toward the living room.

"News about the shark is on all the channels," she said.

*   *   *

Douglas shut his apartment door behind him, stripped off his uniform tunic, pitched it to the couch, and began to loosen his tie. He yawned as he walked into the kitchen. The tie went onto the counter next to the sink, piled with unwashed dishes and glasses. He opened the refrigerator, lifted out a Budweiser, and popped its top. He reached back into the refrigerator, got a second beer, and walked toward the living room.

He unbuttoned his collar, fluffed one of the couch pillows with one hand, and lay down, stretching his long frame out comfortably to try to relax. Leaning his head up to sip the Budweiser, he reached for the TV's remote control on the coffee table at the same time.

The Weather Channel came on. That was the last channel he had viewed before he boarded the helicopter on the first leg of the flight to south Florida. He frowned at remembering how nervous he had been when he had seen the display of the storm front moving across the map toward the waters off the Everglades.

He pushed the channel change button.

On NBC an attractive brunette reported from the Pascagoula River in Mississippi.

Carolyn stood in her brassière and bikini-cut panties in front of the mirror over the bathroom lavatory. She turned to the side and held her shoulders back. "Not too bad," she mumbled, and turned her other side to the mirror.

Seconds later she slipped into a pair of loose khakis and a short-sleeve orange blouse. Before she left the bathroom she dabbed perfume behind each ear and smiled into the mirror.

Martha slipped a thick glove on over her hand and reached into the oven to pull the pan of cornbread out. Her bare hand touched the pan as she laid it on the counter and she mumbled something under her breath.

Carolyn came up the hall.

Martha held her finger up to her lips and nodded toward Alan, lying asleep on the couch. "I told him to lay down and rest his eyes for a minute," she said in a low voice. "That's the last movement he made."

Carolyn smiled as she came into the kitchen. "Where are Paul and Daddy?"

"Out playing with the Frisbee. I ran them outside so they wouldn't wake him. I put the food on the patio so we wouldn't bother him. He can eat when he wakes up."

Carolyn nodded and her mother dumped the cornbread onto a platter and they walked quietly out the door.

"You smell good," her mother said, and smiled a little.

Vandiver covered his head with his pillow as his telephone rang.

It rang a second time.

He groaned, stuck his thick arm out to the bedside table, and pulled the telephone receiver under the pillow to his ear.

"Sir," Douglas said. "You watching television?"

Vandiver slid the pillow off his head and stared at the receiver. Then he moved it slowly back to his ear.

"No, Douglas, I'm not."

"Turn on NBC—they're talking about a big shark."

Paul stood up from the wicker table, pulling his plate with him.

"What do you want?" Carolyn asked. "I'll get it for you."

"I'll be quiet," he said, and walked to the door leading back into the house. He closed the screen door quietly behind him.

Alan lay on his side.

Paul stared at him for a moment, then opened one of the kitchen cabinets, pulled out a clean plate, and opened the drawer to the tableware.

Seconds later, the plate and a fork and knife in his hands, he walked quietly into the living room.

Still quiet, he sat down on the edge of the coffee table and stared for a moment at Alan, asleep a couple of feet away.

"Mr. Alan."

Paul waited a moment. "Mr. Alan," he said again, raising his voice only slightly.

Alan's eyes cracked open.

Paul held out the plate. "We're eating," he said. "I thought you might be hungry."

Alan swung his feet to the floor. "I am. Thank you."

"We're eating outside," Paul said, and looked where Alan's feet had lain up on the couch. "Mother doesn't like shoes on the couch, but I'm not going to tell her."

"Thank you," Alan said.

When Alan stepped out the back door onto the patio, Carolyn looked at Paul. "Did you wake him, honey?"

"No," Alan said. "I was getting hungry."

"Cornbread's pretty good," Fred said. "But not worth the wait."

Martha stared at him.

Paul slid an empty chair over beside his at the table.

Vandiver stared at the TV screen. *A white shark up a river?* Somebody must be smoking something, had been his first thought when he had heard the brunette reporter say that. But the man whose photograph had flashed on the screen was a marine biologist. Surely he would know a white shark when he saw one. And what other shark could be that big? That thought, of course, had made him stop and think. But the tooth found off the Everglades had to come from a megalodon that was a minimum of forty feet at the very least—not twenty-five. Was he missing something?

Alan stood a few feet back from the small wooden dock and looked at the pair of charter boats dimly illuminated in the glow of their running lights as they moved along the channel. One pulled a line downriver, the other craft, passing it, coming upriver. Carolyn came across the yard toward him.

"Paul said to tell you good night," she said as she stopped beside him. She looked toward the river. "We have so many boats we might have scared it off."

"I don't believe it scares very easily."

"Daddy called the hospital and spoke with Armon. A plastic surgeon in town from Dallas heard what Armon did and called the hospital and said that if Armon wants him to he'll remove the scar tissue for free. But Armon doesn't care about that. His main thing was he was worried that the burn on the back of his hand might keep him from boxing. But the doctors said it won't. He's going to have to wait until it heals properly. But then he can do anything he wants. Daddy told him there's no reason not to keep running laps while he waits." She smiled. "That and quit smoking. Would you like a glass of wine?"

"I think I would."

Carolyn walked toward the boat.

"Operator," Vandiver said. "I was given an Alan Freeman's number in Biloxi, Mississippi, and it doesn't answer. Would you check it again for me and see if it is the correct number? Thank you."

Alan held the small plastic cup in his hand as Carolyn poured a second cup half full and placed the wine bottle back into the cooler at the front of the fishing cockpit.

She touched her cup to his, sipped from it, then turned

toward the rail and leaned against it. For a moment she
looked at the section of beef, soft and sagging over the rail.
Then she raised her eyes out across the river to the marshland glimmering a sparkling blue in the bright moonlight.

"It's still beautiful to me."

Alan stepped beside her and moved his hand around her
shoulders. She leaned her face against his shoulder. He
could feel the warmth of her skin through his shirt. He
moved his hand to her hair. It was soft and carried the scent
of her perfume. Her eyes came up to his. He kissed her
forehead gently. She rubbed her face against his shoulder.
He kissed her cheek. She turned toward him and moved
her arms around his neck and brought her lips up to his.
Her lips were soft and slightly moist from the wine, and
warm. He pulled his face back and looked into hers, then
kissed her again, this time harder. She kissed him back and
then kissed his neck at his open collar. He set his cup on
the rail. "Alan," she said. He caught her chin and turned
her face up to his again. "Alan, okay?" She looked toward
the house.

He moved his hands to the sides of her face, kissed her
lightly, and nodded. She leaned back against the rail. Below
her, the water bubbled as a bilge pump discharged into the
river. She caught his cup and handed it to him and then
turned back toward the rail and leaned against it, looking
down at the water.

Paul heard someone coming up the hall, and he jumped
from the window back into his bed and pulled the covers
over him.

Martha pushed the cracked door open and looked at Paul
sleeping.

The scream was shrill and piercing.

Carolyn fought against Alan, pushing him back against the
cabin. She spun to face the rail. He moved past her.

"Alan, don't."

He moved his face carefully out above the rail and looked down at the water.

The dark reflection of a circular cloud, lighter at its wide middle from the moon shining through it, moved softly on the water. He looked back at Carolyn. She had her hands at the sides of her face. He shook his head. "It's a reflection."

Slowly, she stepped forward. She held her body back as she leaned her face forward. She stared down at the water for a moment, then started crying.

Fred dashed out the door of the house. Martha came behind him. Carolyn looked at them and closed her eyes. When Paul came from the house and ran toward the dock, Carolyn moved over the side of the *Intuitive* and walked to meet him.

Paul's face was pale.

She knelt on one knee and caught him in her arms.

"I'm sorry," she said. "It was just a reflection."

She looked up at her father and mother.

"I'm sorry. It was just a reflection."

Alan stared over the side of the *Intuitive* into the water. If it *had* been there, hiding, looking up at Carolyn, observing . . . It had consciously tried to wear down the grass and mud next to Fred and the others, he thought again. Something wasn't right. . . . And he thought for a moment longer, then looked at the section of beef and pushed it off the edge of the cockpit.

It splashed into the water and sunk from sight, leaving ripples spreading out across the river.

CHAPTER 28

Carolyn glanced at her watch, sipped from her coffee, and set the cup on the kitchen table. "We told the Sheriff we were coming back out—and I have to refuel, too."

"What?" Fred asked from the living room without taking his eyes off the TV.

"I said I'm going to have to refuel—you and Armon didn't remember to."

Her father walked toward them with his head turned back over his shoulder toward the TV. "You didn't have a charter scheduled when we were cleaning the boat. I thought I'd get to it later."

Carolyn nodded. "And I didn't think to look when I started her over here. I'd be a fine one to go to sea with."

Her father walked to the back door.

"Daddy, you don't have to go. Why don't you get some sleep here? When I get back I'll pick you up."

"Oh, I don't mind."

Martha spoke from the couch in the living room. "You need the sleep, Fred."

As Alan and Carolyn walked out into the back yard, Martha said in a lower voice: "Maybe they don't want you along, Fred."

He stared toward the door. "Tonight? You have to be kidding."

"I know Carolyn, Fred."

As Carolyn turned the ignition keys to the *Intuitive*'s big engines she looked back at Alan dropping the float off the stern and the line beginning to feed out into the water. She swung the *Intuitive* in a circle wide enough to make certain she cleared the line with more than enough space to spare. As Alan climbed up the ladderlike steps to the flying bridge she straightened the craft down the channel and looked back past the stern again, waited until the line jerked in behind them, and then she pulled back on the throttles until the float was riding gently in a steady pull behind them.

In a moment they were passing a Bertram, illuminated in the glow of its running lights and the bright moonlight and cruising in the opposite direction. Its captain nodded and raised his hand. Ahead of them the Pascagoula flowed directly to the Sound. But after the channel passed under the Highway 90 bridge the river's thousands of years of depositing silt where its mouth widened into the Sound had built shoal water too shallow for any but the smallest boats to navigate. The *Intuitive* had to cross over into Bayou Chemise and follow it into the East Pascagoula and then move down its channel past Ingalls Shipyard into the marked cut leading out toward the Gulf.

Minutes later Carolyn angled the boat out of the channel toward the Intracoastal Waterway and turned west toward Biloxi and the Broadwater Marina.

Ahead of them lay the dark, murky waters of the Sound, to its left the long, broken line of barrier islands, some of them not much more than small isles, and some of them miles long, and to its right, the Mississippi shoreline, some of it brightly lit commercial areas, some of it dotted with condominiums and marinas and yacht clubs, and some of it deserted, dark stretches of sand.

* * *

Nathan stood knee-deep in the Sound. Nettie hadn't left the sand that spread from the water up to the highway. "Nathan," she said, "I'm telling you, that's not real smart."

"Huh?" Nathan asked, cocking his ear in her direction and away from the stiff breeze blowing in off the Sound.

"I said that's not real smart."

"Yeah," he said, and nodded, obviously not hearing what his wife said. He shined the glow from his floundering lamp back down onto the water. He wore a blue windbreaker over his sweatshirt and dark swim trunks and high-top tennis shoes in case anybody had broken a bottle in the water. A flounder's narrow-set eyes glowed in the lamp's beam and he jabbed his gig down into its side.

"Got me a good'un," he called back over his shoulder as he lifted the flat, wiggling fish from the water.

"Huh?" Nettie called. Neither one of them could hear all that well. She had ended up buying a hearing aid shortly after they had retired. He said nothing was wrong with his hearing, if people would just talk plain. And few in Mississippi did to his way of thinking. He had moved there from Peoria, Illinois. He had met Nettie shortly afterwards. With her hailing from the bootheel of Missouri, she could understand most everybody pretty well. They had been married for two years.

"Look at that fool," Nathan said. His thin face was raised out over the Sound past the markers that delineated the channel passing behind Deer Island toward Biloxi Bay. Beyond the markers, a tall spray of water, glistening in the bright moonlight, sped across the surface. "What are those things called?"

Nettie understood him this time. "Wave runners—I think."

"Hadn't the fool heard about the shark?"

"That's what I was just saying about you, Nathan."

"Huh?"

"That's what I was just saying about you, Nathan. Out there in water up to your knees like you haven't got good sense."

"You think a shark is a terrestrial animal, Nettie? How in hell would he get to me here?"

"That's what I'm waiting to see," she said. "I heard insurance companies don't pay off on life policies for seven years if somebody just disappears."

"That's not true, Nettie."

"Well, I'm not taking any chances, anyway. I'm keeping my eyes on you so I can say I saw what happened."

Nathan jabbed his gig down again. "Got another one. Bet you'll want to eat them, too—despite the nagging."

"I'm watching."

"Huh?"

She didn't answer.

"I'll be damned!" he yelled.

"See the shark, Nathan?"

"No. Let the sucker flip off my hand back into the water." He watched the flounder swiftly moving out of sight a few feet away. After a moment all that was left to see was a small dark stain in the water from the blood seeping from the gig wound. In a moment the stain had vanished, dispersed into such small particles it was impossible to see as it continued to move on the receding tide toward the markers, the same direction in which the blood from the flounders Nathan carried in the net bag at his side had been traveling since he had gigged the first one over an hour before.

Beyond the markers, the tall shower of spray glistening in the air suddenly turned in the direction of the beach.

A moment later the shower began to lessen, then disappeared as the thick fin slid under the surface.

Nathan stepped into a hole up to his thighs in water.

"Uh-huh," Nettie said.

The next step he was back up to his knees again. He

looked behind him at the water, but it was too murky to
see what he had stepped off into.

"I'm watching," Nettie said.

"Will you be quiet, Nettie?"

"You can't hear me anyway."

"I did, didn't I?"

"Nathan . . ." There was a change in her tone. She stared
past him toward the near side of the markers.

The moon was brilliantly bright and Nathan had no trouble seeing the dark shape. But even in the bright illumination when he first saw what Nettie stared at he thought
it had to be a boat without running lights. Then it moved
its front to the side and lunged forward a few feet. The
dorsal fin stood out against the clear background of the sky.
The shark began to back into the water behind it. Slowly
it began to sink. In a moment, all that could be seen was
the tip of the thick fin.

And then it disappeared beneath the water.

A few hundred feet beyond the spot, the running lights
of the *Intuitive,* moving west in the direction of Gulfport,
combined with the moonlight to brightly illuminate Alan
steering from the canopy-covered flying bridge. Carolyn
rested her hands against the back of his shoulder. She
kissed his neck softly. He turned his face toward hers and
she nuzzled his cheek. The roar of the hundred-fifty-
horsepower Mercury on the ski boat coming toward them
was loud even over the sound of the *Intuitive*'s twin engines. "I believe Mr. Shark Soup and his friends are on a
new case of beer," Carolyn said.

A woman with her long red hair whipping in the wind
and her legs bare under her light jacket, leaned over the
stocky, dark-haired man at the wheel. Another skinny
woman with short blond hair and attired in a similar jacket
sat across the lap of the thinner, taller man in trunks and a
windbreaker in the craft's rear seats.

The stocky man pointed at the *Intuitive* and the redhead

waved. He said something to her and she dropped her hand. The man in the rear of the boat came to his feet. The stocky man spun the steering wheel and the craft cut toward the *Intuitive*'s bow. He raced across it barely twenty feet in front of them.

Carolyn frowned. Alan looked across his shoulder as the boat sped around the *Intuitive*'s side, bounced across its wake, and came up their other side.

The thinner man came to his feet, facing them. He opened his fingers and cupped his hands toward each other, fashioning a ball.

"Boom!" he yelled loud enough for them to hear and jerked his hands open and out to his sides.

The boat cut across their bow again. *"Boom!"* The hands flew apart. The women were laughing wildly.

"Boom! Boom!"

"Boom!" came back lower to the *Intuitive* now as the ski boat cut toward shore.

"Bo-om," came back, barely perceptible, broken up by the wind now. Alan could see the man still jerking his hands apart as the boat angled toward the marked channel leading behind Deer Island. The blond yanked the man down into the rear seat of the craft. His skinny legs kicked up into the air.

In the ski boat, the skinny legs kicked up once more as the woman chewed on the man's neck. He laughed and pushed her back and reached for the open case of beer in the bottom of the boat. "Howard?" he asked, holding one of the cans toward the front seats.

Howard reached his thick arm back and snatched the beer, let go of the steering wheel to pop it open, and lifted the can to his mouth.

The boat swerved. The redhead grabbed the wheel with one hand and held her other hand back over the seat.

"Peter," she said.

The man slapped a beer into her hand, then came to his feet. "Speaking of peter," he said, "I need some place to take a leak. You all want to shut your eyes?"

The redhead thought that was funny. The blond didn't.

"You better not," she said, grabbing him by his windbreaker and pulling him back into the seat.

Howard suddenly moved his face forward closer to the windshield. "Hey, Peter," he said. His tone was different. "You see what I see?"

Peter looked in the direction his friend stared, but didn't see anything. "What?"

"In the channel."

Peter still didn't see anything. And then he did. Nearly two hundred yards ahead, clearly visible in the mixture of moonlight and the glimmer of flashing lights from the line of tall, brightly illuminated casinos on shore, the thick tip of a dark fin sped between the channel markers leading toward Biloxi Bay.

"Son of a bitch," Peter said. He looked back across his shoulder at the *Intuitive*. "They got our damn dynamite."

"They ain't got this," Howard said, fumbling under his seat. He pulled out a heavy revolver with an eight-inch barrel and held it up in the air. "My madman stopper." He pressed the throttle of the hundred-fifty-horsepower Mercury all the way forward.

The boat jumped in the water and raced for the pass.

CHAPTER 29

Nathan stood at the pay telephone. Nettie stood beside him, looking back toward the Sound.

"Coast Guard," he repeated to the information operator, and then spelled it out, trying to sound as Southern as he could. "C-o-a-s-t g-u-a-r-d. Two words. Starts with a C."

The hundred-fifty-horsepower Mercury roared. Howard waved his "madman stopper" over his head. Peter stood with his hands on the back of the front seats. The ski boat bounced across the water into Biloxi Bay and past the wide, rounded concrete pier fronting the Marine Education Center to their left.

"Where in hell did it go?" Howard asked.

"I'd just as soon we didn't know," the redhead said and looked back at the blond. She nodded.

"There!" Peter yelled. He pointed ahead of them to the Highway 90 bridge running across the bay to Ocean Springs. Near the center of the bridge, the thick fin, barely perceptible in the bright moonlight, moved slowly along the base of the pilings coming down from the high, arched section over the boat channel.

Howard jammed the throttle forward and Peter had to grab the back of the seats to keep from falling.

They quickly closed the distance. The fin kept moving slowly, angling in and out of the pilings. Part of the nose surfaced. Howard raised the long barrel of the revolver over the windshield as the nose moved back under the water.

"Wait'll we get closer," Peter said. "You want to hit him good."

"Wherever a slug from this hits him, it'll be good," Howard said.

The fin sank beneath the water.

"Son of a bitch!" Howard said. They were only a hundred feet away now and he eased back on the ski boat's throttle. The boat slowed. Car lights flashed over their heads from vehicles turning onto the bridge in the direction of Ocean Springs. Small waves slapped gently against the boat's hull.

"There," Peter said. *"There!"*

A hundred feet ahead of them the tip of the fin broke the surface of the water and moved slowly into the marked channel under the bridge. Howard eased the throttle forward. Peter smiled and nodded. The nose broke the surface.

Howard fired, the weapon recoiling in his hand and the sound of the shot deafening. The shark abruptly submerged, leaving the water swirling.

"Hit him right in the head!" Howard yelled.

The boat sped toward the channel.

The wide head exploded up through the surface. The mouth gaped toward them. The body rose ten feet into the air. Howard's eyes widened. "Holy Christ!" Peter said. The body fell forward, splashing big waves out to its sides. And the fin sped out from under the bridge toward them.

Howard dropped the revolver and spun the wheel around, hitting the throttle. The boat jumped forward. The blond and the redhead stared back over their shoulders in shock. "You didn't hit him in the head," Peter said in a voice barely audible over the roar of the motor. "You didn't even see his head."

Spray began to rise to each side of the fin.

Howard glanced back over his shoulder, then ahead of him, and then back across his shoulder again. The spray was rising ten feet into the air now. The fin had already cut the distance in half. Howard jerked the wheel to the right and guided the boat directly toward the pier sticking out from the Scott Marine Education Center. The gap between the boat and the pier quickly narrowed. The gap between the boat and the fin narrowed even quicker. The redhead started climbing over the windshield toward the bow. Peter leaned forward over the seat and caught her around the waist, pulling her backward. She screamed. The blond fought past him toward the front seats.

"Look out!" Howard yelled.

He jerked the throttle back at the last moment. Too late. The boat coasted rapidly in on its bow wave into the side of the pier. There was a loud crashing sound. The front of the boat caved backward. The blond shot forward as though fired out of a cannon. Peter and the redhead, his arms still holding her waist, tumbled through the air toward the pier. Howard slid face first through the windshield into the concrete and rebounded off of it back toward the wheel. Stunned, he came awkwardly to his feet, took two long steps on the boat, and hurdled up onto the pier, wobbled backward at its edge, and dove between Peter and the redhead. The blond scurried past them on all fours.

Behind them, the shark rose out of the water and came down hard on the boat, smashing it beneath the water.

Up and down the Sound, the radios of the charter boats and pleasure craft alike received the Coast Guard broadcast of the shark having been spotted moving in the direction of Biloxi Bay by an older couple out floundering. Carolyn swung the *Intuitive* around to the right and opened the throttles as much as she could without coming to a speed that might pull the section of meat from the big hook trailing the boat. Small waves beginning to build out to the sides of the craft's bow, they moved in the direction of the channel passing behind Deer Island toward the bay.

CHAPTER 30

Alan and Carolyn stared at the flotsam drifting out from the Education Center's pier. The crushed bow of the submerged ski boat bobbed next to the seawall. At the rear of the pier, four figures hobbled slowly in the direction of the brightly lit casinos rising high into the air a few hundred feet in front of them.

"Looks like Mr. Boom-boom is in for the night," Alan said.

Carolyn lifted the mike from in front of her. "Coast Guard, this is the charter fishing boat *Intuitive.*"

"This is Coast Guard Station Gulfport. Go ahead, Captain."

"There's a small boat wrecked on the Scott Education Center pier at Point Cadet. Its four passengers are moving on foot in the direction of the casinos. I don't know if there are any injuries."

The Coast Guard responded by saying they would contact the Biloxi Police and signed off.

As Carolyn replaced the mike she glanced at the four figures again, then turned the *Intuitive*'s wheel toward the Highway 90 bridge and looked over her shoulder at the long line stretching taut in the water behind them.

* * *

Vandiver cradled the telephone receiver against his shoulder as he buttoned his shirt. "The artist's interpretation is what I started thinking about, Douglas—drawing the megalodon's head blunter than a white's is only an artist's interpretation. And what was that interpretation based on? A megalodon is cartilaginous. Cartilage doesn't fossilize, it wastes away—nothing is left from which to interpret. There maybe were a few places where silt formed around a megalodon's body and hardened and left a rough imprint of what it looked like. But that's nothing. Think of the dinosaurs. They did at least leave fossilized skeletons—and there's been many a dinosaur interpretation changed after subsequent finds of new bones. But there's no bones to find of a megalodon.

"And the brown coloring. . . . An artist's conception is all that is too. Hell, nobody really knows what color the megalodon was—it could have been pink. An artist's conception, that's all any of it is. All a guess. The megalodon could look *exactly* like the white of today, at least enough where that marine biologist in Mississippi couldn't tell the difference; perhaps enough alike that nobody can tell the difference. Why not, it's the direct great-grandfather of the white?

"We're going to go look for ourselves. You get out to Andrews and find a flight where we can hitch a ride. You know how we have been catching hell about spending taxpayers' money by using service flights rather than traveling commercial. But we haven't got time to waste with a commercial flight, so find somebody already going that way. If you can't find somebody already going that way, then give them a reason why they should—and I want to take off within the hour."

"Sir?"

"Yes."

"Sir, remember the length of the trench I saw? You said yourself that based on the size of the tooth the megalodon had to be at least forty feet in length. The white in Mississippi is only twenty-five. They said they saw it up close. I don't see how they could have been that far off in their estimate.''

"I've thought about that, too. Why did I say it had to be at least forty feet? Because I used shark teeth of today for a comparison. Who's to say that the megalodon doesn't have teeth twice the size of a similar-length shark of today?''

"Then a megalodon wouldn't look like a white, sir.''

"Teeth wouldn't.''

"The depression I found in the Keys, sir. Its length— over fifty feet?''

"Did you see him lying there, Douglas, or where he had been lying? Hell, how do you know he didn't scoot up the trench so that it looks like he is longer than he really is? He had to settle there, slide into it, come out of it, that would have stretched it some.''

There was no response, and Vandiver waited a moment. Then he frowned. "Douglas, son, I don't know. Okay? You sound just like your mother in an argument; she has to have every damn thing hammered out in concrete before she'll believe it. But bear with me, please. And have that flight ready for takeoff within the hour.''

The *Intuitive* passed under the Highway 90 bridge. Ahead was the old abandoned bridge that once served the traffic between Biloxi and Ocean Springs. Beyond the abandoned bridge was the third bridge crossing the bay, the railway bridge with its open span angling up toward the sky. Ahead of the bridges the moonlight cast the water in an almost daylike brilliance. Alan looked over his shoulder at the running lights of a Bertram entering the bay and cruising past the Education Center.

Carolyn lifted the mike to her mouth. "Kevin.''

The voice came back almost immediately. *"Yeah, Carolyn."*

"Did you see the flotsam?"

"Yeah, what happened?"

"Our friends with the dynamite on the river today—looks like they finally had enough beer. I'm pulling up the channel toward the river."

"Roger, Carolyn, I'll pull straight across toward Ocean Springs."

The *Intuitive* passed underneath the railway bridge.

Ahead of them on the shore off to the left, the big double doors at the rear of the building housing American Aquaculture, Inc. stood open. Bright light from inside the spacious rear half of the building shone out toward the water.

Ho, his long hair hanging down his back, his hands in the pockets of his lab coat, grinned as he stared at the half-dozen mature redfish females circling the sides of the fingerling tank. Flown by private jet into the Gulfport/Biloxi Regional Airport two hours before, the fish were obviously no worse for the long trip from Los Angeles, having taken quickly to their new surroundings and eagerly gone after the food pellets he had dropped into the tank. "Chang know beauties when he see them," Ho said, speaking to himself. Then he directed his words to the fish. "You see soon that you have good job here—all benefits free. And . . ."—he held up a slim finger to make his point—"you never be eaten here."

He turned and walked toward a narrow three-foot-long aquarium sitting in a wheelbarrow by the wide, double doors leading out to the bay. In the water behind the glass a thin rubber hose bubbled oxygen to an eighteen-inch redfish slowly moving its fins.

"You have been good, fruitful mother," Ho said. "Now you go back to your life." Stepping around to the rear of the wheelbarrow, he lifted the hose from the aquarium, then caught the wheelbarrow's long wooden handles and tilted its legs up from the floor.

A moment later he passed out the doors toward the waters of the bay glistening in the bright moonlight.

He stood a few seconds at the edge of the shore staring at the charter boat moving along the channel toward the Biloxi River. Then he lifted a square piece of foam rubber from out of the wheelbarrow and dipped the piece into the bay water at his feet. Next he slipped the section into the aquarium, slid it under the fish, gently wrapped the soft rubber around the fish's body, and lifted the water-soaked section and the fish out of the aquarium to his chest. The fish wiggled, twisted. . . .

"Now, now. Be good woman for moment longer." The fish wiggled again. Water running down the front of his lab coat from the lively bundle, Ho stepped into the bay and waded out from the shore. "Now, now," he was saying as he went farther and farther, the water climbing up his legs.

Soon, he was up to his thighs in the warm water. He took two more steps and, up to his hips now, gently lowered the foam rubber into the water and opened it.

The redfish moved a few inches. Its fins fanned slowly.

"Go ahead," Ho said. "Find friends, and have good life."

With a sudden swipe of its tail, the fish shot forward a couple of feet in the water, slowed a moment, then dove out of sight.

Ho grinned.

The sudden great splash off to his left was as loud as a truckload of lumber falling into the water. He jerked his head toward the sound.

The great shark's back was above the surface, the water line running along under its dark eyes. Ho screamed and stumbled backward, sitting into the water and flailing his arms to regain his feet. The shark shot forward, ground to a sudden stop, twisted its body, swiped its tail hard to the

side, and moved forward again. Ho regained his footing
and moved backward rapidly. His heel caught on a pipe
lying on the bottom and again he sprawled backward,
fought his way up, and came to his feet.

More than half of the shark's thick body was now above
the waterline. The charred section of its wide head con-
trasted vividly with the rest of its gray color. Dark red blood
seeped from a hole in its nose. The pectoral fins, sticking
rigidly out into the water, splashed like giant boat paddles
as the creature rocked from side to side—and scooted forward again.

Ho screamed and kicked his knees toward the shore. The
shark, now squirming frenetically, flicking its tail back and
forth rapidly, could move forward no more. Blood pumped
from the hole in its nose.

Alan and Carolyn had heard Ho's high-pitched scream even
over the loud hum of the *Intuitive*'s engines. Alan had
quickly pulled in the line trailing behind them. Now, white
waves rolling out to the sides of its bow, the boat sped
toward the great shark writhing on the submerged mudflat
forty feet from the bank. Carolyn opened the cabinetlike
doors of the locker built into the bulkhead under the steering wheel. She pulled out a revolver wrapped in an oilcloth.
Alan took it from her and unwrapped it—a thirty-eight-
caliber Smith & Wesson with its lead slugs shaved flat at
the end. Deadly to a man or a five- or six-foot shark, but
next to useless against the twenty-five-foot monster ahead
of them. *He remembered.* "Where are some matches?"

Carolyn looked at him.

"The dynamite, Carolyn—matches, where are they?"

"In the drawer by the stove."

He turned, caught the top of the ladder, and swung down
into the fishing cockpit. A moment later he lifted the heavy
cardboard box up onto the sink in the cabin and ripped it
open. Seconds later he was twisting the tip of an ice pick

around inside the end of a stick of the explosive. He grabbed for the box of percussion caps.

Carolyn looked at the depth sounder, grabbed for the throttles, and jerked them back and put the engines out of gear. The *Intuitive*'s bow rose on its own wave and plowed into the soft mud, shuddering to a stop, throwing her into the wheel and Alan, coming around the cabin with a double handful of the sticks of dynamite, hard against the rail. He regained his balance and rushed around the Zodiac inflatable on the forward deck to the bow.

Fifty feet away, the shark, its wide head charred and blood pumping from its nose, began to slide backward into deeper water.

Alan quickly struck a match and touched it to the fuse protruding from one of the sticks. The fuse smoked. He drew his hand back over his shoulder and whipped his arm forward.

The stick tumbled slowly end over end as it arched through the air and splashed into the water a few feet out in front of the shark's head.

Seconds passed.

The shark slid farther backward into the deeper water.

A muffled thump, the water boiled and foamed, and the shark reared its head and splashed back down into the water.

A second fuse smoked. Alan watched it as it slowly turned brown. He kept waiting.

"Alan."

He suddenly raised his arm and whipped the stick forward. It flew across the water with less of an arch than the first one, hit the shark in front of the dorsal fin, bounced into the air and off to the far side of the thick body—and exploded in a ball of fire and a crescendo of noise.

The shark's head jerked violently away from the explosion. Its mouth gaped wide. The wave of the blast slammed a hard wall of hot air back against Alan. He held the match to another fuse.

With a great shudder of its body, the shark slid backward fully into the deeper water and submerged except for its thick fin. The fin leaned sharply to the side, the great body flipped around in the water, throwing a wave out toward the *Intuitive,* and the creature raced away from the boat.

Alan stared helplessly, then threw the stick as far after the shark as he could. It hit in the water and went under.

The *Intuitive*'s engines roared in reverse. The water foamed around the props. Carolyn jerked the throttles back and jammed them forward again. The boat's stern pulled down in the water. A great dark cloud of silt spread out to the sides of the boat.

A hundred feet behind the racing fin the dynamite exploded with a muffled thump and the water boiled.

Carolyn jerked the throttles back again and then forward once more. Smoke poured from behind the boat. There was a loud sucking sound. The bow moved backward a foot—and then broke loose from the mud's grip.

The *Intuitive* shot backward, its blunt stern pushing a wall of water before it. A hundred yards away now, the fin began to drop lower and lower in the water—and disappeared.

CHAPTER 31

The *Intuitive* moved slowly, Carolyn keeping her eyes glued to the depth sounder as she weaved her way around the mudflats.

Ahead of them the fin had emerged above the surface once more, and now moved slowly as the shark angled toward the marked channel running in the direction of the Biloxi River.

"It's twenty to thirty feet deep where the river connects to the bay," Carolyn said. "If he gets there, it'll be like trying to find him in the Pascagoula all over again."

"*Carolyn,*" the voice said over the radio. "*Where?*"

She grabbed the mike. "Kevin, it's a couple hundred yards ahead of us, south of the main channel, moving toward the river."

Alan looked at the Bertram racing down the channel out to their side.

"*I see it,*" Kevin said. "*I have a rifle if I can get to it before it reaches deeper water.*"

The thick fin began to rise higher. It stopped, edged to one side, rippled backward in the water, and moved in another direction. It came to a halt again, and half of its upper body came up out of the water.

"It's blocked off," Alan said.

The spotlight from the Bertram illuminated the shark's body in a bright, circular beam. The first shots were heard as only light cracks. Tiny sparks of flame jumped from the rifle barrel. The slugs hit in the water around the shark's head and ricocheted toward the shore.

The next two rapid shots slammed into the shark's side, and the thick body jerked sideways into the deeper water. The fin turned and came back the same way it had gone, slowing once, then gaining speed again.

"It's trying to find where it came in," Carolyn said.

The distance between them and the fin began to narrow. Alan stepped to the rear of the flying bridge, caught the rail and swung down into the fishing cockpit.

In the cabin he gathered the coil of fuse, the box of percussion caps, and several sticks of dynamite, and held them to his chest as he came back out the door, up onto the forward deck, and hurried to the bow. Dropping to his knees, he began to work on the end of a stick with the ice pick.

The shark turned toward shore.

Carolyn spun the wheel that way, then grabbed for the throttles and yanked them back. Alan had to press his hand against the deck to keep from toppling forward.

The *Intuitive* coasted forward, then jerked to a full stop as Carolyn threw it into reverse. The water bubbling up in a great, violent torrent out to the sides of the props, the boat began to back away from the mudflat it had approached.

A moment later, Carolyn angled the bow off to the side and eased the throttles forward again.

The shark neared the shore and swung back in the direction of the river.

Alan came to his feet. He held two sticks of dynamite crudely tied together with a length of fuse. Two other fuses projected from the ends of the sticks and were twisted together into one cord. He stared at the fin.

Carolyn watched the depth sounder as she eased the wheel to the right. The water beneath the keel began to deepen again and she slowly moved the throttles forward. The Bertram was working its way out of the marked channel ahead of them and slowly making its way in the direction of the fin.

Flashes jumped from the rifle barrel.

The fin suddenly swerved and, racing now, sprays of water beginning to build out to its sides once more, came directly at the *Intuitive*. Alan watched it narrowing the distance between them. He held two of the matches pressed together between his thumb and forefinger.

A hundred yards.

Ninety yards.

The fin continued straight toward the *Intuitive*.

Eighty yards.

Seventy yards.

"It's going to try to come by us!" Carolyn shouted. She looked at the depth sounder, moved her hand toward the throttles, then stopped it as the water began to deepen again.

Ahead of the *Intuitive* the fin began to sink lower as it sped toward them.

"This is the way it came in!" Carolyn shouted.

Fifty yards.

Alan cupped the small box of matches against his chest to shield it from the wind, held the heads of the two single matches close against the box, and raised the dynamite close to his hand.

Forty yards.

The fin suddenly cut sharply toward shore. It rose rapidly. The eyes came above the surface, the water streaming back under them. Carolyn cut the wheel toward the creature. Fully half of its body was exposed now—and it ground to a sudden stop.

The shark started thrashing, trying to move backward. It bucked violently. Alan struck the matches. They flared brightly and he touched the fire to the fuses.

The shark thrashed its head to the side, tried to turn its long body. Carolyn pulled back on the throttles. Alan lofted the doubled sticks of dynamite into the air.

They arched end over end, landed next to the head, splashing water up across the eye—and exploded in a ball of flame.

The shark's pectoral fin rolled into the air. The head went over on its side into the water.

Another doubled charge arched through the air.

It landed on a side of the wide head, bounced, came down on the head again, and started to slide toward the water.

The explosion blew skin, eye, and meat high into the air in a gory shower.

CHAPTER 32

The twenty-five-foot shark lay on its side, half submerged in the dark water forty feet from shore. Where its eye and a side of its head had been, a four-foot-wide–by–two-foot-deep crater ran blood down into the brown water, staining it a darker shade in an ever-spreading circle. Behind the carcass, lights along the shore had come on at the sound of the explosions. More than one car had stopped in front of the buildings along Bayview Drive. Two teenage boys walked toward the edge of the water. Carolyn said, "It's crazy."

"What?"

"It's crazy," she repeated in a low voice. "But at the last, when I could tell it was trying to escape, I couldn't help but feel sorry for it in a way."

He slipped his hand around her shoulders. She laid her head against his arm. It *had* tried to escape, he thought, not just swimming away from the boats, but consciously trying to find a way into the channel leading toward the river. Consciously, he thought again, the same kind of obvious thinking it did when it tried to wear away the grass and mud where Fred and the others had been trapped. He stared at the body, thought a moment more, then shook his head.

He was looking at it, wasn't he? A white shark. And what else could it have been?

"What?" Carolyn asked, raising her face up toward his.

"It just didn't act like how I would have thought it would have acted." He smiled a little at himself. "But what does an expert in growing fingerlings know?"

Carolyn raised her head from his arm, looked at the body for a moment, then reached for the wheel and slowly eased the throttles forward, turning the *Intuitive* in the direction of the Bertram on its way into the marked channel leading toward the Sound.

Back above the bridges, the first gray light of dawn was beginning to brighten the eastern sky, and soon the wondering was gone from Alan's mind.

Why not? It was dead.

Admiral Vandiver sat among the tall cases of equipment in the belly of the C-130 Hercules. Though all the cargo was securely lashed together, it vibrated like a freezing man's teeth. He frowned at Douglas, sitting against a stack of crates to the side. Douglas looked away. Vandiver leaned his head back against a case, felt his hair start vibrating and, frowning again, sat forward once more. "Real good job here, Douglas."

Douglas didn't say anything.

Vandiver waited a moment. "Douglas."

His nephew's face came around.

"Douglas, why would a megalodon come all the way from the Pacific to the northern tip of the Gulf of Mexico?"

"Sir?"

"Think about it . . . thousands of miles, passing dozens of places quite similar, basically the same water temperatures, the same prey, the same everything. To pass all that up almost makes you think it knew where it was headed from the very beginning, doesn't it? And that doesn't make any sense, does it?"

Douglas started to remind his uncle that all they knew for certain at the moment was that a large white shark had come into the northern Gulf—not a megalodon—but he didn't.

"Then I realized it didn't have to make any sense, Douglas. It doesn't make any sense that the six-gill came to the Gulf."

Vandiver paused at the questioning expression on his nephew's face. "Douglas, when you don't know something just say so. You haven't heard of the Pacific six-gill shark?"

"No, sir."

"Don't you ever even watch the Discovery Channel?"

Douglas didn't answer.

Vandiver shook his head in dismay. "Well, Douglas, the six-gill is another of the deep-ocean mysteries throwing marine scientists for a loop now. I mean that's where all the modern mysteries are coming from—the depths. Why is it that species that for millions of years never rose high enough in the water to even see faintest light are suddenly emerging into shallow waters now? Something is causing it. Pollution? That's doubtful. The ocean floors aren't exactly pristine any more, but to say the depths are polluted in the same sense the land masses are isn't correct. It isn't even close. Deep-ocean temperatures suddenly rapidly changing? We have no indication of that. Yet, for some reason, deep-sea creatures *are* coming up all over the world.

"The six-gill isn't exactly the same kind of case as the megalodon would be, or even the megamouth shark coming up from the depths. Even though no one had ever seen one of the six-gill adults prior to their surfacing, we knew they existed. For years its young came around fish factories along the California coast to feed on what was dumped into the water. A few young six-gills up to eight or nine feet long were caught in some of the deeper bays. But as they

aged they moved into deeper and deeper spots until, by the
time they were full grown, they were in the deepest
trenches—and never rose back into shallow waters again.
That's been true since mankind began. A human had never
seen an adult six-gill. Then, in the seventies, the first
adult—a sixteen-foot female—was caught by a fishing
trawler in relatively shallow water. After that adult six-gills
began to be caught in shallower and shallower waters in
the Pacific. Then, for some unknown reason, they started
migrating, went around the tip of South America and
reached the Caribbean a few years ago. Now they've
moved into the Gulf. One was seen off the Chandeleur
Islands last year—they've gone as far north as they can.
It's as if that's where they were headed from the very beginning. As if that is where the megalodon had been headed
since the beginning. Why?''

Douglas didn't speak. The cargo continued to vibrate.

"Why, Douglas? Why the northern Gulf for the six-gill?
And, maybe, why the northern Gulf for the megalodon?''

Vandiver stared at the young ensign. "Why, Douglas?''

"Sir, I don't—''

"Rhetorical question, son.''

Douglas nodded.

"Important question, too, Douglas.''

"Uh, yes, sir.''

"Make you famous if you can figure out why.''

"Yes, sir.''

"Make me famous, too.''

Douglas nodded. When his uncle continued to stare,
Douglas said, "Yes, sir.''

"Want to know what I think?''

Douglas both nodded and said "Yes, sir'' this time.

"I think it might have to do with the lower Mississippi
River Basin. It's the most ancient, large drainage system in
North America. Been here since way before the last ice
ages. Is home to more so-called living fossils than any other

place in the world—creatures that have existed unchanged for tens of millions of years. The bowfin, the paddlefish, the sturgeon—I could name a dozen species here now that have been here since creatures first existed in the seas. And, if you remember, when I told you about the artist's interpretation I told you that megalodons are cartilaginous, therefore their remains waste away and they don't fossilize like bony animals. So, basically, other than for a couple of full-body impressions in mud that hardened rapidly, only the megalodon's teeth have ever been found to let us know it ever existed. Guess where a lot of their teeth have been found?''

"The lower Mississippi River Basin, sir?''

"That's correct, Douglas. Some of it dry land now that used to be ocean. The teeth have been found all over the upper Gulf Coast. An inordinate amount of remains of other prehistoric sea creatures have been, too; some of them among the largest creatures ever to swim the seas. For one, the basilosaurus—the seventy-foot, giant-toothed whale which would give even the megalodon reason for fear. The Louisiana and Mississippi coasts in particular were a major breeding ground of this creature. Their remains were so numerous that early settlers in those states often used the vertebra for foundation supports for cabins. Many think the same area might have been a breeding ground for the megalodons, too.''

Douglas's eyes tightened. "You mean . . . you're saying . . . you're suggesting the megalodon is acting like a salmon, coming back to where it was bred?''

"That's close.''

"But, sir, the, uh . . . If a megalodon is alive, it wouldn't have been born in the Gulf. There wouldn't have been any born there since man was here. It couldn't be acting like a sal—''

"Douglas, Douglas, Douglas. I said you were close. It doesn't have to be exactly like a salmon. There are many animals, fish, and birds that instinctively go to a place to breed no matter where they were born. Not like salmon going back to the headwaters of rivers, or geese that migrate back to the specific pond where they were hatched, but creatures that, no matter where they are born or live, go back to a particular place at one time in their lives—like birds instinctively migrating south before snow begins to fall. And not just flocks of birds whose migration might be a sign of herd behavior—following the leader—but individual birds flying to certain places the fall after they are born. That's an instinct that has to be passed down genetically—the desire or knowledge has to already be present in the bird when it's born.''

Douglas nodded now. ''You're saying the megalodons went to the deep trenches for some reason. Driven there, maybe. They stayed there until—''

''Correct, Douglas, until something made them move. Like the French explosion in January perhaps. Now they're returning to a place they once instinctively came to.''

Douglas's face twisted in thought. ''You're saying *they*? Something made *them* move. More than one?''

''There can't be only one of anything, Douglas.''

CHAPTER 33

Carolyn sat in the *Intuitive*'s cabin as she spoke on the telephone plugged into the dockside extension. "Did I wake you, Mother?"

"Heavens no, your father got me out of bed when he saw about the shark being killed on the news. We've been up ever since. He woke Paul, too."

"Oh, he shouldn't have done that."

"For once I'll agree with Fred, Carolyn. Paul was so excited. He's playing out on the dock now. I think he's thrilled just to be able to be down at the water again."

"I'll come on in a minute then. I want to see him. I'm going to take a quick shower first."

"Baby, why don't you stay there and get a few hours of sleep? I know you're dead. He's fine. He knows you're okay. If you come over now, you know between his and Fred's questions you're not going to get any sleep here."

"Oh, I'm fine."

"Throwing dynamite around," her mother said, and sighed. "If I would have known that I would have had heart failure."

Carolyn smiled. "I'll see you in an hour or so, Mother."

* * *

At Carolyn's home, her mother looked out the window as she hung up the telephone. Paul was playing on the dock again.

Sitting in the wicker chair on the patio, Fred raised his gaze from his newspaper when Duchess started barking.

Paul pushed the little sailboat he had fashioned from a piece of notebook paper out from the dock and looked over his shoulder at the Labrador at the side of the dock looking down the river.

"It's gone, Duchess."

The Labrador kept staring. She started barking again.

"Duchess, be quiet."

The dog barked faster.

Paul looked down the channel.

"Duchess," he said. "The shark's gone."

Suddenly the Labrador stretched her neck out and looked directly down into the water in front of her forepaws, and barked sharply.

Paul came to his feet. He looked back at the paper sailboat about to move out of his reach and started to lean toward it, but didn't. Duchess was barking continuously now.

Paul stepped quickly off the dock into the yard and called back to the Labrador. Duchess turned and, looking back over her shoulder toward the river, trotted to him.

Paul stared at the water.

Fred stopped beside him. "Duchess see a snake?" He took a step toward the dock.

"No, Papaw," Paul said. "Don't go out there."

Carolyn, dressed in jeans and a short-sleeve blouse and carrying the clothes she had worn earlier, stepped out of the bath house and walked behind the line of charter fishing boats to the *Intuitive*.

She fluffed her hair with her free hand as she came up the concrete walkway and hopped down into the fishing cockpit.

"I feel a million percent better," she said as she stepped inside the cabin.

Alan rubbed the stubble on his cheek with the back of his hand.

A horn sounded outside in the parking area.

Alan stepped from the cabin.

Rayanne sat in her pickup as he walked toward her.

She handed his fresh clothes and a plastic bag containing a toothbrush and razor out through the window. "A mother's work is never done," she said. "Wouldn't it have been simpler for me to have just picked you up and taken you to your apartment?"

Carolyn stepped from the cabin.

"Oh, I see," Rayanne said.

"What in the hell are we doing, Douglas?"

"Sir?"

"The plane is going down, Douglas."

"They have to offload some cargo here."

Vandiver looked at his watch, groaned, and laid his head back against the vibrating crates.

Wearing a fresh white shirt and clean khakis, his towel draped around his neck, Alan stepped inside the cabin. He closed the door quietly when he saw Carolyn, fully dressed, asleep, curled on her side in the bunk. He laid his soiled clothes and towel on the sink and stepped to the bunk, sitting down on its side.

"Carolyn," he said in a low voice.

Her eyes slowly came open. She turned on her back and smiled up at him. "Time to go see Paul," he said. She stared into his eyes for a moment longer, then lifted her hand to the side of his neck and pulled his face down toward hers.

Across the marina, a forty-three-foot Gulfstar Mark IV motor yacht with the sweeping, smooth lines of a sailing vessel began to move slowly out of its slip. The man at the flying bridge was in his mid-fifties, overweight, dressed in swimming trunks, a white dress shirt open down its middle—and had a frown on his face.

"Okay, now?" he called to his wife, a stocky woman dressed in a one-piece bathing suit and standing at the bow.

She didn't bother to answer him.

He looked at his watch. "Six, seven hours and we'll have to start back to Jackson or I won't get enough sleep to go to work tomorrow. I get off an extra day past the weekend and the whole thing's wasted sitting in this damn slip."

A little, blond-haired girl in a two-piece red bathing suit ran up the deck to her mother and looked at the water in front of the boat. The woman slipped her arm around the child's shoulders and looked up at her husband.

"Would you rather have taken the children out and fed them to the shark, Alvin?"

The little girl looked toward the bridge and frowned.

Her twin brother, a curly-haired boy walking toward the bow, looked back over his shoulder and twisted his face too.

They were his stepchildren by his wife's first marriage.

And not only were they the reason that he had been forced to sit in the slip for two days—even though the Gulfstar was way too big to be bothered by a shark of any size—he had also had to sit here since dawn because his wife feared the starting of the boat's big diesel engines would disturb her babies' sleep. He thought about what she had just said about feeding the children to the shark and considered the remark very seriously, then nodded in the affirmative.

Next he looked at the shiny, metallic blue speedboat moving across the water in front of him on its way toward the exit from the marina. Two windsurfing boards with their sails detached and lying beside them projected over the rear of the boat.

A dark-haired boy who appeared to be in his early twenties stood behind the wheel. Dressed in khaki cutoffs with his chest bare, he was the type of lean, tightly muscled youth that would catch any girl's eye. But not as much as the girl standing next to him would catch a man's eye—of any age. Her rounded hips were tightly enclosed in a pair of short shorts, while a narrow pink bikini top strained to contain her heavy breasts. Her long blond hair blowing out behind her tanned figure and whipping back and forth from side to side almost created the optical illusion of her body swaying sexily back and forth. Alvin continued to watch her until the Gulfstar had gone nearly two-thirds of the way across the marina and was about to enter a slip on the other side when his wife said something and he remembered to turn.

Alan pressed his mouth down against Carolyn's neck, feeling the warmth of her skin with his lips. She rubbed the side of his face with hers, and moved her lips across his cheek to his lips. Her hands came around the back of his neck. She spread her fingers and ran them into his hair and up the back of his head, and pulled his lips down harder onto hers.

He stretched out closer to her and she moved forward against him and they kissed again, moving their lips even harder against each other's and holding the kiss for several seconds. Alan slipped his fingers between the top buttons of her blouse, undoing them and pushing the material back to kiss her skin where it began to swell into the top of her breast.

"Alan . . ."

She never finished because of the knock sounding sharply on the side of the cabin.

"Carolyn," Sheriff Stark called.

With his speaking just outside the fiberglass bulkhead, it sounded like he was already in the cabin with them. Alan pulled his face back from hers and looked across his shoulder at the door at the rear of the cabin.

"Anybody home?" Stark called.

Carolyn smiled up at Alan as she buttoned her blouse.

He came to his feet and walked toward the door.

As he stepped outside into the cockpit, Stark hopped down inside the craft from the walkway. "Carolyn," he said, nodding his greeting at her as she stepped from the cabin behind Alan, "I hate to bother you again, but I have a real big favor to ask. The mayor over here wants the shark's body removed. He doesn't like it reminding people what happened here—specifically tourists. Problem is, Sheriff Broussard's daughter is getting married today—to Broussard's chief deputy. Almost the whole damn department is in the wedding party. He called me and asked if I could coordinate the removal for him. With the hours the Coast Guard put—"

The telephone ringing inside the cabin cut Stark off.

Carolyn said, "Just a moment," and stepped back through the door.

When she answered the phone, her father said, "Carolyn, Paul's a little . . . Carolyn, I wasn't going to call you and bother you with it, but Martha insisted. Duchess started barking at the river again and it frightened Paul. He asked when you're going to get here."

"Tell him I'll be there in just a few minutes," she said, and replaced the receiver and walked back out into the cockpit.

"Carolyn," Stark said, "I really do hate to bother you, but with the hours the Coast Guard put in the last couple of days they released everybody from duty but a skeleton crew at the station. They said they would remove the body in a couple of days, but I guess I need to go ahead and do it now—told Broussard I would. I know how much you have already done, but I need a boat with some power and you're the only captain I personally know who I can—''

"Jonas, I'm sorry, but I can't. Paul's worried about the river again, that the shark—''

Carolyn suddenly stopped her words. "Yes, I will help you remove it," she said. "And I'm going to go pick up Paul first. I want him to see that the shark's dead and see us when we take it out and dispose of it. I want him to go with us."

"Thank you, Carolyn. I'll make it up to you some way."

"It's all right. Maybe this is just what Paul needs."

The telephone rang again and she turned back into the cabin.

"I hate this," Stark said to Alan.

"She might be right," Alan said. "It won't hurt anything and it might help him get it out of his mind once and for all."

Stark nodded. "Pretty rough thing for a child his age to have gone through—it'd be hanging on my mind, too." He looked down the line of fishing boats bobbing quietly in their berths without a single captain or mate in sight if a group desiring a charter came by the marina. "Everybody's tired," he said.

Carolyn stepped back into the fishing cockpit. "It was Mrs. Hsiao," she said to Alan. "She said the redfish had to be moved to the spawning tanks before they injured each other, and that she's down there now and can't get the valves or something to work. She said you'd know what she meant. She said Ho had been so keyed up during the night he couldn't sleep and she gave him some sleeping pills. She said to tell you she was sorry to bother you."

"Everybody is sorry," Stark said.

"Go ahead, Alan," Carolyn said. "Jonas and Paul and I can handle it fine. It won't be any trouble."

Vandiver stared at the clamshell-shaped door as it came up to close at the rear of the Hercules.

All that remained in the cavernous sixty-five-foot length of the giant plane's cargo belly was a single small crate sitting conspicuously by itself halfway toward the bulkhead behind the pilot and copilot.

"What's in it?" Vandiver asked.

"I don't know, sir. I got it at the loading dock at Andrews when they were getting ready to put it on a truck."

"You did good, Douglas," Vandiver said.

CHAPTER 34

Carolyn guided the *Intuitive* out of the marked channel toward the body of the big shark lying half submerged on its side in the water. A mixture of small boats surrounded the carcass. Seagulls circled overhead. Two teenagers pushed a rubber raft off the nearby shore and paddled toward the long shape. A skinny man in his late forties stood bare-chested, well over his waist in water as he raised his long arms and worked inside the gaping mouth with a long knife and a pair of big pliers. A tooth, a bloody section of the gum attached to it, came loose, and the man pulled it from the mouth and grinned.

But what Carolyn stared at was the long, gaping slit cut along the center of the shark's belly just above the water line. Parts of the shark's visceral lining, some of it a pale white and some a bloody red, draped down into the water.

She looked at Stark's khaki pants and shirt. At first she thought they were so wrinkled because he hadn't had time to change them from the night before. But now she realized it was because they had been wet in the last few hours. He saw her look, and nodded.

"There was one complete skull, and fragments of the others," he said. "Bones, some of them with the meat still . . . It made me sick to my stomach. The medical examiner says he'll have it all put together enough to positively identify all the victims by tomorrow.''

Carolyn looked at the creature she had felt sorry for the night before, even a moment before, as the man wrenched the tooth from its mouth, but didn't feel sorry for it any longer.

Stark looked back toward the marked channel a couple hundred feet away as the workboat, Deputy Fairley at its wheel and the older deputy at his side, turned toward them.

A thick pile of heavily woven net filled the boat's rear.

Carolyn glanced over her shoulder toward the fishing cockpit. ''Jonas, do you mind if they take the dynamite with them?''

Stark smiled. ''Sure,'' he said. ''Does make a mess when it goes off, doesn't it?'' He raised his hand and signaled for Fairley to bring the workboat to the *Intuitive*'s stern.

''And something else I can do for you,'' Stark said. ''I just thought about it—your ski boat's still sitting in the marshes. I'll have Fairley tow it in and get the prop fixed—compliments of the Jackson County Sheriff's Department.''

The number of people present around the carcass proved beneficial in the ensuing task, several of them joining the two deputies and Stark, in water up to their shoulders sometimes, in slipping the net under the carcass's tail and pulling it partially up under the body. The workboat dragged the net the rest of the way under the body from one side while the *Intuitive* used its big engines to supply the power to the ropes trailing back to the other side of the net.

It took nearly an hour. The last work done was the securing of the net around the top of the carcass as tight as it could be done by human strength and the attaching of the several-foot-tall cone-shaped nuns' buoy Fairley had obtained from the Coast Guard to help keep the dead weight buoyant as it was hauled toward the Gulf.

Still, as they pulled the shark toward the marked channel, it sank low enough that it had to be dragged along the mud with the buoy floating partially submerged above the surface.

As the *Intuitive* came out of the marked safety fairway leading from Biloxi Bay to the Sound, the carcass lifted off the mud for the first time.

With only the buoy's top third showing, Carolyn guided the *Intuitive* in the direction of the barrier islands in the distance. Stark had asked if she minded if he rested in the cabin for a moment, and now was sound asleep on the bunk. Paul stood beside her. When she looked down at him, he smiled up at her and she patted his head.

Behind them, seagulls squawked and dipped low over the buoy. Occasionally one of them dove to the water behind the net to grab a piece of flesh that came loose from the unseen carcass.

The Gulfstar yacht bobbed at anchor a hundred feet behind the small white dinghy making its way toward shore at the northern tip of the Chandeleur Islands. The stocky woman sitting at the bow of the dinghy looked at the water to her sides and said, "That wasn't the only shark in the world, you know, Alvin."

Her husband, holding the arm of the dinghy's small steering motor, shook his head. "The water's only two feet deep here. What do you think a shark is going to do—wade across the shoal and grab us?"

His wife looked across the island to where large waves rolled in to crash against the white sand on the Gulf side of the long structure. "The children aren't going in the water over there," she said.

"Nobody's making them."

The curly-haired boy moved off the single center seat toward his mother. Her broad hips taking up nearly the full width of the seat, the boy had to step to its very outside to sit down. The dinghy tipped slightly to that side and Alvin had to counterbalance it by leaning in the opposite direction. The little blond girl held her hand in front of her face and stared over her shoulder at him.

"The water's blowing on me."

"That happens in boats," he said.

She frowned at the reply and rose from her seat to walk toward her mother's other side.

The boat tipped that way now and the girl tilted in that direction. Alvin thought seriously about suddenly leaning to the same side. But he didn't.

As soon as the bow of the dinghy touched the shore, the children sprinted toward the slight rise at the center of the island. Alvin stepped into the water, caught his wife's arm, and helped her out.

She frowned at the stiff breeze whipping her hair and reached into her purse for her scarf. "I just really would prefer you sold the yacht and bought us a condominium," she said.

He didn't pay any more attention to her saying that than he had any of the other hundreds of times she had said the same thing.

"Momma," the little girl called, "there's somebody here already."

Alvin walked to the rise.

Pulled onto the sand at the far side of the island, with its bow line tied to an anchor planted in the grasses in front of it, the blue speedboat that had exited the marina as they did rocked gently at the waves crashing against its stern.

"I thought this was our island," the little girl complained.

"Just visitors," Alvin said.

"I told you he didn't buy the island," the little boy said.

"You shouldn't be lying to the children," his wife said.

Alvin shrugged.

The little girl dashed toward the boat.

In a moment, she was climbing over into it.

"Honey," Alvin said as he walked toward the boat, "it's

not nice to be on someone else's property without their permission.''

The child frowned back at him and slipped on a ski jacket she found in the boat. Her brother climbed over the back of the seats toward the motor. He held up a pair of short shorts, and then a pink bikini top and bottoms.

Alvin looked toward the trees down the beach. He shut his eyes and dreamed.

His wife frowned. ''We better take the children back to the boat,'' she said.

He nodded and peered through the trees again.

''Alvin.''

He brought his gaze back to the children. ''Come on,'' he said in an unusually gruff voice. ''We're going to find another place.'' He looked back at the trees.

''Alvin.''

His wife wasn't looking at him this time. She was looking out over the water. A hundred feet from the beach an empty windsurfer's board, its sail leaned over in the water, ran up a wave and slid down its near side.

CHAPTER 35

The C-130 Hercules swung down through the light clouds above the Mississippi Sound and circled to make its landing approach across Biloxi to Keesler Air Force Base. Inside the big plane, Vandiver sat on the small box at the center of the otherwise empty cargo bay. He glanced at his watch. A smile of anticipation crossed his face. Douglas didn't like that.

He *hoped* all they were going to see was a white shark—after the locals hooked it. And they might never do that, he knew—what if it had gone back into the Gulf on its way to another area?

Would his uncle want to rent a boat and chase after it? he wondered. And what would they be chasing? Finally he asked. "Sir?"

"Yes."

"Sir, I know you said the length of the depression in the Keys could be due partly to the shark entering and leaving—not really representative of how long the shark was."

"Yes, Douglas, it didn't settle down onto the bottom like a helicopter." He used a motion of his hand laid out flat like an airplane to show the shark gliding into the sand.

"Yes, sir. I know you also said that the submarine soundings that indicated something fifty feet or longer might have appeared that way to you because you weren't as familiar as the technicians with interpreting the soundings.''

''Yes.''

''But, sir, I *personally saw* the slashes in the doctors' boat. I could put my arm down through some of them. Chief Petty Officer Rhiner said the tooth would have fallen through them if he would have let go of it when he held it over them.''

Vandiver didn't say anything and Douglas added, ''So, sir, even if it turns out that megalodons did have larger teeth than comparable-sized Whites of today, and it turns out that the twenty-five-foot shark the people here think is a white is the megalodon that lost the tooth, there's still going to be something else, there's going to be another megalodon with it, isn't there? One bigger.''

''Yes, if they stuck together all the way here.''

''They did at least as far as the Keys, didn't they, sir? The one that lost the tooth, and the one that made the slashes in the hull.''

''Yes, Douglas, it appears they did.''

Behind the *Intuitive* a hundred seagulls squawked and circled over the half-submerged buoy cast in the shadows of the dark clouds overhead. A pair of pelicans flew right at the gulls as if oblivious to their presence, and Carolyn watched the two big prehistoric-looking birds, waiting for a collision. The gulls parted, the pelicans swooped past and on toward Biloxi, and the gulls formed over the buoy again.

Paul saw the first fins. ''Hammerheads,'' he said.

Carolyn looked at the oblong-shaped head that gave the sharks their name as one nosed almost out of the water to bite at the ropes lashing the net to the buoy. The second fin disappeared under the water. Two more fins cut through the water a hundred feet behind the boat as they came toward the net.

*   *   *

Vandiver walked down the ramp formed by the door hanging to the tarmac at the rear of the Hercules. A bob truck already half full of crates, two forklifts and several airmen in fatigues waited to unload the cargo. They came to attention and saluted when they saw his uniform.

He returned their salute and looked around for a ride.

Finally his eyes settled on one of the forklifts.

Alvin guided the Gulfstar from the flying bridge.

"I want to go over there," the little blond-haired girl said. She pointed out toward nothing but water.

"It's shallow over there," he said.

"I want to go over there, too," her brother said.

"Alvin," his wife said, "this yacht isn't *only* for our pleasure."

Alvin frowned and turned the wheel sharply to the right.

The children smiled.

"General," the lieutenant said, "Admiral Vandiver, U.S. Navy, here to see you."

A puzzled expression on his face, the commanding general of Keesler came to his feet behind his desk. "Show him right in, Lieutenant."

As Vandiver and Douglas came through the door, the general politely smiled his greeting. "Admiral."

"General," Vandiver said in return.

"Office of Naval Intelligence?" the general questioned.

Vandiver nodded and gestured with his chin at his nephew. "My aide, Ensign Douglas Williams."

"Welcome to Keesler, Ensign."

"Yes, sir," Douglas said, and tried to come to attention as best he could with Vandiver's two bags of luggage in his hands and a hanging bag draped across his shoulder. He carried his clothes in the small satchel he had tucked under his arm.

Vandiver moved to one of the two straightback chairs in front of the desk. Douglas remained standing, still holding the luggage off the floor. The general slowly settled into his chair behind the desk. He didn't say anything. With the Director of Naval Intelligence suddenly arriving at the base without any advance notice, something big had to be up, he knew. If it was something the Director could openly discuss, he would say so. If it wasn't, there was no use in asking.

Vandiver, for his part, didn't volunteer anything, only asked for a car for transportation and said he would have it back soon. He didn't say when *soon* was, and the general didn't expect him to.

As Vandiver and Douglas walked toward the car brought to the front of the headquarters building for them, the general ran over what he knew in his mind. The Director of Naval Intelligence, not only flying in unannounced with an aide, but in a C-130 that used as a flimsy excuse for its stopping here a single box of cargo . . . It was something *big*. He wondered what was in those two large suitcases the aide had never let out of his hands.

"Sir, you didn't mention anything about the shark to the general," Douglas said after he had slammed the trunk lid closed over the luggage and opened the car's passenger-side door for his uncle. "It's not like we're doing anything wrong."

"No, it isn't. Maybe I've been in intelligence too long, Douglas, but that's my motto: the less anyone knows about what you're doing, the more avenues you'll have to do it. You should think about that."

Douglas did, but the statement wasn't any clearer after considerably longer thought.

*　　*　　*

Vandiver had Douglas stop the car at the first service station they came to. Douglas waited for his instructions.

"The shark, Douglas. Ask them the latest news on the shark."

"You mean if it's attacked any more victims, been seen again? Maybe how they're hunting it?"

"Very good, Douglas."

Douglas was inside the station for such a brief time that it surprised Vandiver when he walked back outside and hurried toward the car.

"It's dead, sir. They killed it in Back Bay. It's lying there close to the shore where everybody can see it."

"Back Bay? Where's that?"

"Oops, sir," Douglas said, and hurried back into the station.

Fifteen minutes later, the car was parked on a weed-grown, graveled area at the front of an abandoned fish-processing plant. Vandiver and Douglas stood at the rear of the building looking out across Back Bay—and seeing nothing but empty water leading all the way toward the bridges and Biloxi Bay.

Vandiver's eyes slowly came around to his nephew's.

"Sir, I'm certain I obtained the directions correctly. It's supposed to be right out there. Forty feet . . ."

As his uncle continued to stare at him, his voice trailed off, ". . . from shore."

Ten minutes later, Douglas hurried back out of a convenience store. He handed his uncle a map he had drawn on a paper bag. He pointed to an X he had marked next to the sketch he had made of the shoreline of Back Bay. He touched his ballpoint pen to the X.

"Sir, we were right here. It's simply not there anymore."

"Get directions to the Coast Guard Station. I know there's one in Gulfport."

The curly-haired boy lowered the binoculars he had been using to look out over the side of the Gulfstar's flying bridge. "I saw a whale," he said, looking back at his stepfather.

"Yeah," Alvin said.

"Alvin," his wife said, "you *could* sound more enthused."

"If he really saw a whale, I would be."

"I did," the boy said.

"Yeah, and you saw an alligator last year in a cotton field in the Delta."

"Alvin," his wife said, "imagination is good in a child."

The boy frowned at his mother now. "I did see a whale," he said. "Right over there."

"I saw it, too," his twin sister said. She was sitting down with her back against the inside of the bridge as she brushed her long blond hair.

Alvin didn't make the effort to respond.

"Maybe they did," his wife said.

"There aren't any whales in the Chandeleur Islands."

"You a marine expert?" his wife asked.

"No, I'm not. I'm not an astronaut either, but I know the moon isn't made of green cheese."

"Well, I want to see for myself," his wife said, and folded her arms in front of her chest. They all three stared at him now.

"Which way?" he asked.

The boy and girl pointed to opposite sides of the boat. When the girl saw where her brother pointed, she changed her finger back in that direction.

Alvin rolled his eyes.

"*Alvin,*" his wife said.

He turned the wheel in the direction the boy had indicated.

The little girl smiled.

The boy picked up the binoculars and began scanning the water.

"Alan," Ho called as he came down the hallway.

"In my office, Ho. You finally get your nap out?"

When the Asian stepped into the office, he couldn't have looked any more nervous if he had just been attacked by the white again.

"Alan, shark's been moved."

"Uh-huh, I know. Are you feeling all right?"

"Man that live across street from where you kill it cut this from mouth." Ho lifted the big tooth in his hand.

Alan stared. Any marine biologist, any marine scientist of any kind would have immediately recognized what the tooth had come from.

"It not possible," Ho said.

Alan kept staring. He would have known it was a joke, either being performed by Ho or by the man who gave the tooth to Ho, except for Ho's nervousness—and part of the bloody gum still attached to the base of the tooth.

"Megalodon," Ho said.

I knew there was something, Alan thought. *Why didn't I examine it? If I had examined the teeth I would have . . .*

And then another sudden thought, He reached for the telephone. "They're taking it out to dispose of it."

He quickly punched in the number of the marine operator.

It took a couple of minutes for the call to be connected. All that time, he stared at the tooth, an off-white or light beige, with its body thicker than a white shark tooth of the same size.

"Go ahead, sir," the operator said.

"Carolyn, where are you?"

There was a moment of silence. *"A few miles south of Horn island. Is there something wrong?"*

"Are you still pulling the shark?"

"Yes."

"Turn around and bring it back. Don't cut it loose whatever you do. You're towing the find of this century—a megalodon."

"I didn't read you clearly, Alan—what did you say?"

"You're towing a prehistoric shark—thought to be extinct for millions of years. I'm on my way out there."

The brown car sped west on Highway 90 toward Gulfport. Douglas drove. Vandiver looked past him toward the dark water of the Mississippi Sound out to their side.

"Douglas, you notice the Sound?"

Douglas glanced out his window. "Yes, sir."

"The water, Douglas, it's silty. I didn't even think about that." Vandiver looked farther out over the water toward the tops of the trees rising above the barrier islands in the distance. "The islands keep the outflow from tributaries along the coast from mixing freely with the Gulf water. That keeps the Sound silty. I wonder . . ."

Douglas looked at him. "Sir?"

"I told you that one of the things puzzling me was why the megalodon would pass up so many similar places, and then come into the Gulf. Then, in particular, stop here—if that's what the white is. It's easy to see now."

Douglas looked out his window.

"The silted water, Douglas. I imagine three or four feet under it and you couldn't see a thing. It'd almost be black."

His nephew looked back at him as Vandiver said, "Maybe the megalodon was simply roaming, happened onto this place. Maybe he likes the dark—it reminds him of the dark where he came from."

As Douglas looked out his window again, Vandiver

added, "Or maybe he's just that smart—knows he can't be seen here."

Douglas looked back across the seat again.

"Keep your eyes on the road, Douglas."

CHAPTER 36

Alan slipped inside the small Robinson R-22 two-seater helicopter and pulled his door shut. The pilot looked across the seats as he started the engine.

"I've pulled a banner asking a woman to marry a man waiting outside her door," he said. "I delivered a guy once who stepped out into his girlfriend's front yard with an engagement ring. But I believe dropping you in the Gulf is going to be one that can't be beat. You are going to propose to her, aren't you?"

Alan looked across the seats. "That might not be a bad idea," he said.

The pilot stared back at him for a moment. A small smile crossed the man's face. "You're getting ready to drop in the water and climb up on her boat—and you haven't made up your mind for certain yet?" He shook his head and smiled again.

A few seconds later, its engine roaring and its rotor blades revolving at top speed, the helicopter lifted off the ground and tilted toward the Sound.

"Atten-hut!"

The seaman working at the bow of the Boston Whaler setting in its berth off to the side of the Coast Guard Station had seen Admiral Vandiver's uniform when he stepped from the car.

Douglas came out the driver's door and nodded his greeting toward the seaman and a seaman apprentice standing at attention in front of the Whaler. Both of the men wore the dark-blue pants and short-sleeve shirt that comprised the unit's summer uniform. "Where's the station commander?" Vandiver asked. "At ease. The station commander?"

"Acting commander is inside, sir," the seaman said, trotting toward the blocky two-story stucco and brick building to the car's far side. As Vandiver and Douglas followed him, he hurried under an overhang made by the building's second level projecting out over the ground floor and opened a door tucked back in the shadows.

"Up the stairs to your right, sir," he said as Vandiver and Douglas moved past him.

Bos'n Mate Third Class Beverly Cowart, wearing the same working blue uniform as the seamen, snapped to her feet behind her desk when Vandiver came out of the stairwell and walked toward her office.

"At ease," he said, and didn't waste any time with formalities. "The white shark that was killed in Back Bay last night—where is it?"

"Sir, it's being taken by a civilian boat into the Gulf for disposal."

"*Disposal!*" Even with all his years of training in the intelligence field he couldn't keep the word from having come out at a half roar. The woman, her eyes widened, stared back at him. He forced his voice lower. "You know the name of the boat?"

"No, sir, but the station commander does. He's at home sleeping right—"

"Wake him up!"

*   *   *

The helicopter hovered twenty feet in the air out to the side of the *Intuitive*. The pilot looked at Carolyn and Paul staring up at the craft from the flying bridge and Sheriff Stark looking up from the fishing cockpit. Alan's gaze was on the long shadowy shapes darting around the form of the megalodon's body, suspended in the net a few feet below the surface of the clear Gulf water. He stuck his legs outside the door and, turning and catching hold of the bottom of the seat, lowered his feet to the landing skid.

"Ready?" the pilot asked.

Alan nodded.

"Wait until I tell you 'Okay' before you jump," the pilot said. "This wind is pretty stiff. Blow me off a little bit and you'll be landing in the water." He looked back at the sharks. "Might not get a chance to make that proposal if you do that." Keeping his gaze fixed on the bridge behind him, he moved his control sticks, sliding the helicopter to the side and as far out toward the front of the boat as he could and still be over the deck.

After motioning with his hand for Carolyn and Paul to crouch down, he began to lower the craft, having some difficulty in keeping it in place against the stiff breeze.

"Get ready," he shouted toward the open door.

Alan let go of the fuselage, grabbed quickly for the skid under his feet, and swung down to dangle below the craft, his shoes a few feet above the *Intuitive*'s bow and slightly out to its side.

The helicopter moved to the left again and down a couple of feet more.

"Now!" the pilot shouted.

Alan released the skid, hit just ahead of the Zodiac inflatable tied to the forward deck, and went to his knees. A moment later he hurried down the rail toward the flying bridge.

Paul, a big smile across his face, met him at the side of the cabin. "Wow, Mr. Alan," he said.

Alan patted him on the shoulder and moved into the fishing cockpit.

"What in the hell is a megalodon?" Stark asked.

"It's what's in that net," Alan answered. For a moment he stood staring at the buoy and the ropes lashed around it securing it to the net. A small, tattered piece of the net boiled to the top of the water, then sunk from sight. There had to be at least twenty sharks around the carcass, hammerheads, white-tip sand sharks, and bull sharks, swarming around the buoy, diving under the water and coming up fighting for the chunks of flesh they were tearing from the body. "We have to drive them away," Alan said. He stepped inside the cabin.

The cardboard box wasn't there.

"Where's the dynamite?"

"Carolyn asked Fairley to offload it," Stark said.

Alan closed his eyes.

"Did she do something wrong?" Paul asked.

Alan shook his head no, and walked from the cabin. A moment later he stepped up beside Carolyn at the flying bridge.

"A megalodon?" she said.

"I don't know how, but it is." He looked back at the buoy, then raised his face in the direction of Biloxi. They weren't even to the barrier islands yet.

"If we don't get rid of the sharks somehow, we're not going to have anything left by the time we get to shore."

"We can shoot them," Paul said, and knelt to open the cabinetlike doors of the storage space under the steering wheel. It contained a flashlight and extra batteries, an emergency position indication radio beacon, and the thirty-eight-caliber revolver Carolyn had handed Alan when they were chasing the shark in the bay.

Stark nodded. "Fresh blood *might* draw them off." He took the revolver from Paul and turned toward the fishing cockpit. In the distance, the helicopter was already beginning to move out of sight.

Alan turned his face toward the radio as it crackled and a voice came over its speaker: "Intuitive. *The charter fishing boat* Intuitive. *This is Coast Guard Station Gulfport. Please come in, Captain.*"

Carolyn reached for the mike.

"This is the *Intuitive.*"

"*Stand by for Admiral...*" There was a moment of silence.

"*... for Admiral Vandiver,*" the female voice said.

"Intuitive, *this is Admiral Vandiver. Are you towing the ... white shark?*"

Carolyn looked at Alan. "Yes."

"*Don't attempt disposal until I'm able to get to you to examine the carcass. This is on Naval Authority. I...*" There was another moment of silence. "*Ma'am, whom am I speaking with, please?*"

"Carolyn Haines."

"*Ms. Haines, this might be important. Could you hold your position until I can get there?*"

"We're already on our way back."

"*Back? You said you hadn't disposed of it yet.*"

"We haven't."

"*Yes, Captain, well, I'm coming that way anyway. Keep coming and I'll meet you.*"

"We have some sharks going after the carcass," she said.

"*Damn. Can you go faster or something?*"

"Not unless we take a chance of the tow breaking loose."

"*Do whatever you can until I get there.*"

A loud crack came from the fishing cockpit as Stark fired the first shot.

Carolyn gave the Admiral her position and replaced the mike on its hook on the radio.

"He knows what it is," she said. "How?"

*   *   *

Vandiver hurried from the building. Bos'n's Mate Third Class Beverly Cowart, carrying an M-16 rifle, trotted along behind him. Across the pavement, all the berths were empty except for the twenty-two-foot Boston Whaler.

"I'm sorry, sir," Cowart said. "Everything is out on patrol. If you want me to call in a forty-one . . ."

Vandiver shook his head as he stepped into the Whaler. "We'll be there before they could get back here."

Cowart slipped on a bright orange life preserver and handed one each to Vandiver and Douglas. Vandiver laid his on the seat and Douglas followed suit. Cowart looked out toward the Sound. It only showed choppy waves, but she knew with the wind as high as it was that the open water beyond the barrier islands would be much worse. "It's going to be a rough ride, sir. You might want to put that on."

Vandiver stared at her.

She turned the ignition key and the seamen pitched the lines inside the boat. Douglas began winding them into proper coils in the bottom of the craft.

The Whaler started backing from its slip.

"*Wait!*" Vandiver yelled, startling everybody.

He stared at the large shark tooth lying on a cardboard box impregnated with a shiny, wax-paper-looking substance.

"Dynamite the sheriff confiscated," Cowart said when she was able to regain her composure.

"No, the tooth," Vandiver said, stepping over the Whaler's windshield onto the bow and hopping up onto the slip. He stared down at the tooth.

The seamen looked at the other Coast Guardsman and then at Vandiver.

"Sir, it's from a big shark killed over in Back Bay last night. A guy cut a couple of teeth out of it. I collect . . . you know, sir, knickknacks. I paid twenty dollars for it."

Vandiver slowly lifted the tooth in front of him. It was an off-white or a light beige in color, its body was rounded more than normal, and it still had some of the gum tissue clinging to its base.

"Sir," Douglas said, "it's shaped just like—"

Vandiver shut him off with a sudden shake of his head and a stare. He slowly laid the tooth back on the box marked **RED DIAMOND BRAND, DITCHING DYNAMITE, 50% STRENGTH**.

"Did you see the shark?" he asked the seaman.

"Yes, sir, before I came on duty."

"It looked the exact same, didn't it?"

"Sir?" the seaman questioned.

"Sir . . . ," Douglas started.

Vandiver stared again. Then he motioned with his head for Douglas to follow him, and walked away from the seamen.

Twenty feet from the boat he stopped and turned back to face his nephew. "What, Douglas?"

Douglas swallowed hard. "Sir, this tooth is the same size as one from a white that's twenty-five feet. If the one that lost the tooth in the Keys came here, too . . . We have to tell them. It could kill somebody else if—"

"You doubted that I was going to inform them, Douglas?"

"Well, no, sir, I guess you were, uh . . ."

"But if you don't mind, Douglas, let me do it in my own way. We start yelling *megalodon* and what happens?" He stared at his nephew as he waited.

"I don't know, sir."

"The sharks cut the tow loose and the megalodon sinks to the bottom . . . maybe they finish devouring the body before we can get somebody down to attach some cables to it and bring it back up. And then let's say the other megalodon is either not in the area or, if it is, leaves without anybody ever seeing it and goes back to where it came from. And even if it is seen, all we're going to have is a sighting of a bigger world-record white. Here we are, talking about a shark extinct for over a million years, a shark that looks exactly like a white, and no proof to show it isn't.''

"The tooth, sir.''

"Didn't I get a tooth from the Keys? We know now it was deposited there at most only months ago. What good has it done? Who's going to say it came from a living megalodon?''

"But we have eyewitnesses to where this one came from.''

"Eyewitnesses, Douglas? Some character saying he cut the teeth out of this particular shark . . . some people saying they saw him do it? An inquiry then, and somebody suggests maybe there's a fraud being perpetrated, says that some character heard about the giant shark and wanted to become famous, so he rushes a couple megalodon teeth over here to say he cut them out of the mouth.''

"Sir, with all proper respect . . . that doesn't make—''

"Sense, Douglas? There's only one thing that makes sense, only one thing that *guarantees* there won't be any doubt. We get to the megalodon that boat's towing and get it back here . . . safe and sound where it can be examined by any scientists the world over . . . anybody that's not going to want to believe it until they see it for themselves.''

"But, sir, you are going to tell them . . . something— warn them.''

"Douglas.''

His uncle's stare kept Douglas from asking anything more.

Vandiver walked to the Whaler and Cowart and the seamen and the apprentice, all of them obviously nervous at how he was acting. He stopped in front of the seaman who had seen the shark himself.

"Son,'' he said, "I have reason to believe that there

might be another white out there. Maybe an even bigger one.''

The seaman's brow wrinkled.

''Yes,'' Vandiver said, ''bigger. I want you to get the word out to vessels in the area, the local sheriffs, whomever you would normally notify, and tell them of the possibility . . .'' He looked back at Douglas standing behind him. ''. . . of the *likelihood* that there is a serious danger out there. Maybe anywhere along the coast.''

The seaman nodded. ''Yes, sir,'' he said, and started for the building.

Sheriff Stark fired the revolver.

A hammerhead twisted off in the water and disappeared below the surface. A few seconds later it appeared twenty-feet farther back behind the buoy, splashed its tail and disappeared again.

Two fins turned in its direction and swam back toward the spot, sinking beneath the surface. Two more long, shadowy shapes rushed under the water toward the stricken hammerhead.

The first shark that had appeared high enough at the surface for Stark to wound had been a five-foot bull shark. It had rolled off bleeding behind the buoy, too, and had pulled some of the others after it. But those leaving the net had more than been replaced by the new ones that had arrived, cutting swiftly across the water toward the buoy from all directions.

Stark fired again, and only nicked the top edge of a fin that had flashed quickly above the water.

A bull shark, its mouth streaming a long, red piece of visceral lining, broke the surface—and Stark pulled the trigger again.

The weapon clicked on an empty cartridge.

''Where's some more ammunition?'' Stark shouted toward the flying bridge.

"That's all there is," Carolyn said. "Just what was in the gun."

Out to the sides of the boat, still more fins converged in the direction of the buoy.

CHAPTER 37

"There!" the curly-headed little boy said.

Alvin stared in the direction his stepson pointed. He saw the spray break over something and, driven by the wind, whip through the air. But only over something. *A long log?* "Give me those binoculars," he said.

"I'm using them," the boy said.

As the boy moved them back to his eyes, Alvin jerked them from his grasp.

"Alvin!" his wife said.

There wasn't a log where he had seen the spray. There wasn't anything. He lowered the glasses and looked with his naked eyes to make certain he had focused on the correct spot, then he moved the glasses back to his eyes again.

Still nothing.

But there had been something.

He turned the wheel of the Gulfstar in that direction.

"Told you," the boy said, and took his binoculars back.

The little blond continued to brush her hair. After each swipe of the brush the stiff Gulf wind whipping across the Gulfstar blew her hair in every direction. "I don't want to see the whale," she whined. "I want to go back to Jackson."

"Alvin, it is getting a little rough," his wife said.

"No, you said that we needed to see if there was a whale."

He pushed the dual throttles farther forward. The Gulfstar began to pound harder into the long swells. The blond looked up at him. The binoculars bounced up and down against the boy's face as he tried to control them. His wife braced herself with her hand on the side of the flying bridge.

He had them in his power now.

Admiral Vandiver, sitting in the front seat of the twenty-two-foot Boston Whaler as it raced south across the Sound in the direction of the barrier islands, looked over his shoulder at his nephew.

"Damn, Douglas, I remembered the name. Chalumna."

"Sir?" Douglas said, and bounced in his seat as the Whaler smashed through a swell.

"The Chalumna River, Douglas. Where the coelacanth was caught off South Africa. Near the mouth of the Chalumna River. I knew it would come to me. I remember something else, too. You know where we are?"

Douglas waited.

"Almost on top of the very area where the Navy tested shark repellents during World War II. They had the whole country in which to find a testing spot and they chose the waters off the Chandeleur Islands. Does that tell you how many sharks there are around here?" Vandiver looked around out over the water and smiled.

"And does that tell you that something here might be especially attractive to sharks?" he added. "Maybe I was correct about the lower Mississippi Basin—drains right into here. Where there have been sharks since time began, maybe? The old home place. How about that?" He laughed aloud.

Bos'n Mate Third Class Beverly Cowart looked out of the corners of her eyes at the Admiral.

* * *

At the Gulfport Coast Guard Station, the seaman sat in the "watch-stander's" chair close to the radio. The apprentice seaman sat in the chair across the desk from him with his feet up on top of the desk. "A *bigger* one?" the apprentice said. "Did that admiral seem a little flaky to you?"

"Petty Officer Johnson seems a little flaky to me."

"Yeah, but that's because your girlfriend dropped you for him."

"I dropped her."

"Uh-huh."

"Mayday! Mayday!"

The seaman grabbed toward the radio.

"Mayday! Mayday! Mayday!"

"Be quiet a moment," the seaman mumbled, "so I can find out where you are."

"Mayday!"

The call stopped.

"Vessel hailing distress, this is Coast Guard Station Gulfport. "What's your—"

"The damn shark's not dead! It's out here! And it's not twenty-five feet! It's twice that damn long!"

The seaman was taken aback.

"Damn it, Coast Guard, are you there?"

"Your position, Captain?"

"The damn thing's chasing me! At the Chandeleur Light! It's almost made up the . . ."

The man suddenly stopped talking, but his thumb remained frozen on the mike button. The sound of his boat's roaring engines could be heard.

Then a scream—a long, wailing, high-pitched scream of a little girl.

"Mommaaaa!" she screamed again. . . . And then a crashing sound.

And then silence.

* * *

Two miles off the northern tip of the Chandeleur chain, Petty Officer Ken Dickinson, in command of one of the Gulfport Station's forty-ones on routine patrol in the Gulf, reached for the radio at the bridge and lifted it to his mouth. *"Station Gulfport, this is forty-one, three sixty-four. We are two miles from Chandeleur Light and en route to the distress call."*

Admiral Vandiver looked across his shoulder at Douglas.

"The second one!" With a chance to see a living megalodon, he ordered Bos'n's Mate Beverly Cowart to break off her route toward the *Intuitive* and turn southwest toward the Chandeleur Light. He knew all that he could do if he continued on to the *Intuitive* was accompany it and its unseen tow back to the Coast Guard Station. There would be time for meeting it there later and having the carcass transported to some kind of refrigeration area where it could be preserved until scientists could arrive to study it. Meanwhile, he had the chance to glimpse a *living megalodon* and he wasn't going to pass that up. As the Whaler turned southeast, he reached for its VHF radio mike and spoke the forty-one's call letters:

"Coast Guard forty-one, three sixty-four, this is Admiral Vandiver, U.S. Navy. Forty-one, three sixty-four, do you copy me?"

"Yes, sir."

"Report immediately to me if you have any sighting of the shark. I say report immediately if you have any sighting. I'm preceding toward the Chandeleurs."

Vandiver looked at Cowart. "How far?"

"Eight miles, sir."

Vandiver nodded. As he looked out over the water ahead of them, a smile crossed his face.

Fifteen miles away from the Chandeleurs, Alan, standing beside Stark in the fishing cockpit of the *Intuitive*, stared back at the trailing buoy riding above the most exciting marine discovery in history. He knew if he left the megalodon's carcass to float motionless in any one spot there would be even more opportunity for the sharks to strip it to not much more than a skeleton.

But from the excitement he had heard in Vandiver's voice when he radioed the forty-one that he was headed toward the Chandeleur Light, there was now no doubt in Alan's mind that the shark reported in the distress call was another megalodon, no less scared of man and no less the same kind of hunter that had claimed five lives that he knew of in four days, and had attacked boats four separate times. With the radio that had made the distress call suddenly going dead, he had no idea if the man making the call had been at the wheel of a small boat that had no chance or a large boat that did. And he didn't know what caused the crashing sound, though he feared he could guess. There had been the child's scream. There might be survivors. The Coast Guard forty-one might find them first—and then they might not. He had no choice. He cut the rope trailing the *Intuitive* and watched the buoy as, anchored by the weight underneath it, it immediately stopped its forward motion and nearly completely submerged on a lifting swell as fins slashed toward it from all directions.

Beside him, Paul stared with his jaw tight. On the flying bridge, Carolyn pushed the throttles all the way forward, and the *Intuitive* rode rapidly up one swell and smashed through the next one. Alan gave a last look at the buoy and then looked in the direction of the Chandeleur Light.

CHAPTER 38

The Coast Guard forty-one slowed as it rounded the tip of the shoal stretching out underneath the water north of the Chandeleur Light. Petty Officer Ken Dickinson, standing at the bridge, lowered a pair of binoculars and stared toward the Gulfstar, hard aground, with its bow angled upward only yards from the rough beach. Fifty feet out from the Gulfstar, a small white dinghy bobbed on the long swells running behind the island.

Minutes later, the bow of the forty-one neared the dinghy, and the seaman at the wheel pulled back on the throttles. Dickinson stared at the cracks running up the side of the Gulfstar's hull, then looked across the island again. A moment later he spoke through the forty-one's loud hailer.

"Attention on the Gulfstar, this is the U.S. Coast Guard."

"There," the seaman said, nodding toward the figures coming out of the trees at the center of the island. There were four of them, two adults, a curly-haired little boy, and a little girl with blond hair. They came slowly toward the shore, but stopped well short of the water.

"Come and get us!" the man yelled, keeping his gaze out over his side across the water as he did.

The two seamen at the forty-one's bow had secured the

dinghy alongside. "I'll go after them in this," one of them called toward the bridge.

Dickinson nodded.

As the dinghy neared shore, the adults and children made no move to come closer to the water.

The seaman beached the dinghy and stepped over its bow.

Alvin shook his head. "I've never seen anything so big," he said.

"I'm not getting back in that," the little girl said, staring at the dinghy.

"You're going to have to," her mother said.

"No."

"Unless you want to stay here," Alvin said.

The girl started sobbing. Her brother tightened his jaw and started toward the dinghy.

"Is that steel?" Alvin asked, looking toward the hull of the forty-one.

Before the Seaman responded, Alvin added, "The shark would have come right through the fiberglass." He looked toward the hull of the Gulfstar.

"Sir, how long did you say the shark was?"

"Fifty feet at least," Alvin said.

"Sir, the world record for a white is only a little over thirty-two feet."

"Then you can get your name in the record books if you catch the one that was chasing me—good luck."

"Sir, I'm only trying to get facts for my report. It would be real unusual for there really to be a shark that—"

"Come on," the little boy snapped. "Let's go. It *was* fifty feet." He was standing close to the bow of the dinghy, but not looking back at them as he spoke, instead keeping his gaze out across the water.

* * *

On the bridge of the forty-one, Petty Officer Dickinson was answering Vandiver's new call. "No, sir, they seem to be okay—there's four of them, two adults and two children. They were on the island. Seaman Brown is bringing them aboard using their dinghy. It was adrift—I don't know yet if there was anybody else in it."

"*We're in sight of the island,*" Vandiver said. "*I want to speak to whoever made that Mayday call as soon as you get them aboard.*"

"Yes, sir."

"*And get in touch with your station and tell them I want to know as soon as that fishing boat gets there with the carcass of the white.*"

Vandiver replaced the radio mike and, gripping the side of the Whaler for balance as it bounced through the growing waves, stared at the forty-one stopped a hundred feet or so to the rear of the Gulfstar. He could barely glimpse the dinghy, lower in the water, making its way toward the forty-one.

He was less than a quarter mile from the forty-one when Dickinson's voice came back over the radio.

"*Forty-one, three sixty-four to Admiral Vandiver.*"

"Go ahead."

"*Sir, the four people were all that were on the Gulfstar. They say there's a speedboat beached on the other side of the island. They had seen it earlier when it left its marina. There were two young adults in it at the time. When Mr. Cunningham . . . that's the name of the captain of the Gulfstar, sir. . . . He says that when he was here earlier he saw the boat and thought the young adults were in the trees. But he looked while he was waiting on us, and he says they're not there. Seamen Brown and Franks have gone back in the dinghy to investigate. Here's Mr. Cunningham—Alvin Cunningham, sir.*"

"*Hello,*" the voice said.

"Mr. Cunningham, this is Admiral Vandiver. You said you saw a shark twice as long as—"

"Fifty damn feet, at least. Yes, sir, I did. And if you see it you'll wish you weren't in that little boat you're in."

"How can you be certain of the size, Mr. Cunningham?"

"Because the damn thing was right behind us. And if it is all right with you, I wish you would tell these people to get us on back to Biloxi while we're talking."

"Certainly. But they're going to have to wait on the two seamen who went back to the island. Now, where did you see the shark?"

"Behind me."

"In which direction?"

"Hell, Admiral, behind . . . Oh, you mean . . . About a half mile west of here. I thought it was a damn whale at first. Then it disappeared and I thought I had just been imagining things. I turned my boat around . . . happened to glance back over my shoulder a few minutes later and it was coming after me. I swear the fin was ten feet tall. If I hadn't glanced back when I did . . . We barely made it anyway. It was almost on us and the water shallowing stopped it. If it hadn't . . ."

Vandiver looked at his nephew. "This isn't a flake talking, Douglas. He's speaking as logically as can be. He saw a megalodon that big—or close to it."

At the word "megalodon," Cowart's brow wrinkled.

"Admiral?"

"Yes, Mr. Cunningham."

"I think it might have gotten that young man and woman. The reason I think that was that there was a windsurfing board floating in the water. I thought they had left it lying on the beach and the wave just washed it off. I pulled it up for them before I left the first time. But there were two boards in the boat when they left the marina. We really need to get on out of here, Admiral. They say this

hull is made out of aluminum—I guess that's strong enough.''

"You're perfectly safe, Mr. Cunningham."

Douglas looked at him. Cowart eased the throttles back and the Whaler quit bouncing so hard as it began to slow. It coasted up one swell and down its opposite side closer to the forty-one.

On the island, the two seamen were walking back toward the shore by themselves.

CHAPTER 39

The workboat was designed with just that in mind—work. Its engine was geared low—for transporting heavy loads or towing. Even at top speed it neither roared like an outboard motor nor hummed like the kinds of diesels found on yachts, but putted.

That's the sound it was making as it turned off the Pascagoula River into the narrow channel running through the marshes and came toward Carolyn's speedboat, still sitting three hundred feet from the river with its bow pushed up into the tall grasses.

Putt. Putt. Putt.

The rhythmic sound make it even more difficult for Deputy Fairley to stay awake. With only a few hours' sleep in the last seventy-two and none in the last twenty-four, he figured that even the shrill loud sound of a train whistle would probably put him to sleep.

And now, with the soft shadows settling over the marshland as the sun dropped below the trees, with the stiff breeze that came off the Gulf slowing to a more gentle warm flow after having reached the land, Fairley was, in fact, for all practical purposes, already asleep. His head nodded, he jerked, his eyes opened again. He neared Carolyn's craft and pulled the workboat's engine out of gear, guiding the bow up into the tall grasses next to the speedboat.

He had to climb over the side into waist-deep water to attach a rope to the bow of the speedboat and then push the craft back out into the middle of the channel. He worked the bow around behind the workboat's stern and looped the rope around a cleat at one corner of its stern. Then he caught the boat's side, tensed his muscles, and sprang up out of the water and over into the craft.

Once again behind the steering wheel, he put the big engine in gear and backed the workboat's bow out of the grasses. A corner of its stern bumped the speedboat, and he grimaced. But the collision left no mark on the smaller boat's fiberglass. He moved the workboat's gear into forward and swung its bow toward the river.

A few minutes later, he entered the Pascagoula and turned down its channel in the direction of the Ingalls Ship Building yard.

Yawning, he leaned back against the seat's tattered backrest. A fly buzzed around his face and he barely flicked his fingers to drive it away.

A thump behind him. The speedboat hung against something for a moment. Its bow rope pulled loose from the cleat at the stern of the workboat and dropped into the water. The speedboat drifted to a stop.

Fairley looked to see what might be floating in the water to cause the bump, but didn't see anything. Yawning, he slipped the workboat's engine into reverse and began to back slowly toward the other craft.

Looking back over his shoulder, he put the gear into neutral and turned and made his way back across the hard, dried blood and animal parts in the bottom of the boat to its stern. The breeze slowly moved the speedboat's bow to the side, swinging the rope hanging from it out of his reach.

He climbed up on a corner of the workboat's stern and reached his arm out. The rope was still a few inches out of his grasp. Catching a firm grip on the stern, he leaned farther forward, putting himself in an unstable position out over the gap in the water between the two boats. Teetering, his grip on the stern about to slip, he reached his hand as far as he could and caught the rope in the tip of his fingers. He worked the rope into his palm and began to pull it toward him. His gaze went to the water below him. Its surface reflected a cloud with a wide, black hole at its center. The outer edges of the cloud shimmered, then blurred.

It took him a moment to realize that the reflection was beneath the surface, not on top of it, and the shimmering was something rushing up toward him.

He tried to yank his body back into the boat. His hand slipped, his fingers barely holding. He pulled hard, and his body wrenched backward as the gaping mouth exploded up through the surface in a rush of water. As his body slid into the boat, his outflung hand didn't come with him. Its fingers still clutching the rope, his hand rose into the air in the shark's mouth. Fairley landed on his back on the hard steel floor of the boat.

There was no pain, only the stub halfway down his forearm, his artery spraying blood up into the air to fall back to splatter on the dried blood covering the bottom of the boat.

Fairley's scream echoed up and down the river and through the marsh. A heron flapped up into the dying rays of the sun and turned away from the direction of the scream.

Fairley cupped the end of the stub with his hand, trying to stop the spurting blood. It sprayed through his fingers and across his face and chest.

He struggled to his feet looking wildly for something to tie around his forearm.

The shark slammed into the bottom of the hull, lifting the boat in the water and tilting it slightly to one side. Fairley's feet slipped in his own blood and he fell forward, crashing into the side of the boat. He tried to rise but his hand slipped down the steel framework of the boat and he crashed hard back onto the floor.

The craft bounced violently. Water splashed out from under it. It bounced again. Fairley pushed himself to his knees. He grabbed the stub and lunged toward the front of the boat and its controls.

One side of the craft lifted, hung, and crashed back into the water. Fairley's shoulder slammed into the controls. He turned toward them, pushed himself off the gear and grabbed its handle. His hand, slippery with his blood, slid off, and he grabbed for the gear again.

The head exploded out of the water, rocking the boat again. The identical twin of the dead megalodon rose a third of its length out of the water and hung there like a dolphin standing on its tail. The mouth gaped wide, exposing rows of shiny brown teeth. The shark moved forward.

Fairley, lying on his back in the seats, saw the boat paddle lying on the steel floor beside him. He grabbed it, forcing himself upright in the seat.

The head towered over him. He pulled his knees under him and lifted his upper body high in the seat. The gaping mouth came down. He slammed the paddle hard into the jagged teeth.

The paddle splintered.

Fairley drew the broken handle back and jabbed it forward. The front of the shark's heavy body came down on the side of the boat, tilting the craft toward the weight. Fairley jabbed the handle into the hollow center of the cavernous maw as the mouth closed around him. He was lifted whole, his feet kicking, and the teeth closed together. His legs went limp.

The shark sank back beneath the surface of the river.

Bubbles rose to the top of the brown water.

The paddle handle popped to the surface.

$$*\qquad*\qquad*$$

The forty-one moved north in the distance toward the barrier islands on its way back toward Gulfport. The Whaler moved slowly across the shallows west of the Chandeleurs. Alan lowered the pair of binoculars he had trained on the Whaler. "That's the Admiral," he said. "Two men in Navy dress uniforms with the Coast Guardswoman. They're looking for the people that were on the windsurfing boards."

Carolyn stared out over the water, then looked down at Paul for a moment before raising her gaze back to Alan's. "They're not going to find them," she said. "I'm going in."

Alan looked back over the *Intuitive*'s stern in the direction of where they had left the net containing the body of the megalodon.

"Carolyn, I . . ."

He stopped as he saw her looking down at Paul again. Then her eyes came back to his once more. He nodded. "Take him on in," he said.

Carolyn looked toward the Whaler.

Alan shook his head. "The Admiral is a big boy. He knows what's going on, too—obviously knows more than we do. If he wants to stay there, that's not our problem."

Carolyn turned the wheel in the direction of the barrier islands.

Stark stared toward the Whaler now. "I first figured that the guy making the distress call panicked with all that had been going on the last couple of days. He saw a shark fin, or what he thought was a fin—and it became a monster to him, I was thinking. But, you're right, that Admiral was on his way to us—he knew what we were towing. And then he became all excited at the distress call, and now he's here. There is a fifty-foot shark out there, isn't there?"

Carolyn looked down at Paul again. She thought of how her father said Paul had acted at the river . . . how Duchess had acted. She reached for the VHF radio and lifted its mike.

A moment later she was in contact with the marine operator.

It took a couple of minutes to connect the call.

"Mother," she said, "I'm not certain what's going on, but I want you and Daddy to stay away from the river—don't go down by the dock."

She listened a moment. "I'm not certain, just stay away from the water."

"And Duchess," Paul said, looking up at her.

She nodded. "And lock Duchess in the house until we get back."

Paul smiled.

"A blooming idiot," Stark said, looking toward the Whaler, now appearing pitifully small in the distance.

Vandiver's eyes were everywhere at once, searching. Douglas looked at the setting sun, now almost touching the horizon. Soon it would be too dark to see and they would *have* to go in. He closed his eyes for a moment, then looked across his shoulder behind them, which he had been doing constantly ever since the captain of the Gulfstar had said the giant shark had come up behind his boat.

Vandiver was on his feet now, his hands resting on the Whaler's windshield, his gaze sweeping back and forth. He frowned when he looked toward the setting sun. "Damn," he mumbled under his breath, "going down like a damn shooting star."

To Douglas, it had never settled below the horizon so slowly.

"Sir?" the Coast Guardswoman said. "If they found one of the windsurfing boards on the Gulf side of the island, it seems like a better chance the other one's in the water over there, too—and any survivor."

Vandiver nodded. "Good chance," he said. "But since we're already over here, let's keep looking for it here for a while."

Keep looking for a fifty-foot megalodon, is what his uncle really meant, Douglas knew. *Fifty feet long and about a half a mile west of the island—where they were now.*

"Over there," Vandiver said.

Douglas's head jerked in that direction. But his uncle was only giving Cowart a new direction to turn. The water out in front of them shimmered brown in the fading light. To the east the sky had already turned gray. Out of the corner of his eyes, Douglas caught a long line of spray whip up into the air in the distance. He didn't say anything, only kept staring carefully at the spot.

Cowart, her bright orange preserver giving her upper body a swollen look, came to her feet behind the steering wheel and peered off to her right. Her eyes squinted.

Douglas quickly swung his face in that direction.

"Sir," she said.

Vandiver looked in the direction she stared. She swung the boat to the right. Douglas still didn't see anything.

Then he did.

A brown fin, a flash of shining yellow . . .

"The board, sir," Cowart said. The sail trailed in the water to the side of the brownish-yellow board, shining in what sunlight was left. The board's end looked little different from a rounded fin. It rode up another swell, its sail acting as an anchor, dragging in the water, pulling the board to the side where it made a tight, sweeping circle on the wave and bobbed up in the air again.

Half a board, Douglas saw now.

Cowart maneuvered them closer.

The place where the rear half of the board had been bitten from the section they now stared at showed great, widely spaced serrations, like someone had taken a saw and cut gaping triangles into the end of the board. Cowart's eyes tightened questioningly. She looked at Vandiver. He raised his face out over the waters surrounding them. Douglas, thinking of the slashes in the hull of the doctors' boat, continued to stare at the board. He closed his eyes briefly, then looked toward the sun again.

"Sir," he said.

"Yes, Douglas," his uncle said without looking back at him.

"It's going to be dark soon."

"Yes, I know."

Douglas waited a moment. He shrugged off Cowart's look back at him, and looked at his uncle again. "Sir, if the shark should come up with it much darker we might not be able to see it."

"I know. I would give my right leg for a flood lamp on the front of this damn boat."

Douglas looked at his uncle's leg.

"Sir, maybe we can come back tomorrow—in a bigger boat."

Vandiver stared back across his shoulder at him, then moved his gaze on toward the twin hundred-thirty-horsepower Johnsons clamped to the rear of the Whaler. "Douglas, if anything *should* come up after us, those motors would keep us as far away from it as we wish. Now keep looking. My eyes aren't what they used to be."

They were all crazy, Douglas thought. Except maybe Cowart. *She had no idea.*

And that wasn't right.

"Sir?"

"Yes, Douglas."

"This is crazy, sir."

His uncle's face turned back across his shoulder.

But that didn't stop Douglas. "Sir, what good is it going to do if we do see it—that still won't be proof. You said so yourself. A giant shark, that's all."

"I don't care," his uncle came back. "I just want it to come up where I can get a close look at it myself—for myself."

"A *close* look at it, sir? Are you out of your damn

mind?'' At Douglas's words, his uncle's mouth fell open. And Douglas's did, too.

Cowart stared at the two, first looking at one of them and then back at the other. And then her eyes suddenly squinted out over the water between them.

Douglas quickly looked that way.

A half mile away and moving in the direction that the forty-one had gone minutes before, a charter fishing boat moved at a rapid cruising speed across the rolling water. Cowart lifted a pair of binoculars from in front of the wheel and stared at the boat.

''Sir,'' she said, ''that's the *Intuitive*.''

Vandiver's face whipped toward the boat.

''Damn!''

He grabbed the radio mike. ''*Intuitive*, this is Admiral Vandiver. Where is the shark you were towing?''

''*We cut it loose*,'' Carolyn replied.

''My God, woman! You don't know what you've done!''

On the *Intuitive*, Carolyn calmly gave Admiral Vandiver the loran coordinates of the net, then replaced her mike.

They watched as a moment later the Whaler made a sharp circle and, a wide wake spreading out behind the Johnson motors revved to full speed, raced in the direction of the coordinates.

A hundred yards behind the Whaler, a fin suddenly broke the surface, and began to rise higher out of the water, gaining speed as it did.

Twin showers of spray climbing higher and higher out to its sides, the fin raced after the Whaler.

CHAPTER 40

Alan and Carolyn and Stark and Paul watched in horror as the thick fin sped after the Whaler. Its speed was incredible, quickly narrowing the distance. Carolyn grabbed for the radio mike.

On the Whaler, Vandiver, frowning, sat with his arms folded rigidly across his chest, bouncing when the Whaler crashed through a swell, but never deviating from his fixed stare in the direction of the loran coordinates. Despite the hard bouncing, Douglas began to relax.

"Admiral Vandiver!" Carolyn yelled over the radio. *"It's coming up behind you!"*

All their faces jerked to the rear.

The tall fin was twenty feet behind them off to the side and angling directly toward the bow. Cowart spun the wheel away from the fin. The boat leaned and cut in a tight arc. Douglas was thrown across his seat, hit the side of the boat with his stomach, and bent over it toward the water. The fin slashed by his head.

The shark swerved in a sharp circle, and came after them again.

Cowart, standing, steering with one hand, tried to reach back across the seat toward the M-16. It bounced out of her reach. Douglas grabbed it, came to his feet with his back against the seats, and raised its barrel.

Nothing happened.

"Inject a cartridge into the chamber!" Cowart screamed.

Douglas fumbled to pull back the weapon's lever arm. A cartridge locked into place. He pulled the trigger. A burst of three slugs sprayed across the top of the fin, and the gun quit firing.

"Release the trigger and pull it again!" Cowart yelled.

A spray of three more slugs cut into the fin, heading directly toward the side of the boat. Cowart jerked the wheel away from the fin again. A third spray of slugs fired into the air as Douglas stumbled backward, hit his rear on the side of the boat, and tilted toward the water. The M-16 flew out of his suddenly upflung hands and over his head. He caught the boat under his buttocks, arched on backward toward the water—and Vandiver grabbed his legs. Douglas was pulled back into the bottom of the craft—as Cowart cut the wheel again and the shark's fin slashed behind them.

Now she guided the Whaler in a straight line toward the Chandeleur Light and the shallow water extending out from it. Vandiver scrambled off Douglas and came to his knees, staring back at the fin.

It quickly closed the distance again and edged out to the right—and spurted toward them. Cowart cut the boat to the left. The fin suddenly swerved back to the left and cut across the Whaler's wake much as a skier would, and came directly toward the side of the craft.

This time too quickly for the surprised Cowart.

Douglas ducked down in the boat. Vandiver stared wide-eyed from his knees. The shark's broad head, ahead of the fin under the water, slammed into the Whaler just as Cowart jerked the wheel in the opposite direction.

The Whaler tipped up on its side, hung for a moment as water poured over its side, and they splashed back down onto the surface—and the motors went dead, drowned out with smoke pouring from them.

The boat rocked.

The fin, having shot ahead of them, made a wide circle and started back.

It rose higher. The wide head broke the surface, the thick-bodied, fifty-foot creature coming at them with water rushing back around its eyes.

Cowart dove for the small storage area under the bow. Douglas grabbed the bottom of a seat and hung on. Vandiver, his gaze directly into the creature's eyes, tightened his hands on the side of the boat.

The shark smashed into the craft, knocking it sliding sideways across the water as if it was on a pad of grease. It slid into a rising swell, tilted—and flipped over.

Vandiver hit the water on his back, ten feet from the boat. Cowart splashed head-first into the water off to his side and was immediately popped right side up by her bulky preserver.

Under the upturned boat, Douglas, his cheeks puffed and his eyes staring through the light-green water, clung to the bottom of the seat.

Bubbles came out of his mouth. He looked toward the sand bottom beneath him. He let go of the seat and paddled madly to the side, hitting his head on the inside of the boat, ducking under it, and popping above the surface with a gasp for air.

Fifty feet away, the shark, nothing showing now but its tall fin, remained motionless as it faced them.

Douglas moved his gaze from the fin to a spot in the water twenty feet closer to them—where the head would be. The fin started slowly forward. They started back-paddling toward the upturned Whaler. The fin suddenly sunk a foot, and spurted forward.

"Watch out!" Vandiver screamed. He dove under the boat. Douglas dove behind him.

Cowart, held above the water by her preserver, couldn't.

She grabbed for the top of the rounded hull, her hands slipped down its side, her feet kicked wildly, and, somehow, she scrambled up on top of the hull. Vandiver and Douglas scrambled up the other side.

The hull rose from the force of the water pushing up from below it as the shark shot underneath the craft.

Carolyn stared down at Paul, caught her lip in her teeth, shook her head, and spun the *Intuitive*'s wheel in the direction of the shark attacking the Whaler, and jammed the throttles forward.

Stark raced up the deck toward the bow.

Alan felt Paul catch his leg and hang on tightly. He laid his hand on the boy's shoulder.

The shark circled sixty to seventy feet out from the overturned Whaler. Vandiver, Douglas, and Cowart were on their knees atop the rounded hull. The fin slowly began to rise. The eyes came out of the water. The wide head began to come slowly forward.

Douglas closed his eyes and mumbled a short prayer. Vandiver continued to stare directly at the shark. Cowart, her jaw tight, tried not to cry out. The shark didn't increase its pace this time. It was fifty feet away.

"It's going to simply pick us off the hull," Vandiver said, his tone almost matter-of-fact.

Douglas swallowed and tightened his jaw. Cowart edged back a little, but there was only the water behind her. She suddenly stripped off her preserver and threw it at the shark.

"Damn you!" she yelled at the top of her lungs.

The wide nose brushed the preserver aside. It bobbed past the side of the head and moved back along the shark's body.

Twenty feet away.

Ten.

Cowart dove off the other side of the boat and started swimming away from it as fast as she could.

The shark's head submerged in a swirl of water. The fin shot forward, sinking.

The Whaler rose on a mound of water as the wide, brown shape swept underneath it.

Vandiver and Douglas looked toward Cowart. She swam frantically thirty feet away. The dark shape swept under her splashing legs. Her shoulders and head suddenly bounced upward out of the water. Her arms flailed as if she were trying to swim up into the air—and she was jerked beneath the surface.

Douglas closed his eyes.

The tip of the crescent tail made a wide sweep out to the side—and the dorsal fin straightened, facing back toward the Whaler. Vandiver looked toward the loud roar of the *Intuitive* racing toward them.

The fin came toward the Whaler.

It began to rise. The wide head broke the surface. The mouth lifted above the water. It gaped open.

Douglas backed down the side of the hull until he was in water to his thighs.

Vandiver didn't move.

The mouth gaped wider, came up above him. He stared into row after row of thick brown pointed teeth.

The *Intuitive* slammed into the shark's side. The bow dug into the thick flesh, bounced higher, and rolled the shark over onto its side, the keel of the boat cutting on across the body.

A propeller shattered against the thick bulk. One of the engines whined.

The shark rolled out from under the rear of the boat. The Whaler spun from the wave slammed against it. Vandiver toppled forward into the water. Douglas was knocked off the far side and splashed frantically. The shark's fin came back above the water as the fifty-foot beast righted itself.

Ignoring the Whaler now, it sped toward the *Intuitive*.

On the *Intuitive*, Carolyn gasped for breath, the wind knocked from her body as she'd slammed into the wheel during the collision. Alan's grip had kept Paul from being thrown into the front of the flying bridge, but he himself had slammed into it with his shoulder and been knocked off his feet, pulling Paul to the deck with him. Stark had come dashing back from the bow as they neared the shark and had dived into the fishing cockpit as they rammed it. He rolled to his back now and, clasping his forearm, came painfully to his feet.

"Hang on!" Alan yelled. He gripped the bridge with one hand and grabbed Paul around the shoulders with his other, jerking the boy tight against him.

The shark's head drove directly toward the bow.

Carolyn kept the boat directly toward the shark's head.

The two came together like a pair of mountain rams slamming head-on into each other. The shark's head was driven under the water as the bow of the *Intuitive* rose into the air.

Carolyn bounced against the wheel again and around it into the front of the flying bridge. Paul's shirt ripped off in Alan's hand. Alan careened back off the wheel toward the rear of the bridge. The bilge pump alarms sounded their high-pitched yelping sound as water streamed through the cracked bow into the interior of the boat.

The shark rolled off to the side. A wide pectoral fin broke the surface and hung for a moment pointed into the air, and then the shark righted itself again. The dorsal fin popped back out of the water, tilted to the side, and straightened.

Stark reached over the side of the fishing cockpit and caught Douglas' forearm. Vandiver came toward them, swimming slow, his head revolving back and forth as if he were dazed. Douglas pushed off the boat and swam toward

him, catching his uncle's flailing arm and dragging him
back toward the boat. It was pulling away from them under
the power of the still-working prop.

Alan jerked the gears into reverse and pushed the throttles forward. One engine whined and did nothing. The other
pulled the stern back toward Douglas and Vandiver in a
slight arc.

Stark grabbed Vandiver and dragged him into the cockpit. Douglas came in by himself and sprawled forward into
the bottom of the boat.

Alan spun the *Intuitive*'s wheel toward the shallow water
extending out around the Chandeleur Light.

Carolyn held Paul close against her legs.

CHAPTER 41

The *Intuitive* limped rapidly on one engine toward the Chandeleur Light. The shark, a hundred feet behind the craft, began to angle out of the wake instead of following directly behind the craft. Alan looked toward the Light, a little more than the length of a football field ahead of them. The water would shallow a couple of hundred feet short of that. The shark began to move faster, still angling slightly out to the side of the wake, but gaining on them at the same time.

"It's going to cut us off," Vandiver said in a low voice. He stood at the very rear of the fishing cockpit, above the water churning from the full power of the one spinning prop.

"And it knows exactly how much time it has before we reach shallow water."

Alan looked at the protruding fin and the dark shape under it. It was coming faster now, but not as fast as it had moved before. Almost as if the shark were playing with them, letting them get closer to safety.

Or moving determinedly, with calculated purpose. *With a plan in its mind?* And then Alan knew that was exactly what was taking place. Its moving out to the side of the wake as it came toward them . . . It had felt the hardness of the reinforced bow. It knew the one, sharp-bladed prop still spun at the rear of the boat. The shark's last charge would be at the side of the craft. The creature's wide head would tear through the thinner fiberglass there as if it were paper. The fin began to move faster.

It was still a hundred feet to the shallow water.

"Here it comes," Stark said.

"Damn it!" Joycelyn Johnson said. She had bumped the cumbersome TV camera into the dash at the front of the helicopter again. The wind whipping inside the craft through the open doorway which had been removed by the pilot before they'd taken off blew her long hair in every direction, stinging her eyes and forcing her constantly to pull it back from in front of her face. She was a reporter, not a damned cameraman. But the only WLOX cameraman working today was up on the Natchez Trace at the forest fire.

"*My God*," the pilot said.

Joycelyn's mouth fell open at the sight of the wide, dark shape speeding into the side of the *Intuitive*.

Though Alan was braced, the crash threw him to the side, nearly jerking the steering wheel from his hands. Carolyn and Paul were thrown into the side of the flying bridge. Douglas yelled his terror. The shark had not slammed into the side of the boat at the waterline, but come up higher, smashing its broad head into the edge of the deck, driving the fiberglass and rail back against the cabin. The great mouth had gaped as Douglas slid across the wet deck into the corner of the fishing cockpit nearest the shark's body.

Vandiver and Stark scrambled to their feet as the head hung above the side of the boat across from them. The shark's teeth clanged together with the sound of a steel trap as Douglas scooted backward on his hands and heels away from the head.

The head rose higher and then came down hard, smashing into the fiberglass like a massive redwood trunk, crumpling the side of the cabin. The flying bridge sank to that side. Paul slid toward the shark. Carolyn grabbed for him and missed. The upper, rounded row of teeth in the shark's jaws pulled the side of the flying bridge toward it. The fiberglass tore loose with a ripping sound. Paul slid through the gap and splashed into the water below the shark's raised head.

Carolyn screamed in horror and lunged on her hands and knees at the gap as the shark's gaping mouth came toward her. Alan caught her legs and jerked her backward.

Paul bobbed back along the shark's side toward its sweeping tail.

Alan pushed Carolyn off the flying bridge into the cockpit and fell after her. She came to her feet, screamed and tried to jerk away from Stark, grabbing her as she pulled toward the side of the cockpit. The shark sank beneath the water.

"NOOOOO!" Carolyn screamed.

Joycelyn Johnson clasped her hand to her mouth in horror. The TV camera vibrated on the floor of the helicopter at her feet. The pilot's face was drained of all color as he watched the small boy drift backward alongside the shark and float out behind the creature on the waves from the great, sweeping tail.

On the boat, the man who had been at the steering wheel raced around the undamaged side of the cabin toward the Zodiac lashed to the forward deck.

The small rubber boat came loose quickly. The shark's massive head again rose high out of the water and lurched forward toward the fishing cockpit. Its occupants pressed their bodies back against its far side as the shark tore a wide section of fiberglass from the boat's other side.

* * *

There was a scraping sound against the bottom of the hull. The *Intuitive* lurched. The scraping sound grew louder, the boat slowed and came to an abrupt stop. The spinning prop began to swing the stern around toward the bow.

The shark's upper body, riding nearly half out of the shallow water, stayed at a right angle to the boat. The eyes stared toward Carolyn and the others pressed against the far side of the fishing cockpit.

Alan wrestled the Zodiac over the side of the boat opposite the shark and dropped it into the water.

Paul was fifty feet behind the shark's crescent tail now. His face white against the silt-colored water, he began to stroke toward the shore.

Somehow he managed to keep his strokes slow enough not to splash.

Hoping the shark wouldn't hear him.

Alan pulled the cord of the small motor at the rear of the Zodiac. The motor immediately caught, roared its sharp, grinding sound, and the Zodiac sped across the *Intuitive*'s stern and shot out to the side of the boat.

The shark's big eye to that side rotated in a line with the movement.

The wide head began to turn.

Paul's eyes came back toward the sound of the Zodiac.

Alan only cut the throttle slightly as he leaned over the side of the Zodiac and reached for the boy.

Paul's arms slapped into Alan's and the boy was jerked out of the water into the small craft.

Alan jammed the steering arm toward shore.

The tall fin raced along out to their side, between them and the shallow water nearer the island.

Alan turned the steering arm out toward open water.

*   *   *

Joycelyn Johnson held both her hands over her face, peering between her fingers. The pilot operated the helicopter's controls rapidly.

"Hang on," he said. "I'm going to try and give them a chance." The craft leaned on its side and swept down toward the Zodiac.

Alan looked up as the sound of the helicopter overpowered the sound of the Zodiac's motor. He stared directly into the pilot's face. The landing skid to that side moved toward Alan. He wrapped his arm tightly around Paul, already clinging to his neck. The shark put on a burst of speed. Alan came to his feet, swayed as he tried to keep his balance, and reached for the skid, just out of his reach.

The downdraft from the spinning rotors battered the Zodiac. The steering arm began to turn. The craft's bow moved slowly around, then turned abruptly to the side. Alan grabbed the skid, locking his elbow over it as the helicopter swung hard to the side. He was jerked forward out of the craft and to the side. His feet splashed into the water. Pain tore through his shoulder. Paul had his eyes closed, his face buried into Alan's neck. Alan's arm slipped. His elbow came up at a right angle to the skid. The helicopter couldn't lift the combined weight of the two people inside it and the two hanging on beneath it. Alan's feet splashed against the water again. The shark's head, five feet behind them and racing, began to rise higher in the water.

The helicopter jerked upward. Alan revolved on the skid, his arm wrenching. The shark came by under their feet. The helicopter turned toward shore. Alan's arm slipped off the skid. He fell a foot, his hand, somehow, still clasping the damp metal of the skid.

Two hundred feet to the island.

His hand slipped loose, and they plummeted the fifteen feet to the water, slammed into it hard, skipped across it, and disappeared under the surface.

*   *   *

The *Intuitive,* racing as fast as it could with only one prop and its hull filling ever deeper with the water seeping into its interior, came toward them in a direct line paralleling the shallow shoal extending out from the island.

Alan splashed frantically toward shore, Paul hanging onto his neck with one hand and trying to help swim with the other.

Spray mounted above the shark's fin as it drove directly toward them. The head rose above the water. It rose more as the hard shoal underneath the creature's stomach angled sharply upward.

Forty feet between them.

Thirty.

Twenty.

The shark's stomach scraped bottom. It lunged ahead.

Ten feet.

The bow of the *Intuitive* slammed into the creature's side. This time, with the shoal against its stomach, the shark wasn't forced down into the water, but rolled hard over onto its side, the *Intuitive* riding up on the thick body. The craft's heavy tonnage, made even heavier by the hundreds of gallons of water filling its hull, crushed down into the shark's body, and the bow angled up above the creature, the ribbed keel cutting deeply into the thick skin.

The shark, pinned under the boat as the craft slammed to a stop atop it, flopped on its side like a fish lying on dry land. The *Intuitive* bounced as if juggled nervously in a giant, moving hand. The boat leaned sharply to the side.

The shark flopped violently.

The hull's bottom caved in, sat back down onto the thick body beneath it, then leaned sharply to the side and began to turn over as the shark flopped a last time and moved out from under the craft.

*   *   *

"Dive! Dive!" Alan shouted from where he stood chest-deep in the water toward the island.

Carolyn shot from the boat in a racing dive. Douglas splashed into the water behind her. Vandiver didn't leave the cockpit.

The shark rolled in the water, hit its side hard on the bottom, and rolled back upright. It leaned to the other side. Blood seeped from its mouth and from the long gash across its back and flank.

Douglas looked back over his shoulder at his uncle and quit splashing toward shore.

"Dive!"

The shark slipped backward into deeper water. Its head began to submerge. The fin slowly turned off toward the rear of the *Intuitive*.

Alan caught Carolyn's hands and pulled her toward him.

She grabbed Paul into her arms and nearly went under before her feet touched the shoal.

The fin moved in a straight line now, toward the tip of the island a hundred feet out in front of the shark. It moved slowly, a dark stain spreading out behind it.

A minute turned into two, then three as the fin kept moving slowly in the same direction, leaving an ever-widening dark stain in the water behind it.

They stared silently now.

The fin began to rise. The upper body rose above the surface, the water dropping farther and farther down its sides. The shark came to a halt.

"It's grounding itself on the shoal," Carolyn said.

The shark lay there, not moving, then slowly began to move its tail back and forth until, with a last sideways motion of its thick trunk, it turned and faced back toward the boat.

"It's coming back again," Douglas said.

"It's dying," Carolyn said.

The stain in the water around the creature continued to widen.

A white film settled across the black eyes, leaving them only a blurred shadow behind the film.

The mouth slowly cracked open.

A barely perceptible, high-pitched sound began to rise from deep within the creature.

It grew louder, growing shriller as it mounted in intensity, until finally the air was filled with a sound not unlike a baby's piercing, crying scream of pain.

They were walking toward shore now, up only to their knees in water, but Douglas stopped, feeling the same kind of chill pass over him as he had experienced when his uncle had played the tape from the submarine.

Then the sound began to lessen in volume. The mouth slowly closed. The dorsal fin tilted slightly to the side.

Alan saw Paul looking at him with a questioning expression on his face.

Alan nodded.

"My God!" Douglas suddenly exclaimed.

Two hundred yards beyond the shoal, out in the deeper Gulf water, a fin stood stark and enormously thick in the dim twilight. Already twice as tall as the fin of the shark lying silent on the shoal, it continued to rise into the sky.

Alan felt Paul's hand clasp his trousers.

It still rose.

Sixty to seventy feet in front of the fin, the water mounded, as if a great bubble of gas were lifting it from beneath. A gigantic head broke the surface, water pouring down its sides. Black eyes as big as truck tires and set thirty feet apart rose above the water. The swells rolling in from the Gulf caught against the creature's sides and broke into foam as if they had run into a two-hundred-foot-long cliff suddenly emerging from the water. The giant head moved forward. Douglas stepped back involuntarily.

"Damn," Stark said in a low voice, almost a whisper, and looked toward Vandiver, now up on the *Intuitive*'s partially demolished flying bridge and looking toward the head.

A sound.

Coming from the giant.

Barely perceptible at first, then rising in volume, something like the sound the shark on the shoal had made, but deeper in tone.

The sound rose, became louder and louder until, finally, it filled the Gulf air with its intensity, sweeping across them like a giant's groan broadcast over a loudspeaker turned to its highest volume.

Paul moved his hands to his ears.

"Look," Carolyn said.

The shark on the shoal had moved. Slowly, its tall, crescent tail began to swipe sideways. The head moved. The trunk arched to the side now, and the tail swept with a greater motion. The body began to slip backwards, and then to the side. The tail swept again.

The blood that had dwindled to a slow seep from the wound across its back began to run down the dark body again. The shark moved farther sideways on the shoal, its actions stronger now. It twisted again, and slipped sideways into deeper water. The body began to move forward toward the giant two hundred yards out in front of it. The giant's head began to move slowly backward. The distance between the two gradually closed.

The helicopter moved above the pair.

In minutes, the smaller fifty-foot shark was passing to the side of the giant's head. And then the giant turned behind it.

They moved slowly in the direction of deeper waters, the helicopter keeping pace above them.

Another minute.

The giant head slipped lower into the water and sub-merged with a rush of water and the surface swirling into a whirlpool, only the towering fin remaining in sight.

Soon, it, too, slipped under the swells.

The smaller fin remained visible for a moment, tilted to the side, straightened, then itself slid beneath the green water.

"Mother," Paul said. He was looking back toward the *Intuitive,* past it in the direction of the barrier islands.

Moving toward them was the Coast Guard forty-one, its bow throwing wide white waves out to its sides. Everyone looked toward it.

Except Vandiver. He continued to stare at the spot where the giant head disappeared. In his mind he was looking at the captain who told in 1963 of seeing a shark over eighty-five-feet long pass under his freighter. And he was listening in the presence of David G. Stead in 1918 as the fishermen told him of the shark over a hundred and fifteen feet long that had swallowed their lobster pots. And he was paddling with the Polynesians who looked from their dugout canoes to see monster sharks nearly a hundred and fifty feet long slashing through the waves in front of them.

And he had bested them all.

A faint smile crossed his face . . . then went away as he looked back over his shoulder at the bright orange life preserver floating alone behind him.

CHAPTER 42

The workboat and Carolyn's speedboat floated empty, side by side down the Pascagoula River. The twenty-five-foot twin of the shark that had been killed by the dynamite had already left the river, responding to the deep call that had vibrated through the water from off the Chandeleur Islands.

Ahead of the twin, in the twilight dimness at the bottom of the Gulf floor south of the barrier islands, long, shadowy shapes slashed in and out around the carcass contained in the ripped and gaping net. Hammerheads, sand sharks and bull sharks, their mouths agape, repeatedly smashed into the great bulk, shaking their heads violently as they bit down.

Suddenly, they began darting away from the body to disappear quickly in the twilight water beyond the carcass.

In only a moment nothing could be seen but small particles of flesh suspended in the water slowly settling to the sandy bottom.

Stillness ensued.

At the fringe of the dark green curtain fifty feet from the carcass, a rounded nose tapering back to a streamlined head appeared. With pectoral fins set to its sides like airplane wings, one of the first Great Whites to reach this northern-most part of the Gulf in years swam slowly into sight.

Able to know that its quarry was dead by the first scent that had reached its nose a mile away, the sixteen-foot adult dispensed with the stealth it would have shown in tracking a live victim, swimming directly toward the carcass.

A magnificent creature, king of the seas for hundreds of thousands of years and neither instinctively nor consciously fearing anything that swam temperate waters, the white kept all its senses directed at the carcass.

Its nose lifted and its bottom jaw dropped, its great mouth unhinging so that it could take as large a bite as possible. Gleaming white, razor-sharp serrated teeth set in rows in its gums reflected the dim light.

From out of the dark to its side came a shape swimming so rapidly as to appear almost blurred. The twenty-five-foot twin, its mouth gaping, its great teeth a shiny brown, plowed into its cousin of a million and a half years' distance, driving the White sideways through the water, biting it nearly completely in half with the first crushing pressure of its jaws.

Then, gulping the moist, bloody meat down its cavernous gullet as it turned, the megalodon came back to bite off and swallow a second large portion of the body before the White had time to settle next to the carcass of its ancestor.

Moments later, the twenty-five-foot twin put on a burst of speed toward the south.

CHAPTER 43

The buoy was found late that night by a forty-one conducting a search. Neither the net nor carcass of the twenty-five-foot megalodon was ever found. Maybe someday somebody would discover one of the teeth that for one reason or another wouldn't be quickly covered by silt being spread out toward the Gulf's depths by the many tributaries draining the lower Mississippi Basin. But Vandiver knew that would prove nothing to the surprisingly large number of skeptics who still insisted on discounting the evidence of the teeth that had been cut from the megalodon's mouth and couldn't be dated as anything but of recent origin. And, with the WLOX reporter having let her camera slip out the helicopter door into the Gulf, and thus no video around for proof, very few scientists put much stock in the report of a two-hundred-foot giant. Not that the scientists doubted his or any of the others' honesty. But it had been twilight, nearly dark, at the time of the sighting, the skeptics argued, and it would have been possible for a whale to have momentarily visited the northern Gulf—though of course, not a two-hundred-foot whale. Again, it was nearly dark.

But Vandiver didn't care about the skeptics. For that matter he didn't care about the many who did believe. As far as he was concerned, he had all he really wanted out of the incident, to know for certain what he had always felt.

"Sir?"

At his nephew's voice, Vandiver looked toward the computer terminal on the far side of the office. Douglas had brought up the artist's rendition of the megalodon and was looking at the creature, its mouth gaped and its pectoral fins spread wide to its sides, facing out from the screen as if it were about to swim into Douglas's lap.

"Sir, did you do this?"

"The changing of the body color?"

"Yes, sir."

"Uh-huh, hit the control and C key together and you can have your choice of a brown to grayish-brown upper body and dirty-white underbody, or blue to bluish-gray with white below—but not solid brown anymore. The same colors of whites of today. I thought about making one pink, too, just for the sake of argument. But that wouldn't be honest, would it?"

"No, sir. Sir, do you think they'll come back again?"

"Certainly. They have for centuries. Give them another fifty to sixty years and somebody will be reporting seeing them again."

"But they've gone back to the depths now?"

"They always have, haven't they?"

"The megamouth and the adult six-gill haven't, sir."

"No, they haven't, Douglas."

"You think something might be different this time, sir?"

"Like what?"

"I don't know, sir—maybe whatever made the megamouth and six-gill come up to stay."

"I wouldn't say the megalodon is exactly the type to play follow the leader, would you Douglas?"

"No, sir. I don't guess so, sir."

"Well then, let's just assume they have gone back, Douglas—in case I have to send you scuba diving somewhere again."

His nephew looked back across his shoulder.

And Vandiver chuckled.

*   *   *

Three months later, Carolyn was leaning against Alan's arm as they stood at the bow of the *Intuitive II* anchored off the Chandeleur Light. Alan stared out toward the open Gulf.

"You know," he said, "I was thinking about Fairley drowning . . . especially with his body never being found. You remember how Duchess acted that morning? I wonder if there's any chance that there might have been another—"

"I don't want to know," Carolyn said.

"And I've wondered—if there were only the two—if one was a male and one was a female, and if we were witnessing the last remnants of a magnificent species."

"I don't want to know that, either."

"Mr. Alan," Paul called as he came up the deck from the fishing cockpit after taking his nap, "don't you want a sandwich?"

Carolyn looked back at him. "I'll fix you one in a minute, Paul. But come here right now. I have a surprise for you I think you're going to like."

She held up her hand with the engagement ring that now took the place of her old wedding band.

"What do you think about this?"

"I already knew," Paul said, and smiled. "He told me first."

At that moment, several hundred miles beyond the mouth of the Gulf, the fifty-foot megalodon and the twenty-five-foot twin dove at a sharp angle down through the clear, blue water of the Atlantic. Ever deeper they sped, the light beginning to fade around them. They slowed as they approached the pair of great long two-hundred-foot giants swimming side by side, and turned in beside them.

Staying close to the bottom that angled ever deeper, the four swam slowly toward the dark curtain in front of them, and out of sight.

*   *   *

"Like I said, give them fifty or sixty years," Vandiver said as he walked out of his office with Douglas.

Douglas's mother, her broad back to the office door, stood in front of the receptionist's desk. Vandiver quickly slipped his arm around his nephew's shoulders, startling Douglas.

"Fine boy, sis," Vandiver said. "Didn't know you were in town."

His sister folded her thick arms across her chest and smiled at the friendly scene.

The receptionist stared, too.

"What in the hell?" Norman "Bubba" Fitzwald said. He was thirty-five miles south of the Chandeleurs, on one of the oil-well platforms anchored in the clear waters of the Gulf. Smoking was strictly forbidden on any of the platforms and he had moved down the inclined metal steps circling one of the round legs supporting the platform to escape from being seen as he puffed on a Marlboro Light. What he saw now was the long shadow—a hundred and fifty feet long, at least—of something moving beneath the water close to the surface a couple of hundred yards out from the platform.

Then he looked up toward the bright sun. A thin, long cloud moved slowly across the sky. He looked back at the shadow, smiled at his imagination, flicked the stub of his cigarette out toward the water, and turned and started back up the steps.

Behind him, the long shadow abruptly changed direction.

A moment later, gaining speed, it moved rapidly in the direction of a Russian freighter on its way out of Gulfport with a load of frozen Mississippi chickens.

Six months after that, people began swimming in the Gulf again.